Pay The Penance

The final book in The Mechanic Trilogy

Rob Ashman

Print ISBN 978-1-912175-47-5

For Karen, Gemma and Holly

Also by Rob Ashman

Have you read the first two books in The Mechanic Trilogy

Those Who Remain

In Your Name

Chapter 1

Fabiano Bassano was watching baseball in his man-cave. The room was full of excited chatter as the additives from the fizzy drinks and chocolate snacks began to kick in and the kids went a little crazy. He liked nothing better than watching the game with his five grandchildren. They were mad about baseball and mad about Grandpa.

Whenever they got together it was always the same. The kids talked over the commentary, walked in front of the TV, and bombarded him with questions about the rules, but that was fine. For Fabiano Bassano, enjoying the ball game with his grandchildren had nothing to do with the ball game.

'Hey, what's going on,' he cried, holding up an empty beer bottle. 'Who's on bar duty?'

One of the children reached up, snatched it from his grasp and dashed into the kitchen, returning a minute later with a frosted replacement, courtesy of Grandma.

Zak, the youngest, snuggled on to the chair alongside him.

'Grandpa, why do you have this silly picture?' His shock of black tousled hair hid his face as he gazed at a silver framed photograph in his tiny hand. He looked up, his moon face and bright eyes waiting for his favourite playmate to respond.

'Yes, that is a silly picture, isn't it?'

They both laughed.

'What is it?'

'I don't know. Someone gave it to me. I like it, don't you?'

'Yes, I like it too.'

'It makes me smile.'

'It makes me smile too, Grandpa. Who gave it to you?'

'A friend of Uncle Chris.'

'Is he the one who died?'

'Yes. He died when you were small.'

'I like it.' Zak turned the picture over in his hands and the frame caught the light.

'I'll let you into a secret.' Fabiano bent his head and whispered into the child's ear. 'Do you know what today is?'

'No, what?'

'Today is its birthday.'

'Its birthday?' Zak was fixated, not taking his eyes off the image. 'How can a picture have a birthday?'

'Well, it's one year ago today that the photograph was taken.'

'Wow, then it does have a birthday.' Zak and his grandpa sang Happy Birthday. But Grandpa struggled on occasion to get his words out. When they finished he dabbed his eyes with his sleeve.

'Now put it back and we can watch the game.'

Zak shuffled off the chair and placed it on the shelf.

It was an odd photograph.

Chapter 2

Mechanic bumped the front tyre of the Vespa scooter against the kerb and parked up. From her cliff-top vantage point the view across the Bay of Naples was stunning. She watched as the sun dipped below the horizon and mirrored the sea with the burnt pink of the sky. The salt breeze cut through her shirt, cool against her skin. It was the perfect evening to kill a stranger.

The Italian resort buzzed with the excitement of three thousand pilgrims visiting for the Easter festival. She had flown into Naples International, taken a rental car and driven the fifty-two kilometres south, down the A3 to Sorrento. The car was parked at the hotel, the only way to get around was by scooter, and everybody had one. They buzzed around town like wasps at a picnic and were just as annoying. Mechanic turned off the ignition, kicked down the stand and put the keys into her pocket. She slipped on a thin cotton fleece, swung a black backpack onto her shoulder and headed for the centre.

Mechanic's face was tanned gold and her short hair streaked blonde from the sun. She looked like any other carefree tourist in search of religious tradition and culture. The truth was very different. She had only arrived the day before, the effects of the sun came from running in Balboa Park, San Diego, and she was in search of a man who had something she wanted.

Piazza Tasso was the beating heart of Sorrento, a beautiful square full of cafés, bars and restaurants, with a web of small roads radiating from it. She sat outside Fauno's café, ordered an espresso and watched the throngs of people milling about.

Today was Maundy Thursday, and the procession of Our Lady of Sorrows had taken place earlier in the afternoon. Hundreds of people dressed in hooded white robes had marched through the narrow streets. Mechanic was waiting for the later, much larger, procession, commemorating the Madonna's mourning when she found her son dead.

She lifted a newspaper from her bag as her coffee arrived.

'Grazie,' she said, stirring in dainty cubes of sugar.

Thousands of fairy lights burst into life, piercing the dusk with pinpricks of colour, while waiters busied themselves lighting candles in jars. The heat of the day was fast disappearing and Mechanic zipped up her jacket.

The coffee was strong and the mountain of sugar masked the bitterness. She flicked through the pages and scanned the headlines, not paying the slightest attention to what they said, concentrating instead on the middle-aged man taking his seat four tables away. He was dressed in a white linen suit and brown sandals. His skin had the appearance of worn leather and he sported a white Fedora hat, which made him look like a Bond villain.

Fedora man clicked his fingers and a waiter scurried across. Without looking at the menu he ordered food and a bottle of wine in fluent Italian.

Mechanic followed his lead, but with iced mineral water and no finger clicking.

The clock face said 11.30 and the square was packed with people eager to see the Madonna's statue carried aloft, supported by the hundreds of white-robed figures.

Fedora man wiped his mouth with a napkin, clipped a handful of notes into the bill folder and left his table. Mechanic had already left the café and was sitting across the square on a low wall watching the swelling crowds. She followed him as he meandered his way along the side streets. He frequently stopped to browse the tourist mementos outside the shops and doubled back on himself several times. Mechanic kept her distance, she was used to dealing with textbook anti-surveillance measures.

There was an eruption of singing and the sound of a band striking up in another street. The procession had begun.

Fedora man quickened his pace and weaved his way towards the music. At the end of the road Mechanic could see a gathering of white-robed people all jockeying for position behind the holy statue. Fedora man ducked through a doorway into a bar.

Mechanic darted into a dark alley opposite, opened her backpack and took out a white hooded robe. She flattened out the backpack, pushed her arms through the straps and pulled it tight. She slipped on the white robe and watched the entrance to the bar as the minutes ticked by. A man wearing an identical costume emerged from the bar. He was minus his hat but recognisable all the same. He jerked the hood forward and pushed himself into the throng of people.

Mechanic kept her eyes firmly targeted on Fedora man and joined the tight knot of people. She weaved between the worshippers and in less than two minutes he was in front of her, his brown sandals clearly visible beneath his robe. Mechanic mingled with the sea of white, keeping within six feet of her target. The singing grew louder as more people joined the throng, walking down Corso Italia and winding their way through the narrow lanes.

Fedora man veered off to his left and started talking to someone. Mechanic couldn't hear what was being said, but they were definitely having a conversation. Fedora man lost his footing on the cobbled stones and stumbled. The person to his left stepped forward and grabbed him around his waist. His right sleeve rolled back as he did so and Mechanic could see a man's arm. There were audible exchanges of *grazie* and *prego*.

That was it, the exchange was made.

Fedora man slowed his pace allowing people to pass him. He was now level with Mechanic and going backwards as the people marched on through the streets. She ignored him and kept her focus on the new guy wearing bright yellow running shoes underneath his robes. The procession stopped outside a church, and some people broke off and went inside. Yellow shoes guy stayed put.

After a short ceremony the parade moved onto the next church, and the next. Each time was the same. At the sixth church Mechanic saw the man in yellow shoes drift to the edge and when the parade stopped he entered the church. Mechanic followed.

The inside had a traditional layout, with a central aisle leading to an altar with a tall stained-glass window behind. Either side of the aisle were rows of wooden pews with kneeling cushions on the floor. The place was half-full, with people crammed into the front rows and the priest standing at the front. The figures in white sat amongst the congregation and the priest started speaking. Mechanic watched her target take a seat at the back against the wall. She shifted her place in the queue and sat beside him. No one else joined them.

She pulled back her hood, glancing to the side. The man was in his mid-thirties with angular features and pale skin, which blended into the whitewashed wall. The service started and everyone stood – he was taller than Mechanic with a slender build. His hands were fidgeting in front of him.

The priest chanted and people mumbled in return. The soulful sound of an organ reverberated against the vaulted ceiling and the congregation sang. Mechanic glanced down at the order of service. Her Italian wasn't good but she could understand enough.

She could see the word *preghiamo*.

The priest was intent on making up for the empty seats and bellowed out the song like Pavarotti. He particularly enjoyed the end of the chorus and gave full vent to the high notes, which he could barely reach. Mechanic counted down the verses, waiting for the final chorus.

The man beside her sang under his breath, his eyes searching the pews, his hands still fidgeting. She slid her right hand through a side slit in her robe and drew the gun tucked into her belt. The silencer made the weapon difficult to manoeuvre under the material. The priest built himself up to a rousing finale and blasted out the final line of the hymn.

The gun spat.

The .22 hollow-point shell made a small neat hole just below the man's ribcage, then flattened to the size of a dime as it tore through his body. Mechanic wound her left arm around his waist and gripped him tight. The second round entered through the same hole and ripped into his heart. He went limp.

Mechanic supported his weight against the wall. He was heavy and she jammed her body against him to keep him upright. The singing stopped.

The priest looked up from his book and said 'Farci preda'. The entire congregation sank to their knees in prayer, clasping their hands in front of their faces.

Mechanic lowered the man to the floor. She raised his arms and propped him against the pew in front, flicking the hood over his head.

As the church filled with the sound of murmuring prayer, she patted her hands against his body and felt the slim package tucked into his shirt. She removed it and pushed it inside her own.

The congregation stood up and started filing out. Mechanic didn't move. She kept her head bowed mimicking her colleague, both of them kneeling in the act of silent worship. The red stain on his robe was getting bigger and blood was pooling at his right knee. When the last of the people shuffled past, Mechanic eased away from the body and joined the line of people exiting the church, pulling her hood forward.

Outside she merged into the crowd and after walking a short distance broke away into a side street. She stripped off her robe and bundled it into the backpack before walking back to Piazza Tasso where her scooter was waiting. The key turned in the ignition and she drove away.

She reached the hotel and parked, just as a parade of a different sort was starting up. Two police cars thundered down the main road closely followed by an ambulance.

Mechanic had no idea what was in the package, even less why it was worth killing a man to get it. But two things she was sure of: in fourteen hours she would be back on American soil, and she'd be a damn sight wealthier than when she left.

Chapter 3

When the sniper's bullet exploded his wife's head into a thousand pieces, it shattered Lucas's life into a thousand more. The shock took away his ability to function, rendering him unable to do the most basic of tasks. And being unable to cope, Harper took over.

Dick Harper, a man famously unable to get through the week without causing himself significant harm, stepped up to the plate. He looked after his friend in his own inadequate way. He made the arrangements for the funeral and sorted out Darlene's affairs, while Lucas spent his days sitting in a chair staring with moist eyes into the middle distance.

Lucas did have one searing burst of emotion which tore him from his grief-induced stupor. He met Heather Whitchel at the funeral.

Heather Whitchel, the woman who had given his wife a place to stay when she finally snapped and left him. The woman who had confirmed all of Darlene's grievances and told her she was doing the right thing. The woman who had acted as his wife's self-appointed guard dog, repelling his attempts at a reconciliation. The woman who had got her rocks off by playing judge and jury on whether or not to hand over the phone.

Heather Whitchel, the woman who had denied Lucas his last chance to speak to his wife before her life was snuffed out.

At the funeral, the room was full of polite chitchat over tea and sandwiches. Heather spotted Lucas and made a beeline for him, wanting to give her condolences. Up to that point Lucas had dismissed her attempts to contact him, she was the last person in the world he wanted to talk to. Harper had played the guard dog role by blocking her calls, but she was slow on the uptake and was not taking the hint.

But under these circumstances she had direct access, and if she was foolish enough to persist, then Lucas wasn't going to hold back.

She slithered up to Lucas dressed in a stick-insect trouser suit and a starched plain white shirt that matched her face. She oozed simpering remorse.

She put her hand on his arm.

'I'm *so* sorry.' She layered an amateur dramatic emphasis on the word 'so'.

Lucas placed his hand on hers. It was the touching reunion she had dreamed of.

'You know, Heather, every night I wish I could turn back the clock.'

'I know, I know,' she nodded, a crocodile tear welling in her eye.

'And every night, I wish it was you who took that bullet, and not Darlene.'

Lucas pressed his hand on hers.

'But all I mean is …' She glanced down at her trapped hand.

Lucas pulled her close.

'What did Darlene say, Heather, the last time I called? What did she say?'

Heather tugged at her hand.

'I don't know, please let me go.'

'No, and neither do I. And why is that, Heather?'

'Please let go.'

'Because you wouldn't let me fucking talk to her,' Lucas hissed in her ear. 'So when you're lying in bed tonight, staring at the ceiling, trying to work out why your life is such a car crash, think about me turning back the clock and picturing your brains splattered over that car park floor.'

Lucas released her and stepped away, leaving Heather with a pink complexion and an open mouth.

That certainly did the trick and Lucas hadn't seen or heard from her since.

Unfortunately, that was his only show of emotion in a morass of numbness. Afterwards Lucas went back to sitting for days staring at nothing a thousand yards away.

In the early days he couldn't bring himself to stay at his house. He hated everything about it. Every room reminded him of a time when his wife filled the place with warmth and laughter. Now it was full of nothing. It was too painful, so he filled a bag with clothes and moved in with Harper, which was a mixed blessing.

Harper wanted to play host and slept in the spare room with a mattress on the floor. Lucas took Harper's bed, with broken slats in the base. The sagging mattress gave Lucas the feeling of being sucked into a black hole every night. Eventually his back hurt so much he made Harper swap.

Another peculiarity of living with Harper was his refrigerator, which could simultaneously keep things cold at the bottom and room temperature at the top.

'Don't put food in the top of the refrigerator,' Harper told him. 'It's not cold.'

One day Lucas suggested it might be a good idea to buy a new one.

'What for?' Harper rejected it out of hand.

Also, the freezer defrosted itself whenever it felt like it, which meant mealtimes were a constant round of feast or famine. They either had to cook enough food to give a horse a heart attack or not enough to feed them both.

With the help of this absurd normality, Lucas started to get back on his feet. He gradually spent more time at his home and after three weeks waved goodbye to Harper's hospitality and moved back in. Which was a blessed relief for both of them.

The bereavement counselling provided by the force was the best on offer, but it didn't help. They met every Tuesday evening, a sad collection of people struggling to come to terms with the loss of a loved one. It was led by a young woman whose police officer husband had died in a road traffic accident.

She was good, but Lucas felt little benefit from attending. On reflection, this was probably due to him meeting up with Harper after the counselling sessions and spending the remainder of the evening drinking himself into oblivion. When he woke the next morning he couldn't recall a thing the woman had said or anything about the class.

It had been almost a year since he laid his wife to rest in Roselawn Cemetery. Lucas ghosted from day to day achieving the mundane – laundry, shopping, watching TV and drowning himself in a vat of whisky and beer every night. He ate all the wrong foods and drank enough alcohol to give three people liver failure.

Harper had well and truly fallen off the wagon and Lucas was fast joining him in the gutter.

The force offered to pension him off, so Lucas accepted early retirement, and the gross misconduct charges evaporated with no further action. His boss was fantastic after Darlene's death, which pissed him off. The man was a total dick. Why did he insist on being generous, caring and supportive at the very time when all Lucas wanted was someone to hate.

The various payments from his wife's life insurance policies meant Lucas didn't have to work, which was just as well. His life was a collection of nondescript days where nothing happened, and forgotten nights where he drank until he blacked out. It was a sad sequence he repeated over and over again. Everytime he tried to break the cycle his resolve clattered to the floor. Try as he might the scabs kept coming off his life, exposing the deep wounds below, and preventing the healing process taking place. His life was in a flat spin and he couldn't pull out of it.

The phone rang. Lucas picked it up.

'Hello.'

It was Chris Bassano's father.

Chapter 4

It was testament to the depth of his decline that Lucas no longer minded meeting Harper in the worst café in Florida. In fact, over the past year, he was at risk of being considered a regular.

There was a time when he would physically recoil from his suits if they hadn't made it to the dry cleaners following a visit to the café. Nowadays the reek of stale smoke and bad hygiene permeated his clothes and he put them on without even noticing.

Lucas shoved open the door and was enveloped in the stench of a hundred wet dogs. The neon signs buzzed behind the bar and grey smog clung to the ceiling like rain clouds. The guy behind the counter looked up and acknowledged him, not with a 'Good morning, sir, I will be your server today' type of greeting, this was more of an imperceptible nod of the head.

Harper was in his usual spot, with a steaming mug of black sludge in front of him. He looked up and raised his hand. Lucas moved between the tables and chairs, which looked like the leftovers from a yard sale, and pulled up a seat. Their usual topics of conversation eluded them.

'I can't believe it,' Harper said.

'I can,' Lucas replied. 'Mechanic was never going to stop at killing Darlene.'

'Are they sure it's her?'

'No, they haven't a clue. But it's Mechanic alright, her signature is all over it.'

'How did he …'

'Massive blood loss, the autopsy report said he died in minutes. She attacked him in an alleyway outside a club. It was some kind of singles night, a masked ball with over three hundred people there. No membership required, just buy a ticket and turn up. You know what Chris was like, she probably came onto him and he swallowed the bait. She took him outside and sliced him up.'

'Did they find …' Harper hesitated again.

'No, the SOCOs tore the place apart, but didn't find his cock and balls. I can only assume she took them.'

'They're probably in a jar taking pride of place on her dressing table.'

'She did that before with the military guy who raped her, remember?'

'Yup, she called an ambulance for him though.'

Lucas clenched his fists on the table.

'Bassano's family are devastated. His father called to break the news.'

'They get their kid back on his feet only for this to happen. What have the police said?'

'It looks like they got jack shit. No CCTV, no forensics, and of course from their perspective, no motive.'

'And if we give them the motive, we open ourselves up to a whole world of pain.'

'Exactly.'

The two men sat in silence. The guy behind the counter appeared carrying a mug and slopped it down in front of Lucas.

Harper waited until he had retreated out of earshot. 'We gotta kill this bitch.'

'Agreed. If we don't, it's you or me next.'

'Are you up for it? I mean you've taken a beating and I wouldn't blame you if you needed more time.'

Lucas put his hand on Harper's arm. 'I want her dead. I want to videotape the life draining from her eyes, so I can watch it over and over again.'

'Yeah, I get that, but are you up for it? Grief is a funny thing, man. It hits folk in different ways.'

'You sent me that letter containing the sugar packets because I needed something to fight for, something to stop me hitting the self-destruct button. I hated you for doing it but you were right. Well, I reckon it's time for me to get off my ass and fight again. She's taking away the people I hold most dear and I have to stop her. And besides she can't kill you, you're the only one I have left.'

'You are in one sorry-ass state if I'm the only one you have.'

'Yes, I am.' Lucas held up his mug. 'To killing the bitch.'

Harper held up his drink. 'Let's kill her good.'

They drank the hot, bitter coffee and both reached for the sugar bowl.

'The question is, where do we start? She could be anywhere,' said Lucas.

'While you've been out of commission, I've been doing some digging.'

'What have you got?'

'I figure there's no point trying to look for Mechanic. We know how good she is at disappearing and if the cops can't find her, we sure as hell won't. But we do have a new piece of the jigsaw which we didn't have before.' Harper reached into his jacket pocket and pulled out a sheet of paper.

'What is it?' asked Lucas.

'Are you sure you want to do this?'

'Do what? What have you got? What new piece of the jigsaw?'

'The bullet that killed your wife.'

It stopped Lucas in his tracks. His head went down and he closed his eyes.

'You okay?' Harper asked, knowing this would be difficult. 'That's why I haven't said anything before. Are you sure you're ready for this shit?'

'I'm fine, go on.'

Harper flattened the page on the table. 'The bullet which killed Darlene, and the rifle that fired it, were serious pieces of kit, real high-end stuff. I got an extract from the ballistics report, this was military grade ammunition. It's not your weekend warrior weaponry. You don't use this to shoot squirrels with your buddies, this is designed to kill people, from a very long distance.'

Lucas picked up the paper. 'This is specialist kit. It says here it has a boat tail narrowing at the bottom of the shell. That's proper sniper gear.'

'Yup, purely limited edition, this is latest issue ammunition.'

'Where the hell would Mechanic get her hands on that? Not to mention the rifle to fire it.'

Harper folded away the paper and put it back into his jacket.

'That's not the right question. The question is *how* would she get her hands on it?'

Lucas considered the nuance carefully. 'That's right. Because it's obvious where it came from. It came from the military. But *how* would she get her hands on it?'

'The only thing I can think is she's got a contact currently serving in the armed forces. Maybe someone she's worked with in the past?'

'That would fit. And if we find that person, we get a lead on Mechanic.'

'Kit like that isn't going to come cheap.'

Lucas tapped the table, catching up fast with his friend's train of thought. 'And what do we always do when that happens …'

'Follow the money.' Harper finished the sentence.

Lucas got up from the table, motioned to the bartender, and sat on a stool as a telephone was placed in front of him.

'Who are you calling?' Harper asked.

'Moran,' Lucas replied punching in numbers.

Harper threw his hands in the air in protest but it was too late.

'Hi, can you put me through to Detective Rebecca Moran, please.' Lucas cupped his hand over the mouthpiece. 'Trust me on this one. I know what I'm doing.'

'Detective Moran,' she answered.

'Moran, this is Lucas.' He paused. 'Mechanic has killed Bassano and we need your help.'

'Fuck off.'

The line went dead.

Chapter 5

Detective Moran had spent the last twelve months trying to rebuild her life and behave like a normal person. The trouble was she no longer knew what that looked like. If her dealings with Lucas and the plot to catch Mechanic became public knowledge, she was dead meat. She would not only lose her career but her liberty as well. The call from Lucas had ignited her worse fears. It wasn't over.

The hit on Darlene was unimaginably cruel. But as far as the cops were concerned, it was a one-off incident, probably the work of an ex-con with a grudge. In the police interviews which followed, no one mentioned kidnapping Jo Sells, the motel killings, the adverts in the paper or the link to murdering Bonelli. Lucas kept his mouth shut and Moran stayed well clear. That was the way it had to be.

After Darlene's murder Moran severed all ties with Lucas, Harper and Bassano and refused to return their calls. She froze them out, she had to. She wanted to forget it ever happened and move on. What she didn't need was Lucas dredging it up again.

In her quieter moments Moran still craved the prospect of catching Mechanic but she had to put that ambition behind her. Her immediate priority was to keep out of trouble and bury anything connecting her to the bitch.

In the months following Darlene's death, Moran had continued to work with Mills on the motel murders and the drug killings, but neither investigation had gone anywhere. Mills had screwed up both of them, which suited Moran just fine. Thankfully, under his leadership, no one had managed to join the dots and work out that the same killer was responsible for both crimes. And, come what may, Moran was not about to put her head on the chopping block and point that out.

After a while both investigation teams were scaled back and Moran was transferred to another case. This one involved the shooting dead of a police officer while making routine house-to-house calls in the hunt for Jessica Hudson, Harry Silverton's bodyguard. The evidence suggested Jessica was lying low after the Bonelli killings, and it was critical to Moran that she remained off the grid. After all, Moran was the only person in the force to know that Jessica Hudson and Mechanic were one and the same, a piece of information she had to make disappear if she was going to protect herself.

The shooting dead of the officer took place in Vegas, in a small apartment which was rented to Mrs Nassra Shamon. She was an Omani woman in her mid-forties and had moved in only days before, paying one month's rent up front in cash. Her paperwork checked out and the rental agency had the relevant photocopies of her ID and visa. There was nothing to suggest the shooting was linked to the other cases.

The bathroom window at the apartment had shown signs of being forced, and Moran concluded the most likely scenario was that the officer disturbed a burglary in progress. When he intervened he was killed. The other likely scenario was Shamon came back, found him dead, panicked and did a runner. Immigration records showed she had not left the country, but try as they might they couldn't locate her.

It appeared straightforward but for two worrying facts which bugged Moran: whoever killed the officer took the time to dig the slug out of the wall before leaving, and the whole place had been wiped clean of prints.

* * *

Moran arrived at the station early and set about her work. It had been three days since Lucas called and there had been no further contact. Her blunt response had obviously had the desired effect.

Moran heard Mills' voice booming across the corridor.

'Yes! You little beauty.' He was ecstatic about something. 'Got you, you tricky bastard.'

What the hell was he doing in at this hour? Moran left her desk and followed the noise.

Mills sat in an adjacent office in front of a flickering monitor. He was moving a thumbwheel back and forth on what looked like a giant video recorder.

'What is it?' Moran asked.

'I've been ploughing through these all night. It's taken the best part of a year to get hold of them.' He pointed to a wall of VHS cassettes stacked on the table.

'What are they?'

'They're not blue movies, that's for sure. They're the CCTV footage from the street where Ramirez was killed. You know, the one who got his throat cut and pushed out of a car.'

'Yes, I remember, but so what?'

'We've been working on the premise that whoever was inside the car killed him and dumped his body on the sidewalk. Our problem is that we have not been able to ID the car or the people in it. We've got a street full of shoppers and no one sees a damn thing.'

'I remember the witness statements were pretty flaky.'

'Yeah, plus the fact those useless suckers at the city council managed to lose the damn tapes. Well, watch this.'

Mills turned the wheel and reversed the tape. Moran saw a car pull up at the kerb, and then the two guys in the front got out and walked away. The camera angle wasn't good but she could just make out Ramirez sitting in the back, leaning out of the window.

'So the first thing we got is a BMW 3 series with a good shot of the plates. Got that?' Mills was like a schoolboy demonstrating a magic trick to his friends.

'Yup, that's clear.'

He turned the thumbwheel the other way and the action on the screen went into fast forward.

'Watch.'

The people on the screen fizzed around Charlie Chaplin style as the film sped forward. Moran could still make out the sequence of events unfolding before her. The BMW was parked at the side of the road and a woman wearing long robes and a hijab approached the vehicle with her hands outstretched. People on the sidewalk did their best to avoid her. She stopped in front of the back window and Ramirez waved her away. It looked like the woman was begging for money. She moved in close, her back to the camera. She stumbled as though he had pushed her. She straightened up, turned and walked away.

'Watch now,' Mills said as he wound the wheel back with his thumb and slowed down the film.

The two men returned to the car carrying grocery bags and jumped in. The car pulled away and then came to an abrupt stop. The passenger leapt out, flung open the back door and Ramirez toppled out onto the sidewalk, his throat sliced open.

'Gotcha,' said Mills hitting the freeze-frame button and zooming in. He jabbed his finger on to the screen, pointing at the man next to the car. 'At last you and me are going to have a little talk.'

Moran wasn't looking at the man, she was looking at the beggar woman shuffling up the street towards the camera. She was looking at Nassra Shamon.

She tried desperately to make sense of what she was seeing. Why would a woman who paid a month's rent in cash be begging for money on the street?

'When was this?' Moran asked.

'April 27. Time stamp 1.15pm.'

Moran swallowed hard. That was the same day the police officer was shot dead.

Her instincts were in overdrive and it didn't feel good. This was all wrong.

She kept Mills chatting a little longer and congratulated him on finding the footage. Every muscle in her body screamed to get back to her desk while the image was fresh in her mind. She gave Mills a 'well done' pat on the shoulder and left.

Opening the file, Moran flicked through the interview notes and SOCO reports. She pulled the grainy photocopy of the rental agreement from the wad of papers and stared at the picture. Sure enough, staring back was the face of the beggar woman at the scene of Ramirez's murder.

Moran went back to join Mills to be certain. By now a small gathering of early risers were crammed around the monitor with Mills stabbing his finger into the man's face on the screen.

'I know that scumbag,' said one of the onlookers. 'His name is Jerome Wilson, he works for Bonelli.'

'Okay, guys, let's get to it. We got the car and we got a face, bring them in.' Mills was up and running.

Moran stared at the image on the screen. The hijab was different and her complexion was a little darker but it was her. The same question hurtled around her head: Why would a woman who could pay a month's rent in cash be begging on the street? This was wrong, very wrong.

Mills had seen what he wanted to see, and the alternative interpretation for Moran made her feel ill. She sat at her desk nursing her third coffee of the morning. She excelled in joining the dots and looking for patterns, and whichever way she joined them up, Moran reached a terrifying conclusion.

Ramirez had his throat ripped open in broad daylight having moments earlier been face to face with Nassra Shamon. The same day a police officer was shot through the head while conducting house-to-house enquiries at the apartment of – guess who? – Nassra Shamon.

This is a 44-year-old woman from Oman visiting on a short-term visa. She appears out of nowhere, pays a month's rent in cash, begs for money on the street, features in two murders and then disappears the same day.

Moran ran the what-if scenarios in her head.

What if the goons in the car didn't kill Ramirez? What if Nassra Shamon slit his throat? The two guys returning to the car panicked and Ramirez ended up on the sidewalk. What if there was no burglary at Shamon's apartment? What if it was staged to look like one? The police officer turns up at the place and accidently stumbles onto the secret world of Nassra Shamon. And she kills him in order to do her disappearing act.

Her head was spinning. There were more dots to join up.

Ramirez was travelling in a car with two of Bonelli's men. Now who has a penchant for killing Bonelli's guys? The answer to that is Mechanic. Who has the skills necessary to slit the throat of a hardened mercenary on a crowded street in the middle of the day? The answer to that is Mechanic. And who has the ability to simply disappear into thin air? The answer to all three questions was Mechanic.

'Shit.' Moran slopped coffee into her lap. This was getting worse.

If Nassra Shamon was Mechanic, then this latest turn of events brought her back in play. It was only a matter of time. Moran coughed as the taste of bile filled her mouth.

She got up from her desk and walked to the water fountain. The physical act of moving stopped her from shaking, and she needed to get rid of the taste of panic. She tried to maintain her composure, when in truth she was falling apart in full view of the office. The mail arrived, which gave her something to do other than prop up the water dispenser.

She busied herself allocating letters to people. A plain brown envelope addressed to her stood out from the rest of the corporate junk. Moran ripped it open. Inside was a set of black and white photographs.

One showed her standing outside her car, the second showed her with Lucas, and the third was of her, Lucas and Harper deep in conversation. All three were taken in what looked like a car park. The date stamp at the top said *Christchurch Mall, 8th floor, camera 3, 28 April, 05.13am.*

Scrawled across one of the images in red marker pen was written, 'Want to explain these to your boss?'

Moran managed to make it back to her desk before her legs gave way.

Chapter 6

Moran struggled to breathe. The pain in her chest felt as if she was having a heart attack and the thumping in her head was deafening. She tried to suck air into her burning lungs. She gripped the photos in disbelief. Panic tore through her body.

Who the fuck sent these? It was external mail but the postmark was illegible. She stuffed them back into the envelope and rammed them into her desk drawer.

Mills burst into the office barking instructions.

'Okay, listen up. I got new work orders. I want Jerome Wilson picked up. Get out there and bring him in. I want this car found.' He waved a wad of magnified screen shots from the CCTV in the air and slapped them down on the desk. 'And I want the name of the driver. Let's hustle people.'

Moran took one and spent the rest of the morning touring the streets looking for Wilson and the car. But her thoughts were a million miles away, wrestling with the implications of the mailed pictures. After her third near traffic collision of the day, she thought it best to abandon her search and return to the station. Her head was a mess. The office was empty and she sat at her desk, the car park screen grabs in her hand.

The phone rang.

'Detective Moran.' She cleared her throat.

'I assume the mail has arrived by now.' It was Harper.

'I'll tell you what I told Lucas. Fuck off.'

'Do you really want to play that game?'

'It's not a game, Harper. I'm not interested in getting dragged into this.'

'But you're already in it, Detective, right up to your neck.'

'No, Harper, it's over.'

'It's over when I say it is. And what you've been looking at this morning proves you're still very much engaged. I have hundreds of pictures of you, me and Lucas at that multi-storey at five in the morning, and I'm dying to send them to your boss. I'm not sure what he'll make of them, but it does take one hell of a lot of explaining.'

'Listen, you piece of shit. I'm not doing this.'

'Never play hard ball with a man who has nothing to lose, especially when you have everything to lose.'

Moran tilted her head back, tears of frustration in her eyes.

The silence of a hundred years passed between them.

Moran eventually broke.

'What do you want?'

'I want you to be more cooperative. And you were rude to my friend, which was mighty discourteous of you.' Harper was determined to make the most out of having the upper hand.

'How did you get the photos?'

'I bought them from a guy who knows a guy who works as part of mall security. I wanted us to have a record of killing Mechanic, you know something to tell the grandkids about, but that wasn't to be. I kept them anyway as a kind of insurance policy if things took a turn for the worse.'

'What do you want?'

'I told you, I want you to play nice.'

'Cut the crap. What specifically do you want?'

'Mechanic killed Bassano which would suggest me or Lucas is next, and not surprisingly we want her dead before that happens.'

'I'm sorry about Bassano but I don't see how I can help.' Moran was still trying to sound defiant, even though she knew her position was hopeless.

'You have access to information and we want you to get it for us.'

'Go on.' Moran reached for a pen and paper.

'The hit on Lucas's wife was a professional job.'

'You mean Mechanic contracted it out?'

'No, she did it alright, but the equipment she used was military grade. This wasn't something you find at the local gun club, it was state-of-the-art weaponry.'

'So how do I come into this?'

'Gear like that doesn't come cheap, it would cost a ton of money. When in Vegas, Mechanic used the name Jessica Hudson. We need you to look for sizeable money transactions from her account, anything out of the ordinary. It's a long shot but it's a start.'

'Follow the money to find the supplier?'

'That's it.'

'Then target the supplier to find Mechanic.'

'There you go. See, you are a clever detective.'

Moran bristled.

'Leave it with me.'

'Oh, and one more thing, don't think about screwing with me. Remember, I have nothing to lose and I will burn you.'

Harper replaced the receiver and walked back to his regular table. Lucas sat there ignoring his coffee.

'That was Moran,' Harper said.

'No point talking to her, she cut me dead the last time we spoke. Told me to fuck off.'

'It looks like she's had a change of heart.'

* * *

Moran pulled Jessica Hudson's financial records from the file. She remembered running them through the system before and nothing unusual had jumped out. There was rent, utility bills, gas and grocery shopping. The incomings were slugs of money consistent with her working personal security. The transactions were normal everyday items and nothing on the list said 'One day's rental for a sniper rifle'.

Then the image of Nassra Shamon barged its way into Moran's head. She fed the details into the system and ran a bank search. Sure enough, her name came up and it was a very different story.

Shamon had no credit card transactions just a series of large cash deposits made into a recently opened account. Moran recognised the outgoing amount for the apartment rental, and there were numerous small withdrawals. The financial picture was totally in keeping with someone living a cash-only lifestyle.

However, three transactions stood out like the balls on a bulldog. They were bank transfers of two thousand dollars each made to Helix Holdings. The last instalment was made on April 27, then the remaining money was withdrawn and the account closed.

April 27 was the day before Lucas's wife was murdered.

Chapter 7

Mechanic lived in the fashionable Gaslamp Quarter of San Diego. Located in the top corner of a restored factory building, the large furnished apartment was an open-plan space on two levels with wood flooring throughout and modern appliances. The sun poured through the wrap around windows showcasing the stunning views of the historic heart of the city.

The money from her work with Silverton had set her up comfortably, even discounting the cash she gave the Huxtons. She didn't begrudge them the overpayment, they had looked after her sister well, and Mechanic considered it a thank-you bonus.

After the hit on Darlene Lucas, Mechanic thought it best to disappear for a while. The advantage of San Diego was that it was a big city within driving distance of Vegas and with excellent flight routes in and out of the international airport.

There was another reason to choose San Diego. When they were young, her father was stationed there and moved the family to Canyon View naval complex. This was where it all went wrong for the young Mechanic. Moving back was an attempt to exorcise the demons that had haunted her and to draw a line under that painful chapter in her life. After all, she only had herself to consider now – her sister was dead, her whore of a mother was thankfully dead, and her father was probably living in drunken squalor somewhere. She could finally concentrate on herself, and where better than the beautiful city of San Diego.

Mechanic didn't attend her sister's funeral, she didn't even know when it was. It would have been too dangerous to show her face in Vegas. She had to assume the Nassra Shamon cover was compromised and she only had one false ID left. So, with the cops looking for her and Bonelli's men wanting to slice her into tiny pieces, the sensible option was to stay away, however much that hurt. Jo would have understood.

Mechanic missed her sister with a sadness that would corrode her to dust if she let it. But she wasn't going to let it. The responsibility of caring for Jo had been lifted from her shoulders and she could think about what she wanted to do. It's funny how things turn out, even for psycho serial killers.

Captain Mark Jameson had been so impressed with the way Mechanic carried out the hit on Darlene Lucas that he decided to do a little business diversification and offer a select line in contract killing. This work was far more lucrative than his Mr Fixit assignments and his relationship with Mechanic gave him the perfect partner.

When Jameson had a job, he would contact Mechanic and thrash through the outline operational plans. He would build the necessary intelligence reports and procure the equipment, and Mechanic would supply her skills and expertise. She had carried out three contracts in seven months and each time the bank balance got fatter.

She enjoyed working with Captain Mark Jameson, it was an uncomplicated relationship. He worked in military intelligence and could lay his hands on anything and deliver it direct to your door. He could compile intelligence reports on the movements of your favourite pet if you asked him. The man was a legend.

Mechanic had saved his life when a covert op went wrong, and when an ex-Navy Seal says he owes you, he means for life. He was eye-wateringly expensive and very good. He preferred to be paid up front, but where Mechanic was concerned he always took a part payment transferred directly into his account and the rest to be paid in kind.

He had a liking for having the shit kicked out of him during sex, a service Mechanic was only too pleased to provide. He had pulled out all the stops on the Darlene Lucas hit and she had promised him an extra-special something the next time they met. She told him to invent a cover story and book a few days' emergency leave. He was going to be in a no fit state to go to work afterwards.

Mechanic enjoyed delivering the penance, it was everything Lucas deserved. But that did not eliminate her need to avenge her sister's death. All three had to pay the ultimate price. The score stood at one down and two to go, she had two more pounds of flesh to collect.

The chance to kill Bassano came out of the blue. She had instructed James onto compile intel reports on all three of them, and discovered Bassano's liking for the monthly masked singles night. Mechanic saw the potential immediately and it was too good an opportunity to pass up. She booked her ticket to New York and went hunting.

The hit was straightforward. There were no special requirements, just an invitation, a mask, a sharp blade and a seriously flawed personality. The beauty of it was that if the opportunity didn't work out all she had to do was walk away. It was a shot to nothing. Mechanic wanted it to be a hands-on kill, which sent a clear message to Harper and Lucas: you're next.

* * *

She had returned from Sorrento several days ago and had spent her time decompressing and keeping in shape. Today was a day for relaxing, nothing to do and all the time to do it in.

It was 10.40am and Mechanic shouldered her way through her front door with two brown paper bags of groceries and dumped them on the worktop. The TV blinked into life at the press of a button and the news channel came on. There had been no mention of the killing at the religious festival on the World Service or any other channel. For some reason it wasn't newsworthy.

Mechanic never found out what was in the slim package lifted from the man in the church. As instructed, she'd dropped it into a luggage locker at Naples airport and mailed the key to an address in the city. It didn't occur to her to ask if she was killing a bad guy or a good guy. All Mechanic cared about was the successful completion of the contract and getting paid.

She knocked the top off a bottle of tonic and unloaded the bags, putting items into the refrigerator. The big advantage of having her own place was she could ensure she ate the right foods and stayed healthy. She needed to be in top condition for her line of work.

A door slammed.

Mechanic scanned the apartment. It had six doors and she could see four of them from where she was standing. All were slightly ajar. She remembered closing the front door with the back of her heel, so it had to be the bathroom door, which was around the corner.

Mechanic reached across and drew the long chef's knife from the block.

She skirted the centre island in the kitchen and dropped to a crouch. She could see the door reflected in the hall mirror. It was closed.

Mechanic stood up, the knife clenched in her right hand, and made her way across the hall. She could hear the sound of soft murmuring, someone speaking. A gentle voice was whispering something which she could not catch.

Mechanic reached the door and gripped the handle. There was a bang as another door slammed shut. She spun around, thrusting the blade out in front of her.

Mechanic glanced around the rooms. The front door was shut and the others were still open. She turned back to the bathroom. The voice floated around, as she twisted the handle and burst inside, plunging the knife into thin air. It was empty.

Toiletries and folded towels lay in exactly the same place as when she'd left to go to the store. Mechanic spun on her heels and ran to the bedroom. Her shoulder thumped into the wood and she clattered inside. It too was empty. The next bedroom was the same, along with the laundry closet.

Another door slammed.

She whirled around, the blade slicing through the air. All the doors except the front door were open. Mechanic held her breath and listened to the distant whispering. Another door slammed. To her horror Mechanic realised the noises were coming from inside her head.

The razor-sharp point dug into the wood floor as Mechanic let the knife fall from her grasp. She rushed to the kitchen, switched on the gas hob and rummaged through a drawer. She found what she was looking for – a metal barbecue skewer.

The steel crackled in the blue flame. Mechanic sank to the floor, tears running down her face as she held her breath.

Listening.

Heavy footsteps pounded around the labyrinth in her head, the unmistakeable sound of voices echoing off the walls. Doors banging and slamming.

'No!' she cried seizing the hair either side of her head.

The silver-coated metal turned carbon black in the heat. Mechanic tore off her top, wound a dishcloth around her hand and grabbed the skewer.

She could smell the hot metal.

The skewer hovered just above her stomach. Tiny hairs on her skin singed under the heat. A dozen old scars were slashed white across her flesh where the pigment had been burned away.

Mechanic held her breath, listening.

Her whole body shook causing the tip of the metal to kiss her skin. It hissed, sending cotton wisps of smoke into the air. Mechanic winced, the sweet smell of scorched flesh filled her senses.

Mechanic tensed every muscle to control what had to happen next. The skewer wavered above her skin.

As quickly as they had appeared, the voices subsided and the footsteps stopped.

She tossed the skewer into the sink. It sizzled against the wet stainless steel. Mechanic slumped forward, drew her knees to her chest and put her head in her hands. Her shoulders rocked back and forth as she sobbed.

Daddy was back.

Chapter 8

Lucas boarded the early morning flight bound for Newark
Liberty International where he planned to rent a car and
drive the fifty-nine miles to Darian, Connecticut. There
a tree-lined remembrance garden overlooking the expensive
Noroton Heights district was to be the final resting place of Chris
Bassano.

Lucas had a knot of nervous tension in his stomach the size of
Ellis Island and was dreading the day. Not just because his friend
was being cremated, but he was nervous as hell about meeting his
parents.

He had met them several times in the past and they had
got on well, their son liked Lucas, so they did too. But when
Bassano was attacked by Mechanic and had to leave the force,
their attitude towards him changed. The atmosphere was
decidedly hostile. Lucas had tried to contact Bassano when they
took him back to the family home to recuperate, but the parents
kept him at a distance. They needed someone to blame and held
Lucas responsible. It was an absurd assertion, but Lucas allowed
them to hate him. After all, their actions confirmed his own
feelings of guilt.

The Bassano family were well off. His father was a partner
in a law firm in Manhattan and could never understand why his
son was drawn to the dirty and less well-paid end of the business.
Chris was one of five brothers, and to their father's permanent
annoyance, not one of them had chosen to follow in his footsteps.

Lucas drove away from New York heading for the Hutchinson
River Parkway and I-95 north to Darien. The funeral was being
held at Oakland Cemetery in Fairfield, one hundred acres of the

most beautifully landscaped grounds and manicured lawns. He rolled through the front gates and up the driveway. The keen wind was cold enough to blow right through your coat and the grey sky was threatening rain. Ideal weather for a funeral.

Lucas stepped out of the car and fumbled around in his jacket pocket. He produced a black tie and swept it around his neck. The last time he wore this suit and tie combination, he was committing his wife to the ground. He could see his reflection in the driver's window and his hands were shaking.

After several attempt she straightened the knot, flattened down the collar, and walked across the granite paving to the chapel. Lucas saw a cluster of people milling around outside and in the centre was the minister dressed in black robes with purple edging. Lucas stood on the periphery of the group and surveyed the faces. He knew no one.

Without anyone giving a noticeable signal, they filed in through the dark oak doors to take their seats. The chapel was large with plain white walls and a high vaulted ceiling. Rows of wooden chairs lined both sides of the wide central aisle. A red ribbon of carpet ran the entire length of the building and flowers adorned the sandstone altar at the front. Pamphlets had been placed on each seat giving the order of service, and on the front cover the smiling face of Chris Bassano beamed up at the congregation. Lucas felt a lump rise in his throat as he picked it up and took a seat. He choked it down.

He gazed at the floor and his eyes stung with tears, as the memories of burying his wife shuddered through him. The indistinct strains of soft music washed through the chapel, along with the sound of muted conversation.

The family entered and people rose to their feet, craning their heads to get a look. The minister led the way with his head bowed, followed by the father and mother. He had his arm wound tight around her waist, as if to steady them both, and she had her hands out in front clutching a small posy of flowers. Both wore dark glasses. The coffin came next, carried high on the shoulders of the brothers, four strapping guys each one the image of Chris, each one with watery eyes. Two men from the funeral directors followed the cortege in their sombre suits and with sombre faces. It was a heartrending scene.

Lucas continued to stare at the floor as they passed. The coffin was slid on to a staging at the front of the chapel and the family helped each other into the first few rows, sitting amongst their wives, girlfriends and children.

The service was mercifully short, a couple of hymns plus a few prayers, and a eulogy given by one of the brothers which had everyone dabbing away the tears. There is something catastrophically sad about saying goodbye to someone taken too soon.

At the end the minister said a prayer, as a curtain drew around the coffin obscuring it from view. The front pews emptied out first, followed by the rest of the congregation filing past the shrouded casket into a walled courtyard.

The family lined up to shake hands with the mourners, who in turn cried on their shoulders in a show of mutual grief. Lucas hung back. Bassano's father had spotted him in the crowd and turned away. Lucas was determined to pay his respects so kept his place in the thinning crowd.

By the time Lucas reached them the family had dispersed, talking with relatives, doing their best to console each other. Bassano's father stepped out of nowhere and offered his hand.

'Thank you for coming,' he said.

Lucas shook it and placed his other hand on his shoulder.

'I'm so sorry for your loss.'

Fabiano Bassano nodded as though any words he said could never express what he felt. He held onto Lucas's hand and pulled him in close.

'Did she do it?'

Lucas was stunned by the question.

'I'm sorry, who?'

'Did she kill Chris? That fucking maniac bitch who took his arm. Did she do it?'

'I haven't worked the case, but from what I know, there is no evidence to indicate who did it.'

'Yes, I know, that's what the police told us. But I'm asking you, did she do it?'

Bassano's stare pierced through Lucas, his eyes welling with grief and pain.

'Yeah, I believe she did.'

Fabiano Bassano released Lucas's hand and hugged him tight.

'Can you do me a massive favour?' he whispered through clenched teeth.

'I'll try, what is it?' Lucas tried to move away from the forced embrace, but he was clamped solid.

'Can you track her down and kill the murdering bitch. And then call me when it's done. I have money and there is nothing better I want to spend it on. All you need to do is ask.'

He released Lucas from his bear hug and gripped his shoulders with both hands.

'Can you do that for me?'

Lucas nodded his head.

'It will be my pleasure, Mr Bassano.'

The fight was on.

Chapter 9

Lucas was finishing breakfast in the kitchen when he heard the familiar sound of alloy wheels striking concrete. It was 9am. and Lucas always knew when Harper had come to visit. Harper had swung his car around in the road and clattered into the kerb. It happened every time.

Lucas had got back late from the funeral and was waiting for his third cup of coffee of the morning to blow away his muzzy head. Harper had left him an excited message on his answer machine, something about the information Moran had turned up and what they had to do today. At least that's what Lucas thought he said, it was difficult to tell as Harper was both excited and drunk. At least arriving home late last night had brought with it one advantage. Lucas didn't have a hangover.

Harper waited in the car and Lucas dumped his weary frame into the passenger seat. 'How was it?' he asked.

'It was shit.'

'How were his folks?'

'They were shit.'

'You okay?'

'I feel like shit.'

'Shit all round then, eh?' Harper said, impressed by his friend's descriptive powers.

They set off, heading for town. Neither one felt like talking until Lucas broke the silence.

'His father offered me money to kill Mechanic.'

'Did you tell him we're gonna do it for free?'

'No, but I told him it would be my pleasure.'

That broke the verbal dam. Harper babbled on about the information provided by Moran. He talked about Jessica Hudson and how that had proved a dead end. He talked about Nassra Shamon and how Moran believed this was Mechanic using a fake ID. He talked about the money transfers from Shamon's bank account and banged on about Helix Holdings.

'Where are we going?' Lucas interrupted Harper's flow.

'To the public records office.'

American companies are registered at state level and must provide four principal officers. Typically, these are a president, a vice president, a secretary and a treasurer, although one person can fill multiple roles. Helix Holdings just happened to be registered in Florida, so Harper had told Moran he would take the information and see what he could dig up. Moran was relieved he was leaving her out of it but she feared that would not last long.

They arrived at the imposing stone-fronted public building and went inside. It was like a vast library with company records held on five floors, each with its own silent study area and a set of IBM computers. Harper strolled up to reception and spoke to the woman behind the desk.

'We'd like to trace a company which is registered here in Florida.'

'Certainly, sir, all records are stored alphabetically starting with A at the top left of the building.'

'The company is Helix Holdings.'

'That's on the fourth floor. Come out of the elevator and turn right.'

'Thank you.'

The coffee had finally kicked in and Lucas felt quietly positive. Harper was on a high, behaving like a crazed bloodhound.

Turning right out of the elevator they were confronted by an enormous room stacked to the ceiling with row upon row of files and bound documents. A young man with glasses approached them as they stared at the lines of shelving disappearing into the distance.

'Anything out of reach, guys, you only have to holler and I'll get it down for you.' He breezed past into the opposite hall.

'Cheeky little shit,' Harper said.

'He's just being helpful.'

'He's just being a cheeky little shit, that's what he's being.'

'Come on, old man.' Lucas went inside.

It was truly needle-in-an-alphabetical-haystack time. They split up, each one looking for 'H'– if only it was that easy. After forty minutes Lucas strode over to Harper, who was halfway up a ladder busy proving a point to the cheeky shit in the glasses.

'I have good news and bad news.'

He was holding a fat buff-coloured file in one hand and a thick book in the other.

'Fantastic.' Harper climbed down and they both headed for the soft-seated area. 'So what's the good news?'

'I found it,' Lucas said handing Harper the overflowing file. 'Helix Holdings, the president is a man named John Stringer.'

'That's great. We can feed that to Moran and find out where he lives.' Harper hesitated, 'You said there was bad news.'

'Look at the paperwork.'

Harper flicked through the sheaf of official-looking documents and read out some names.

'Cut Above?'

'That's a hairdressing business,' Lucas said.

'Crazy Catering?'

'As the name suggests, it's a catering business.'

'Fender Benders?'

'A panel beating and car repair business.'

'What the hell are these?'

'They are all companies.'

'But we want Helix Holdings not a sandwich maker and a garage.'

'That's right, we do. The bad news is they are all Helix Holdings.'

'I don't get it.'

'Neither did I, so I asked the cheeky little shit and he gave me this.' Lucas held up the book. 'Helix Holdings is a damn shell company, or holding company, or parent company, or whatever the hell it's called. There are so many definitions in this book I don't know which one fits.' He tossed it to Harper who struggled to catch it. 'What I do know is, it's not a single entity, whatever they choose to call it.'

'You mean all these businesses are part of Helix Holdings?'

'Yup.'

'What does that mean to us?'

'It means, my friend,' Lucas leaned forward, 'when Mechanic pays money to Helix Holdings it's anyone's guess where it ends up.'

'But doesn't it go to this John Stringer character?'

'Not necessarily. Each company has its own governance and its own board, it could be any of them.'

'What, any one of these?' Harper fanned through the pages and raised his eyebrows.

'I think so.'

'Shit, man, there's a ton of businesses named in here.'

'Yes, it's a lot, but significantly less than when we started.'

* * *

Searching through the complex structure of Helix Holdings was like playing a game of Russian dolls. Every time they located a company, that too owned a company, which owned another, and another, and so it went on. They worked through the morning and into the afternoon, forgetting about lunch. By 4pm they had identified twenty-three separate companies along with the names of sixty-six people who were involved in one role or another.

Lucas tried to structure their findings by mapping out a company tree showing how the businesses linked together. But even that got confusing. By the end he had six pieces of paper taped together, with what looked like a child's badly done homework scribbled on it.

'Are we done, I'm starving,' he said.

'I guess so, I've come to the end of the line and you stopped a while ago to draw a map of the subway, so I figure we are. Copy those names into your sheet, I need to make a call.' Harper handed Lucas more paper.

Lucas set to work listing the owners and their associated companies.

Harper stood in one of the soundproof phone booths in the lobby.

'Detective Moran, please.'

'Moran speaking.'

'We have the names of people associated with Helix Holdings. It's not an exhaustive list, but a start.'

'Okay.' Moran was in an office full of people.

'Give me a fax number and I'll send it over. I want you to run each name and see what comes up.'

'Give me your phone number and I'll call you back,' she said in a light and airy manner.

Harper read off the number and hung up. Two minutes later it rang.

'I did what you asked, now fuck off.'

Moran was obviously in a place where she could speak more freely.

'You did, and now you need to do more.'

'Go to hell.'

'Don't be a hero, I have you over a barrel and we both know it. Now stop pissing around and give me the fax number.'

The line went quiet for a minute and then Moran returned. She gave him the number and hung up without waiting for a response.

By the time Harper got back, Lucas had completed the list. Harper had the number written on his hand.

'Just gonna send this off to Moran,' he said scooping the papers from the desk.

'Isn't it great that she's on board?'

'Yup, sure is.'

Harper walked off in search of a fax machine.

Chapter 10

Mechanic watched the first rays of the sun wash a burnt orange glow across the walls of her apartment. She was sitting hunched in the corner with her knees tucked under her chin, her arms hugged around her ankles pulling them in tight. She'd been like this all night.

The attack had taken her by surprise. There had been no warnings, no feelings of uneasiness, nothing. As the night hours ticked by, her head raced, searching for the trigger which had brought it on. The only thing which made sense was moving back to San Diego. Maybe it was a step too far. Instead of exorcising the demons that blighted her, it had brought them back to life.

Mechanic had managed to doze a little but spent the rest of the night wide awake, listening for noises inside her head. Thankfully none came. The skewer was still in the sink, a physical reminder, if she needed it, that it was not a dream.

She was shattered and scared.

Scared that she would once again descend into a world where she had little control of her actions, driven instead by the insane desire to sacrifice lives to satisfy Daddy: the vicious merry-go-round of planning and killing, only to have to plan and kill again. The prospect had frozen her to the spot.

She watched the shadows shift across the floor as the sun rose higher in the sky. The daylight felt better. She got to her feet and stretched out the cramps in her legs, not sure what to do next. Carrying on as normal was her only option, she could hardly keep herself huddled in a corner forever.

The phone rang.

'Hello.'

'We got another one.'

It was Jameson.

'Okay, usual pick-up?'

'Yup, I sent it yesterday. Get back to me as soon as you can, these guys want to move fast.'

'I'll collect first thing this morning.'

After a pause Jameson said, 'Have you given any thought to when we might meet?'

'Have you lined up a few days' emergency leave?'

'It's all in place, I can push the button whenever you say.'

'Then push it.' She hung up.

Mechanic poured herself a glass of cranberry juice and went to the bedroom to get changed. She had to clear her head of last night's troubles. And the thought of beating the crap out of Jameson while getting herself fucked to a standstill was just the type of normality she needed.

* * *

Ten minutes later Mechanic left her apartment and ran across the road towards Horton Plaza. She decided the longer route along Market Street and First Avenue would be good, a distance of a little over a mile.

She arrived at the post office, clicked her watch and leaned against the wall to catch her breath. Her legs and face were red, she was radiating heat and her hands shook. She had pushed the pace hard and did it in well under six minutes. Mechanic sucked in air and linked her fingers together at the back of her head. The exertion had certainly blown away the cobwebs of an awful night.

She allowed herself time to cool down, joined the queue inside and waited her turn.

'Box 508, please,' she said to the woman behind the counter and handed over a key. An anonymous PO box made an ideal drop location. Paid for on a monthly basis in cash, it was perfect. A couple of minutes later Mechanic pushed the fat envelope under her vest and ran home.

Back at the apartment, she dumped it on the table and headed for the shower, feeling considerably better. She had to carry on as normal. What the hell else was she going to do?

Mechanic sat with her breakfast of hot, sweet coffee and mixed fruit. She tore open the envelope and retrieved the papers inside, spreading them on the table.

The briefing packs were always concise, containing details of the target, an itinerary of recent movements, and the most important thing, when and where the hit was to go down. This always took the form of a photocopy of a diary entry, which made it look like a meeting. The time and place was merely a suggestion from Jameson. Mechanic trusted his operational judgement and when Jameson provided an initial view it made for good planning. But if she didn't like it, or could see a better alternative, then it was always up for discussion.

The one thing not in the pack was the fee, a sensible omission should it ever fall into the wrong hands. This was agreed over the phone along with the finer details, such as method of entry, extraction, specialist kit and logistics support.

This hit was a walk-by kill, a riskier scenario than a sniper shot. Mechanic got a buzz out of getting up close when murder had a personal motive, but in contract killings she preferred to be at a distance. This job was all about making the right approach, executing cleanly and exiting fast. Controlling the environment would be fraught with uncertainty – however meticulous the planning, it had to be supplemented with a slice of good luck.

Elaine Cooper was a regular night shopper who bought her groceries from a 24-hour store in a suburb of San Francisco when everyone else was tucked up in bed. Maybe she was a shift worker, or an insomniac, or preferred to shop with no lines at the checkout. Mechanic liked to play a game and try to fathom what people did from the briefing information. Perhaps she had an embarrassing deformity or was having an affair with the guy at the store. The possibilities bounced around in Mechanic's head. Either way it didn't matter, Elaine Cooper had managed to upset someone enough to want her dead.

Chapter 11

Moran's day was going to hell in a handcart. She was freaked out by Harper's call and was still trying to maintain her resolute position of not getting involved. But the situation was hopeless and Harper was not a man to be taken lightly. He was right, she was well and truly screwed. If he carried out his threat to send the CCTV pictures to her boss she was finished.

She had the list of names from Harper and was considering the best time to run them through the system without arousing suspicion when Mills stuck his head around the door and shouted, 'Full meeting, drop what you're doing.'

Shit, what now, Moran thought. She picked up a pad of paper and followed the procession into the conference room.

Her case investigating the fatal shooting of the police officer was running out of steam and her time was being prioritised into other areas, which suited her fine. The less focus there was on it, the less chance she'd be forced to declare something she didn't want to. There was a strong whiff of the case becoming old news.

Mills stood at the head of the table with a large image projected onto the wall behind him. It showed a freeze-frame of the man opening the back door of a car as Ramirez toppled out.

'Jerome Wilson.' He tapped the wall with a long stick. 'We brought him in for questioning on the suspicion of killing Ramirez Sanchez.' He moved the point of the stick to indicate the guy falling to the sidewalk. 'Not surprisingly he kept his mouth shut, as did the driver of the vehicle, a local hood by the name of Samuel Torte.' He tapped the stick against the grainy outline of the man in the driver's seat. 'Both men said they had borrowed the car from a friend, which checks out, though for friend substitute the words "a member of the same drug gang", and ...' Mills paused and turned to the people crowded around the table, 'they both insisted Ramirez already had his throat ripped open when they got back to the car.'

'Surprise, surprise,' said one of the older guys.

Moran looked at her pad avoiding eye contact with Mills. She knew what was coming next.

Mills continued, 'Annoyingly, the forensics report on the car supports this. It says the amount of blood found on the seats and floor was consistent with the victim bleeding out for at least a minute and a half. The time between the suspects getting into the car and Ramirez ending up on the sidewalk was twenty seconds. It also says the blade entered the left side of Ramirez's neck and was slashed forward, severing his jugular and trachea. He died almost immediately. It would be difficult for Wilson or Torte to make that move from the front seat. The most likely scenario is the cut was made from outside the car through the window.' Mills pushed the button on a remote control and the image changed.

The hairs on the back of Moran's neck stood on end and her chest tightened. Projected on the wall was the image of Nassra Shamon.

'This woman can be seen approaching the car.' Mills clicked the button and a montage of screen grabs appeared. He tapped the stick on each one in turn. 'Here is Ramirez peering out of the back passenger window, here the woman leaning into the vehicle, and here she's walking away. The next we see Ramirez, he's spilling claret all over the sidewalk.'

Mills indexed the slide show forward. 'So, ladies and gentlemen, does anyone know this woman?' Moran stared at the three-foot-high picture of Nassra Shamon. There was nowhere to hide.

'Sir, she looks like the woman who rented the place where the police officer was shot dead. It's not a great match but she looks similar.' She had no choice but to call it out.

'Do you have a current mug shot?'

'Not current, it's the one lifted from her driving licence.'

'Get it down to the lab and let them take a closer look. Remind me, we never found her after the patrolman was found dead in her apartment, did we?'

'No sir, she disappeared.' Moran was trying to sound matter of fact and professional on the outside, when inside she was crumbling to dust.

'Chase this through and let's see if we can make a connection. Anyone else got a fix on who she might be?' Mills asked. Everyone looked around and shook their heads, everyone that is except Moran, who was too busy avoiding eye contact.

'Good work, Moran,' Mills said walking from the room. She grunted.

Moran took the photocopied image to the lab and spent the rest of the day processing the list of names Harper had given her.

She wasn't sure what the female equivalent was, but running every name through the system was a balls-aching job. Sixty-six data entry files to complete, followed by the system spewing out sixty-six personal profiles, there was a mountain of information to sift through. She had reached number forty-three when she got a call.

'Come down downstairs, we got something interesting.' It was the technician.

She entered the lab, which was a very different working environment to the one upstairs. To start with, it was clean and air conditioned and had a medical feel to it. The benches were stacked with complex-looking equipment being used by white-coated people who were busying themselves with test tubes and chemicals. Mills was already there, looking through a large lens.

He tapped the table. 'See what you think.'

Moran looked through the optic at the grainy print of Nassra Shamon's face. The lab tech removed the picture and replaced it with a still from the CCTV footage. There was no doubt in her mind, they were identical.

'Not sure,' she said trying to cast an element of doubt.

'Really?' Mills elbowed her out of the way to take a second look. 'They look remarkably similar to me.'

She looked again. 'I suppose it could be the same person.'

Mills picked up the picture. 'So this woman slits Ramirez's throat, returns to her apartment, and three hours later a police officer is found dead, shot through the back of the neck. If we can make the connection and prove it, I reckon we'll blow this case wide open.'

Moran's day was not yet over but it was certainly on its way to hell, being transported unceremoniously in a handcart.

Chapter 12

Lucas and Harper sat patiently by the fax machine, or to be more accurate, one half of them did. The other half fizzed with irritation.

'She said 10.30am.' Harper looked at his watch.

'It's only 10.40.'

The public records office was almost empty as they waited for the paper-spewing machine to bring good news.

'She said 10.30.' Harper was not going to let it go.

'What else did she say?'

'She didn't say much. She said she'd collated the results and would fax them through.'

'Had she found anything?'

'She didn't say.' Harper mentally recalled that Moran actually had a lot to say, most of it blunt and to the point, bordering on abusive.

The machine whirred into action and the sheets rolled off. Lucas looked at the number in the LCD display window.

'It's her,' he said, recognising the Vegas dial code. Page after page churned out, thirty-two pages of densely printed names, addresses, previous convictions, known associates and bank details. Lucas gathered them together and put them in a file, paid the beady-eyed woman behind reception one dollar sixty cents and then headed to the fourth floor.

'She's done a thorough job,' said Lucas scanning through the names and addresses.

As they stepped out of the lift the young guy in glasses breezed past.

'If there's anything you can't reach give me a shout and I'll get it for you.'

Harper gave him his best scowl.

'He's only doing his job,' Lucas said.

'I'll do a job on him, cheeky little—'

'It's strange how Moran has done all this work and yet didn't offer an opinion on what she'd found,' Lucas interrupted. He fanned the pages through his thumb and forefinger.

'Not very chatty, I suppose.'

'When I talked to her she was adamant she was having nothing to do with it. And then she produces all this.'

'Yes, very odd,'

'How did you persuade her to help?'

'I said it would be good if she could lend a hand.'

'Lend a hand? This is a little more than lending a hand. What exactly did you say to change her mind?'

'Nothing, I guess she just decided to help out.'

'Wait a minute.' Lucas had first-hand experience of Harper being evasive. 'What have you done? How does she go from telling me to fuck off to this?' He waved the papers in front of Harper.

Harper turned and faced Lucas with his hands held up in a sign of surrender.

'I blackmailed her, okay?' he said, as though it were the most natural thing in the world, which to him it probably was.

'You did what?'

'Blackmailed her.'

'But how? With what?'

'I acquired the CCTV tapes from the multi-storey the morning we planned to take out Mechanic. I sent her pictures of you, me and her together, and suggested it would be better if she cooperated.'

'Or what?'

'Or I would send them to her boss. She could either deal with us or deal with him. She chose us.'

'I don't believe it. Why didn't you say something?'

Harper slapped his hands to his sides.

'Because you'd get all self-righteous and stop me. That's why.'

'Damn right I would. You can't go around blackmailing serving police officers.'

'That proves my point, doesn't it? We got a head start here. We got these names and addresses because she's decided to play ball. The ends justify the means and I can sleep at night.'

'You sleep at night because you're drunk.'

Lucas was not sure what to make of Harper's actions. On the one hand he was horrified, on the other he was impressed.

'How did you get the tapes?' he asked.

'That was easy, I just—'

'I don't want to know. It's difficult to work out who's more ruthless, you or the crooks we used to catch.'

'There was a time when that was definitely me but now I figure it's honours even.'

Lucas handed Harper half the papers.

'Look through these and see if anything unusual jumps out.'

They separated and each found a quiet spot. Harper could hear Lucas tutting from across the room.

The next hour passed quickly, both of them trawling through the papers. Lucas was so engrossed he didn't notice Harper standing in front of him with two Styrofoam cups.

'Coffee?' he said handing one of them over. 'Have you found anything?'

'Not much, there's nothing that jumps out, what about you?'

'Not sure what I was expecting but it's all mundane stuff. A handful of speeding fines and parking violations but nothing says 'arrested for running arms out of Nicaragua'. However, I do have one that's different.'

'Different how?'

'Every company has multiple people holding different roles, agreed?'

'Yeah, that's what I have too.'

'Some are family members and others are business associates, but there's always multiple people.'

'That's what I've got.'

'Well, I have one company where all the roles are held by one person, a man named Gerry Vickers. I don't know if that's significant but it does stand out from the pack.'

'What is the business name?'

'Sheldon Chemicals.' Harper handed Lucas his list with the name circled in red.

The young chap with glasses walked by.

'Excuse me,' Harper said putting out his hand to stop him. 'Could you help us locate this company's records?' He snatched the page from Lucas and handed it to him.

'Do you know it's registered here?'

Lucas and Harper looked at each other blankly.

The young man realised he had reached the end of useful conversation. 'I'll take a look, sir, won't be a moment.'

'Nice kid,' Harper said.

Lucas shook his head.

A couple of minutes later he returned with a dog-eared manila file stuffed with papers.

'Here you go, sir, Sheldon Chemicals.'

Harper nodded a thank you and spread the papers on the desk. After a while Lucas leaned back in the chair and sipped at his coffee.

'That's odd.'

'What?'

'Why would you register a company in Florida and operate it out of San Diego? And Gerry Vickers should be businessman of the year.'

'Why?'

'Take a look at the annual report.' Lucas handed Harper a glossy pamphlet.

'Okay, wise guy, it might surprise you to hear I've forgotten everything I learned at Harvard. What does it say?'

'The company runs a chemical procurement and distribution business. It has a steady turnover of about a million dollars a year and buys all its chemicals from one company. It has six customers and does its distribution through a third party called Decklan Logistics.'

'What's unusual about that?'

'Look at the other documents. Gerry Vickers must be superhuman because according to this he runs the whole thing single-handed.'

'Maybe the guy's a genius.'

'Let's find out.' Lucas picked up the annual report and walked off in the direction of the payphone.

Harper waited, pretending to read the other documents relating to Sheldon Chemicals.

After fifteen minutes Lucas returned.

'Well?' asked Harper.

'I rang the supplier and the haulage company. They both stopped trading with Sheldon Chemicals three years ago when it went into liquidation.'

'So it's not a real business?'

'No, I figure Gerry Vickers is using it to launder money.'

'How's he doing that?'

'I know a little about this from my time in Chicago. If I'm right, it's a classic case of placing, layering and integration. You place dirty cash into the company and move it around to create confusion. Then you bring it back in as clean money.'

'Let me get this straight. They buy non-existent chemicals, sell them to non-existent customers and pretend to collect the money from them.'

'Yup, they pay taxes to the IRS on the income and the money is clean.'

'Wow, and they bag about a mill a year?'

'That's what it says.'

'If we can connect the money transactions from Nassra Shamon to Sheldon Chemicals we have game on.'

Lucas nodded and cracked a smile.

Harper continued, 'We need to dig deeper into our new friend Gerry Vickers, because a thought occurred to me while you were off playing IRS investigator.'

'What's that?'

'We're looking for someone who can lay their hands on the latest military hardware, right?'

'Right.'

'So, San Diego is homeport to the Pacific Fleet, the biggest US naval base in the States.'

Chapter 13

The Nassra Shamon bandwagon was gathering pace. Mills had failed to make headway with the hotel murders or the drug-related killings and his reputation was crumbling around his ankles. The discovery of Nassra Shamon had given him a face he could chase, even if he had no idea where the woman was.

Mills was determined to crack this one and was throwing his weight around. Moran, on the other hand, was busy trying to work out how to stop her career from being tossed onto the bonfire. How could she distance herself from the investigation into the killing of Ramirez? If she was right, and Nassra Shamon and Mechanic were the same person, then arresting Shamon could bring Moran's employment and liberty to an abrupt end. However, if she was right, then she also held the trump card. The chance of Mills getting anywhere near Shamon was virtually zero.

'New work orders,' Mills barked as he entered the office. 'I need to shuffle people around to cover the bases.' He allocated new roles and tasks to the team. 'Moran, I want you on the money. Find out about Shamon's financial affairs.'

Shit, she knew exactly what she was going to find. She was backed into a corner and could see no way out.

The phone rang, it was Harper.

'Give me your details caller and I will ring you back,' Moran said fighting the urge to tell him to go to hell. She made her way to a side office and closed the door.

'What do you want now?' she spat into the receiver.

'Good morning to you too.'

'Look, Harper, I did what you asked. Give me a break.'

'You did, and that proved very useful. And now you need to help us again.'

'What is it?'

'We want you to run a name through the system: Gerry Vickers. He owns a business called Sheldon Chemicals operating out of San Diego. Turns out it's a subsidiary of Helix Holdings. He came up on the list you sent.'

'What's so special about him?'

'He's different, that's all.' Harper was keen not to give anything away.

'What am I looking for?'

'The usual – last known address, any previous, known associates, that kind of thing.'

'I gave you that before.'

'Run it again. There has to be more to this guy than what you sent us.'

'This has to be the last time. Things are hotting up around here and I'm struggling to keep a lid on this.'

'Hotting up how?'

'They've identified Nassra Shamon as a possible murder suspect and have launched an all-hands investigation.'

'Murder? Who did she kill?'

'A man called Ramirez. With the spotlight on her it's only a matter of time before the forensic accountants are all over Helix Holdings, then your guy Gerry Vickers will be next, and the direct line to Mechanic will be dead.'

'Shit, you need to bury it.'

'Don't talk stupid. All that whisky must have rotted your brain. I can't bury information like that.'

'We want Gerry Vickers to ourselves, you need to find a way to delete those records.'

'Are you out of your mind? The woman is a murder suspect, do you honestly believe that's possible?'

'It doesn't matter what I believe, what's important is what are you going to do about it?'

Moran fell silent, beads of sweat forming on her upper lip.

Harper continued to turn the screw. 'You told me that you believed Nassra Shamon and Mechanic were the same person. If that's true, and it increasingly looks like you're right, you don't want your uniformed friends getting to Vickers first. If they do, I will be the least of your troubles.'

'I can give you seventy-two hours max, then that's it. After that, I will have to give up the account details. That's the best I can do.'

'I need the info about Vickers fast.'

'I'll get you what you want. Give me an hour and I'll fax anything I find to the usual number, but this has to be the last time.' She banged the phone down.

Sitting alone in a side office she could hear the noise of intense activity taking place outside. Mills was whipping the troops, and himself, into a frenzy. She had to get creative if she was to buy herself seventy-two hours.

* * *

An hour later the fax machine in the public records office churned out a single page. The lady behind the desk said, 'Twenty cents, please'. Lucas fished around and put the coin in her hand.

He and Harper sat in the quiet zone reading the document.

'Is that it?' said Harper.

'Suppose so.'

'You sure you've not left more on the printer?'

'No, that's all of it.'

'We got a name, an address and a driver's licence. That's not much to go on.'

Lucas was thinking, then the obvious went off in his head like a grenade. 'We have everything we want right here.'

'But there's jack shit to go on.'

'Precisely. It's like this guy exists in name only.'

Harper had the same grenade moment.

'A fictitious company run by a fictitious man.' Harper paused. 'There's something else.'

'What.'

'Moran said we gotta move fast because the cops are looking for Nassra Shamon in connection with a murder. She will delay giving them the financial records but she figures we have seventy-two hours tops. I told her to delete them but she won't play ball.'

'Better get a move on and book a flight.'

* * *

Moran perched on the corner of a table and glanced at her watch: 7.15pm. Her desk looked like a fire hazard with paper sprawled into every corner. The office was deserted. In front of her lay a computer printout with the three payments to Helix Holdings highlighted in yellow, the last one made the day before Shamon killed Ramirez and the cop. The line below was the entry for the following day, it said Account Closed.

She stared into the middle distance playing with scenarios in her head. How could she put the brakes on? How could she delay without making it obvious?

The conference door across the hallway banged against the doorstop snatching her from her thoughts, Mills blundered in.

'Hey.'

'Hey.'

'Didn't know anyone was still here.'

'Yes, I'm still here.'

'How you getting on with the Shamon accounts?'

Moran slid the printout under the mound of paper.

'There's something screwy with the transactions. I remember looking at this before, when we first investigated the cop found dead at her apartment. It was all in order, but now the account has been corrupted with a bunch of weird shit. I need to get hold of the bank first thing tomorrow to straighten it out.'

'Okay. You sound tired, get yourself home.'

'Yeah, I was just packing up.'

'Me too.' Mills swung his arms through his jacket and picked up a briefcase.

'Fancy a beer?' Moran blurted out.

Mills looked like she'd asked him to lend her a million dollars. Moran could see the cogs spinning as he tried to make sense of the request.

'Er, well, yes, I suppose so.'

It was not the enthusiastic 'Oh, yes please' response she had expected.

'Look, if you're busy that's fine, I didn't fancy going home straightaway.'

'No, listen, that would be good. I could do with a beer.' Mills was recovering well.

Moran grabbed her bag and he held the door for her.

'You have a favourite place?' he asked.

'No, not been here long enough.'

'I know a bar that's nearby, it does fantastic ice-cold beer with chips and salsa.'

Moran walked down the corridor, making small talk, clutching her bag to her chest. If she was going to delay spilling the beans on the Shamon account, she needed to be on the right side of the guy who was going to ask for it. She was not looking forward to the evening, no matter how cold the beer or good the chips and salsa.

Chapter 14

The taxi door swung open and Mechanic looked out across the hotel concourse. The concierge stared at her legs as they emerged from the back seat, the hem of her dress rising ever higher as she slid out. The sequined material shimmered under the spotlights piercing the darkness above. She towered over the gawping man in her stripper's heels.

Two men in monkey suits swished open the double glass doors and Mechanic made her way through reception, her heels announcing her presence as she crossed the marble floor. Business types stopped their inane chatter as she slinked into the lounge bar. The throw around her shoulders hid little of her cleavage and her legs seemed to go on forever. Her short blonde hair was now long and auburn while the green contacts electrified her eyes.

The hotel smelled of honeysuckle as the air conditioning pumped its corporate brand of scent into the air. The inside was a collage of marble, chrome and deeply upholstered leather. Expensive people draped themselves on expensive chairs, and expensive carpet supported their expensive footwear.

Mechanic was met by the maitre d' who was falling over himself to be of service. After a brief discussion he showed her to a seat at the bar and then clicked his fingers to attract the attention of the tuxedo-suited barman. He bowed as he left her, probably to get a closer look at her lack of skirt.

The bar was long and plush. The mirrored wall behind magnified the effect of the dripping chandeliers. Mechanic inched herself onto the bar stool and crossed her legs. When she moved, the light caught her drop earrings and, with her lips the colour of cherry cola, the barman was falling over himself with eager attention.

'Wild Turkey on ice, please.'

The barman looked surprised, expecting an order of Moet or Krug rather than Kentucky straight bourbon with a kick like a mule.

'Certainly, madam.'

The bar was noisy with dinner-suited men and the occasional glitzy woman. The guys were putting on a pitiful show of not looking at the new arrival. Mechanic glanced down the bar at the solitary guy at the far end. He was dressed in a grey suit and an open-necked shirt. He looked up for a moment, then continued to stare into his glass.

She sipped her drink and the ice chimed against the crystal. She toyed with the glass on the bar and spun it round on the coaster.

The guy in the open-necked shirt was standing beside her.

'Can I get you another?' he said in a slow southern drawl.

'Maybe,' she said, 'when I've finished this one.'

The bar went quiet. The raucous chat was replaced with a 'Did you see that!' silence.

He raised his glass and she chinked hers against it, downing the fiery liquid in one.

'It's finished,' Mechanic said and held the glass for him to take.

He leaned forward and ordered two more.

'You here for business or pleasure?' he said, turning and placing both hands on the bar. His suit creased tight across his arms and shoulders. Even leaning forward he stood about six feet tall, with chiselled features and the celebrity look of a NFL linebacker.

'Both. How about you?'

'Both.'

The drinks arrived.

The man lifted them from the bar and gave one to Mechanic.

'To both business and pleasure,' he said offering a toast. She chinked his glass and downed it in one. He did the same.

'Two more, please,' he said to the barman who hadn't moved from his spot directly in front of them.

The men at the bar had a collective look of 'lucky bastard', while the women had their faces set with a look that said 'frigging hooker'.

'What business are you in?' the man asked.

'The people business,' she replied motioning to him that the drinks had arrived.

He picked them up and handed her one.

'That sounds like fun. What kind of people?'

'All sorts.'

She held her drink in the air. The glasses chimed as he struck the rim and they sank the whisky.

Mechanic held out her hand. No words were necessary. He fished a room key from his pocket and placed it in her open palm. Mechanic slid from the barstool.

If the bar was quiet before it was deathly silent now. The tuxedoed men were nodding their heads in a mutual show of appreciation that said 'nice one'. After a few seconds the women continued talking in an 'I'm not interested' kind of bluff. Despite their different perspectives, all eyes were fixed on Mechanic's ass as she sashayed out of the lounge.

The guy with the open-necked shirt ordered another Wild Turkey and pulled up a stool. He could see the reflection of fifty gawping faces staring back at him in the mirror behind the bar. The drink arrived and he knocked it back. He signed the bill and headed for the elevator, hitting the button marked Executive Suites.

The doors dinged open and he walked the short distance to room 906. He tapped on the door. Mechanic opened it wide and ushered him into a huge suite. It was comprised of two lounges, with steps leading to a massive bedroom, and a bed big enough to hold a game of baseball.

Mechanic opened the mini bar and fixed two glasses of Wild Turkey. She held one out for him to take. He removed his jacket and tossed it on a chair.

He took the drink and chinked his glass against hers.

'So, are we drinking to business or pleasure?' he asked.

His hand snaked around her neck and pulled her close. He kissed her and tasted hot liquor in her mouth. She wound her arm around his waist. She could feel him hard against her.

She dropped her right hand and stroked the front of his pants. 'I said both.'

She grabbed his balls and squeezed. She felt them squish in her hand as she twisted and tightened her grip.

The drink fell from his grasp while his legs buckled. She released him and hammered her right knee into his balls. He doubled over, clutching his crotch.

Whisky slopped from Mechanic's glass and onto her dress.

'You've made a mess,' she said.

'Jesus,' he croaked, staggering around.

Mechanic shoved him and he toppled over backwards onto the floor. He writhed on the carpet, his hands between his legs.

Mechanic sipped her drink and stood astride him.

He looked up. She had her hands on her hips allowing him to feast his eyes on the view. Her underwear was discarded on the bed.

'I said, you made a mess.'

She stamped her heel into his chest. The jagged point tore through his shirt and blood erupted against the white material.

A torrent of air rasped from his throat.

She shifted her weight and ground her heel deep into his flesh. His mouth opened and closed as his skin shredded.

He brought his hands up and seized her foot to alleviate the pressure. Mechanic leaned further forward. He gurgled as her weight tore the air from his lungs.

She held the position until he could take no more, then stepped back to survey her handiwork.

'Roll onto your front.' She kicked him in the side.

He complied, still gasping for breath, his hands clasped to his chest.

Mechanic retrieved something from the table.

She straddled his back, leaned forward and forced a ball gag into his mouth. There was a click as it located itself behind his front teeth. He shook his head and tried to free his hands trapped beneath his body. The leather strap pulled tight across the back of his neck and he retched as the gag was drawn deep into his gaping mouth.

Mechanic tugged his arms from under him and secured them behind his back with a noose tied above his elbows. She stood up and retrieved something else. The man twisted and turned against his bonds, saliva drooling from his mouth. Out of the corner of his eye he could see her approaching, her legs and heels filled his vision.

'I'm going to count to ten.' She circled around him.

'One, two …'

He craned his neck to see what was in her hand but lost her from view when she stepped behind him.

'Three, four …'

His body tensed.

'Five, six …'

He was shaking with anticipation.

'Seven …'

Mechanic reached down and forced a thick plastic bag over his head, yanking a drawstring cord tight around his neck.

He let out a stifled scream as the clear plastic clung to his face.

She laughed and downed the last of her drink, the man choking and squirming at her feet. Mechanic fixed another Wild Turkey and picked up a hunting knife.

She squatted down in front of him and waved the blade across his field of vision. He could see the steel glinting through the condensation which fogged the inside of the bag. The point of the blade picked at the cotton threads of his shirt as she drew the knife down the length of his back. He struggled beneath her, fighting for breath.

'Mind you be still now,' she whispered in his ear. The blade flashed severing the shirt away from his skin.

She shifted forward, drove the blade under the waistband of his pants and slashed it upwards. The material gave way with a tearing sound as the sharp edge cut through his suit.

Mechanic got to her feet, seized his clothing and yanked it down, lifting the bottom half of his body clear of the ground. His suit pants and underwear were now wound around his ankles.

She made her way back to the drinks cabinet and cracked the top from another miniature. She watched as the bag around his head inflated like a balloon only to shrink back encasing the contours of his face. His semi-naked body convulsed for oxygen, his lungs burning. She downed the drink in one and picked up the riding crop.

He heard it swish through the air.

'Now let's see how long you last.'

Jameson had booked three days' emergency leave but it looked like he'd clearly underestimated.

Chapter 15

Lucas looked out of the window at the apartment block across the street. The cool bay air blew through the drapes and he could smell the sea. The windows of apartment number forty-six Maple Crescent were alive with the dancing shadows from the TV. His watch read 3.15am, but it was fifteen minutes after midnight San Diego time.

The flight had been easy to arrange but tiresome to endure. They flew United Airlines out of Tallahassee International to San Diego, a six hour flight with a one hour stopover at Dallas. The time difference meant the journey took only four hours and, if Moran was right, they needed every hour they could get.

Lucas passed the binoculars to Harper.

'Vickers' place is on the fourth floor, third room from the left, starting at the fifth window along.'

Harper panned across the front of the building.

He could see both windows of the apartment. One was large, probably the living room, and the other was smaller, maybe a bedroom or kitchen.

A light flicked on in the small window. 'Someone's home,' he said.

'You did well to get us in here,' said Lucas, referring to the two-bedroomed serviced apartment they were standing in. It was perfect for keeping the Vickers place under observation.

'Yeah, a little better than being cooped up in a rental car.'

'We need to stake out Vickers for awhile, see where he goes, who he meets, that kind of thing. We got his mug shot from his driver's licence, so let's see what he does in the morning. Time to turn in, we got an early start.'

'We're on a tight deadline, you know. How about we go over and knock on his door?'

'How about we don't. How about we do this properly and find out about the guy first? You know, like we used to do when we were cops.'

'When I was a cop I would have kicked the door in,' Harper said studying the flickering lights in the window.

'That's why you're not a cop anymore.'

Harper skulked off to his room to grab a few hours' sleep.

* * *

The sun cascaded early morning shadows across the street as Lucas leaned against the wall on the opposite side of the road to Maple Crescent. His eyes were set on the front door. The sky was flawless blue and the gentle warmth of the morning was a welcome change from the chill of Darien. Harper was around the back at the underground car park, clocking the tenants as they left for work. It was 6.30am.

People busied themselves with briefcases and pull-along bags. Some wore suits, while others wore casual business attire, and some had a look that said 'I work in a place where we sit on beanbags all day and drink coffee with soya milk'. None of them was Gerry Vickers.

The morning rush kicked in at 7.15am, when people flooded out to catch public transport or miss the morning jam. Lucas struggled to eyeball every one and had to move in closer. Harper had a much more orderly line of motorists waiting for the exit barrier to lift on the underground car park. Some had passengers but most were singles. None was Gerry Vickers.

By 9.15am Harper appeared at the front, he waved at Lucas and cupped his hand to his mouth signalling 'I need a coffee'. The parade of people had all but dried up and there was little point standing around any longer.

Ten minutes later Harper handed Lucas a brown paper bag containing hot coffee and pastries. Lucas was walking on the spot stretching his leaden legs, he wasn't built to stand around for three hours' straight.

'Maybe he works from home,' Harper said snapping the lid off the coffee.

'Could be any number of reasons, but one thing's for sure, he didn't leave this morning.'

'I suppose knocking on his door is a little too direct?'

'Until we know more about him, I say we stake it out first.'

Lucas devoured a whole apple lattice in two bites. Staring at strangers was hungry work.

* * *

The stakeout routine lasted all day and into the night. They swapped positions to counter the boredom and ate fast food. By the end of a very long shift one thing was clear, Gerry Vickers had not left the building today.

They were back in their apartment and Lucas once again had the binoculars trained on the TV shadows dancing across the windows opposite.

'Maybe he's a hermit and that's how he runs the business single-handed,' he mused.

'He must have an enormous phone bill 'cause he hasn't left that building today.'

'Your turn.' Lucas went to hand the glasses over to Harper when a light came on in the smaller window. 'What time is it?'

'It's a quarter after midnight.'

'I'm sure that happened yesterday.'

'What did?'

'That light came on at the same time.'

'Maybe his favourite TV show finishes now and he needs to pee.'

Lucas scrutinised the windows.

'Why doesn't he close the drapes?'

'Maybe he's an exhibitionist. Let me see.' Harper took the binoculars. 'Now you mention it, they haven't moved since we've been here.'

Lucas took back the binoculars.

After a while he said, 'You know what? I don't think Vickers is at home. I reckon the sneaky bastard has the lamps and TV operating off a timer.'

'So now can we knock on the fucking door?'

* * *

Seven hours later, after a fitful night's sleep, Harper stood in the doorway to their apartment with his shopping consisting of two plastic bags and a toolbox. He dumped them onto the bed and changed into blue overalls, safety shoes and a peaked cap. He swaggered into the living room carrying a clipboard and the toolbox.

'What do you think?' he said to Lucas who was eating breakfast.

'You look like something Stephen King would write about.'

'You got a better idea?'

'Nope, and I sure as hell can't match them duds you got there, boy.' Lucas mimicked a hillbilly drone.

They had decided a more innovative approach was in order given their discovery the previous night, and hadn't done the early morning stakeout. Which was a welcome change of plan.

'Let's go,' Lucas said. It was 7.15am, rush hour at Maple Crescent apartments.

Harper crossed the road and timed his run to perfection. A young woman hit the green release button and pushed open the glass door to leave the building. She politely held it open for Harper to step inside carrying his toolbox and clipboard. The lobby was kitted out with wall-to-wall fake marble and chrome with a large glass-topped concierge desk against one wall. The desk was unmanned. The elevators were located five easy strides away across the shiny floor. Lucas took up his usual position on the opposite side of the street, leaning against a wall nursing a coffee.

Harper stepped out of the lift on the fourth floor and found door number forty-six. The corridor was bright and smelled of fresh paint. This was where you lived if you had a good job or wealthy parents.

He rapped his knuckles against the door – this was the risky part. If they were right then no one would answer, if they were wrong, Harper would have to make up a story about a maintenance issue and leave. He knocked again but no one came.

Harper knelt down and opened his toolbox. A man burst out of the apartment opposite, and Harper kept his head down.

'Can I help you?' The man was dressed in running gear with a backpack slung across one shoulder.

'No, I'm fine, sir. Just here to fix this lock.'

'Where's Bernie?'

'It's not a job he can do, so they sent for me.' Harper guessed Bernie must be the regular maintenance guy.

The man slammed his door behind him and rattled a key in the deadlock.

'You ever see the person who lives in this apartment?' Harper asked. 'He said he would be in, but there's no one home.'

'No, never seen him, or her, or whoever lives there. And I've been here two years now.'

'Oh well, I'll just get on with it.'

The man walked past Harper and headed for the elevator. What's the point of using the elevator on your way to your morning run? Harper thought.

He opened a small leather pouch and got to work. After a couple of minutes, the picks did their job and the lock sprung open. Harper tended to travel light, but wherever he went, his lock picks came with him. He stepped inside and put the lock on the latch.

The apartment opened up into a small hallway that led to a large living room with a sofa, two easy chairs and an oversized TV.

'Hello!' Harper called. 'Maintenance guy. Anyone home?'

The place was silent apart from the hum of the refrigerator.

Harper moved from room to room. The apartment was empty. He crossed to the window, pulled one of the drapes closed and then opened it again. A signal to Lucas which said 'Get your ass up here'.

The rooms were immaculate with not a coaster out of place. The cushions were puffed up on the sofa and the kitchen work surfaces were clean. Harper opened the refrigerator, it was empty. He opened the cupboards to find rows of matching crockery but no food. He stepped on the pedal bin to reveal a black plastic bag with nothing in it.

The front door edged open and Lucas bustled into the apartment. He closed the door and placed a clipboard on the table in the hall. Harper tossed him a pair of blue surgical gloves.

'It's empty. I don't think anyone lives here,' Harper said in hushed tones.

Lucas moved into the bedroom and opened up the closet, a row of empty hangers dangled from the rail. He looked behind the bedside table.

'As we thought, the lights are on timers,' he said spotting the timing device plugged in the socket.

'So is the TV,' Harper replied. 'Vickers doesn't live here, or if he does he cleared the place out before a long vacation.'

They checked the drawers but found nothing.

'It's as clean as the day he first took the keys.'

'It is, but take a look at the dust. It's undisturbed, no one has moved a thing in this place for some time.'

Harper lifted the corner of a magazine on the coffee table to see the outline imprinted on the surface below.

'He might be the tidiest guy in San Diego but he should sack his cleaner. I checked the mailbox downstairs, there were takeaway food flyers sticking out, but nothing else.'

'Why would you go to this much trouble to make the place look lived in?' Lucas said opening the cutlery drawer.

'Maybe he's on vacation?'

'I suppose he could be. He might be the nervous type who goes overboard to make it look as though the apartment is occupied.'

The toilet flushed.

Lucas ducked against the bedroom wall putting his finger up to his lips. Harper drew his gun. He motioned to Lucas who crossed the living room to the bathroom. He put his ear to the door. All he could hear was the sound of water filling the tank.

Lucas wrapped his hand around the handle and counted down with the fingers of his other hand– three, two, one.

He threw open the door and Harper charged inside, his weapon levelled at head height. It was empty.

Harper lowered his gun and the two men looked around.

The bathroom was in the same condition as the rest of the apartment, with one notable exception. The top of the toilet was missing and a small solenoid valve was connected to the plunger. Two wires ran from the top of the valve to a socket on the wall. In the socket was the same make of timer used in the bedroom.

'Not seen one of these before,' Lucas said, allowing his heart rate to die down.

'Putting your lights on automatic is one thing but wiring up your toilet is extreme. Why would you do that?'

Lucas rubbed his chin. 'It solves the problem of whether or not he's on vacation.'

'How come?'

'This tells us he's not on vacation.'

'How are you so sure?'

'He's done this to use water,' Lucas said. 'He doesn't live here so the water usage would be zero. This way he consumes water and it shows up on his utility bills.'

Harper looked at the timer. 'It's set to go off every two hours. Vickers might not be businessman of the year but he sure as hell is a clever bastard.'

'He's gone to an awful lot of trouble to make people think he lives here, but unfortunately for us the place is clean, there is nothing here.'

'What next?'

There was a knock on the door and the sound of a key in the lock.

'Shit!' Lucas said as he rushed from bathroom, just in time to hear the front door open.

'Hello … hello!' bellowed a gravelly voice from the hallway.

Lucas came into view.

'Who are you?' said an elderly man dressed in a tracksuit, sporting five days of growth on his chin and a trilby hat. 'Max said you were here to fix the lock?'

'Max?' Lucas was stumped.

Harper emerged from the bathroom closing the door behind him.

'No, sir, that's me. I'm the one fixing the lock. I guess Max is the neighbour in the running gear.'

'Yeah that's right, he said there was something wrong with the lock. First I heard about it.'

'The person who owns the apartment called us direct. This is my supervisor.' Harper pointed at Lucas. 'For some reason he thinks it's necessary to check up on me from time to time.'

Lucas acknowledged the old man with a nod of his head then picked up the clipboard and lifted the front sheet.

'Yeah, very funny.' Lucas gave Harper a sideways look. 'We got a call from Mr Vickers saying his lock was sticking and could we take a look.'

'I'm the janitor and I don't know nothing about it.'

'Well, as I said, Mr Vickers called us direct. We didn't think to check with you first,' Lucas said.

'Oh, okay, I suppose,' said the old man, 'but I don't see how he would know that.'

Lucas and Harper flashed a glance at each other.

'Don't see how he'd know what?' replied Lucas.

'That the lock was sticking.'

'Why wouldn't he?'

'Because he hasn't been here in months. How he'd know it needed mending is beyond me.'

Lucas shrugged his shoulders. 'He called the office and asked us to sort it out.' Lucas consulted the blank clipboard again hoping the old man didn't ask to see it. 'He told me to put the invoice into his mailbox downstairs, so he must pick up his mail sometimes?'

'He gets his mail okay.'

'That's good, would hate for him to miss it. So Mr Vickers comes to collect it?'

'No, some kid does it for him, comes in every Wednesday morning and takes it away. The kid must have a forwarding address.'

'We are about done here, sorry if we've caused any inconvenience,' said Harper picking up his toolbox and making for the door.

Lucas thanked the old man and headed out, with Harper in hot pursuit. They needed to revise their plan. It was 9.20am and today was Wednesday.

Chapter 16

Lucas sat in the reception of Maple Crescent. He had persuaded the janitor to allow him to wait until the mail was picked up to ensure the invoice went to the right place. A thin excuse for loitering with intent but it worked all the same.

The reception was decorated with minimalist flair, with a bank of silver-fronted mailboxes built into the wall opposite, each with a gold number and a lock. Number forty-six had a bunch of takeaway menus poking out of the top, as did the majority of them. Lucas read the free newspaper and drank his coffee.

Harper had gone back to the apartment to change, not wanting to spend the rest of the day dressed as a comedy maintenance man. He stood outside the entrance, leaning against the wall, also reading a newspaper. It was 10am.

For Lucas the passage of time was slow. The three clocks mounted on the wall behind the desk telling the time in London, New York and Paris ticked in unison, marking every second as it rolled by. For Harper the passing of time was a far more pleasurable experience. He had long since stopped reading his paper and was happily admiring the view. The women in San Diego sure knew how to dress for work.

At 10.35 a kid, who must have been about fourteen, stopped at the doors to the apartment block. He bent down and fiddled with the laces on his sneakers, then rummaged through a bag slung across his body, then went back to attend to his laces. Lucas saw him. Harper saw him.

A man in a blue suit came out of the elevator and hit the exit button. The door released and he strode out onto the sidewalk. The boy straightened up and caught the door as it began to close.

He stepped inside. The same door dodge as Harper had used hours earlier, perfectly executed.

Lucas made eye contact with Harper over the top of his newspaper.

The boy stood in front of the mailboxes with his back to Lucas. He was doing something with his hands and stuffing paper into his bag. Lucas moved forward.

'Hey son, do you have a minute?'

The boy swivelled round and stared at Lucas with a look of horror on his face. He snapped his bag shut and darted for the doors. He struck the green button and squeezed himself through the gap as they started to open.

The boy ran up the street closely followed by Harper. Lucas no longer walked with a stick but a brisk stroll was all he could manage, so he quickly gave up the chase. Harper wasn't faring much better. In a race between a fourteen-year-old boy scared for his life and a fifty-seven-year-old alcoholic, there was only going to be one winner. Harper was fine over the first thirty yards, then his body yelled stop. He was panting like a porn star and about to be reacquainted with his breakfast when he stumbled into the road. A yellow cab screeched to a halt. The driver wound down his window.

'Hey, buddy, you gonna get yourself killed.'

Harper opened the door and fell into the back seat, a much better option than falling in the gutter.

'That kid stole my wallet.' Harper gasped for breath.

'Which one?' the driver yelled over his shoulder.

Harper was trying not to have a heart attack.

'That one, the boy running,' he said between gulps of air. 'The dirt bag stole my wallet.'

'Punks are ruining the neighbourhood and the cops are nowhere to be seen when you need them.'

As an ex-cop Harper bristled at the slight on his profession but was too grateful to retaliate.

The driver sped away, continuing his rant. 'One of them lifted my wallet last month, cash, credit cards, driving licence, the full shebang. Took me ages to sort out. And where were the cops then? Nowhere, that's where. But when my buddy ran a red light, oh boy they came down on him like a ton of bricks.'

Harper nodded, not wanting to waste precious air on trying to speak. He could see the boy darting between the other people on the sidewalk. The boy swung his head around, slowed, and came to a stop, convinced no one was after him.

The driver pulled the cab over to the roadside and shouted through the passenger window.

'I know you, you little shit.'

The boy's head jerked around as if God was talking to him. Harper opened the door but the boy spotted him. He ran off again, weaving his way up the sidewalk. Harper shut the door and the driver gunned the engine.

The boy changed direction and cut across the road between the traffic and darted down an alley.

'Damn!' Harper exploded. 'We lost him.'

'The fuck we have.' The driver put his foot down and the cab lurched forward. About a hundred yards further on he made a sharp right and slammed on the brakes.

'Chances are the punk is running this way,' he said looking in his rear-view mirror. 'You gonna be alright, man?'

'I'll be fine,' Harper said throwing ten bucks from his pocket onto the front seat. 'I'll be just fine.'

'No need, man.' The cabbie held up the note for Harper to take back. 'Give him one from me.'

'No, you take it, buy a new wallet.'

Harper bailed out of the back. He was at the head of a T-junction, with the street the boy was travelling along running right to left in front of him. He pressed his back to the wall and risked a peek around the corner. Sure enough the boy was walking towards him with his head down. Harper gave the driver a thumbs up and he reversed the cab back up the road to join the main drag.

The boy drew level.

Harper grabbed his arm and swung him into the wall. He jammed his right forearm across the boy's chest pinning him to the brickwork. He let out a shriek.

'Why did you run?' Harper said into the boy's face.

'I don't know, let me go.' The boy kicked his legs but Harper held him firm.

'You were picking up mail, weren't you?'

'Yes. Let me go.'

'What do you do with it?'

'I stick it in a dumpster.'

'And when does it get collected?'

'I don't know.'

'Which dumpster?'

'It's up there, let me go.' The boy nodded up the street.

'Show me.' Harper released him and gripped his upper arm.

'Shit man, you're in dead trouble for this,' he hissed, trying to pull free.

'Yeah, I'm sure I am. Now where is it?'

The boy pointed to a group of industrial trash bins set off to one side.

'Show me what you do.'

'What?'

'Which one, show me which bin.'

'Any one of them, man, I take the flyers from my bag and put them in the trash.'

'What flyers?' Harper screwed his face up.

'These flyers.' The boy shook his arm free and unclipped the flap on his bag. He reached inside and pulled out a fistful of takeaway menus.

'Where is the mail?'

'What mail, there is no mail. I clear out the flyers from the mailboxes.'

'What?'

'I take these from the boxes.' The boy thrust a fistful of menus into Harper's chest. There were Chinese and Mexican takeaway menus and pizza delivery flyers. 'I take these out of the mailboxes and put them in the trash.'

'Why do you do that?'

'So when Mr Milano puts his pizza menu in their mail they will buy from him and not these.' The boy threw the flyers in the air to emphasise his point.

Harper gawked at the glossy paper as it fell around him. The boy saw his chance and bolted. Harper could see the white flashes on the underside of his trainers as he sprinted away. He was making one-fingered gestures over his shoulder and shouting something about Harper being a dead man. Which, given his unexpected bout of vigorous exercise, he very nearly was.

* * *

Lucas was enjoying a leisurely walk in the sun. He had returned to Maple Crescent when he lost the boy. His pathetic attempt to catch him ensured he only had a short walk back. From the description he gave, the janitor didn't recognise the kid who'd picked up the mail. So, in the absence of being able to help Harper, he stayed put. A strategy which paid off.

Ten minutes later Lucas was sitting in his usual place in reception when a different boy turned up. He headed over to the mailboxes and Lucas could hear the sound of a key being inserted into a lock and the rustling of paper. Then Lucas had his first piece of luck of the day – the boy dropped the mail. When he bent down to pick it up, Lucas could see the door to number forty-six flapping open. Proof positive, this is what they had been waiting for. The boy locked the box and put the envelopes into his backpack.

Lucas didn't fancy his chances with another foot race so decided against a direct approach. The boy left the building, and Lucas filed in behind, following him at a safe distance.

They sauntered down the street and the boy hung a right into the park. He found a bench and sat down, removing the mail from his bag. Lucas stopped at the park entrance and pretended to wait for someone. There were three letters which the kid laid out on the seat, along with a large brown envelope. He placed the letters inside and sealed the flap. Lucas noticed the stamp on the top right-hand corner.

The boy took a pen from his bag and wrote on the envelope. Lucas had to get closer to have any chance of reading what was written. He strolled over, but after four strides the boy got up and walked back to the park entrance.

Lucas stared straight ahead and the boy passed to his right, pulling a set of earphones from his bag.

Lucas allowed the boy to leave the park, and then doubled back and followed him along the street. The boy's head was bopping to the music in his head.

Then Lucas saw it.

A slate grey USPS mailbox about fifteen feet ahead and directly in the boy's path. He was heading straight for it. Lucas quickened his pace and was closing on the boy.

Fifteen feet, ten feet, but the kid was getting closer.

Eight feet, five feet, the box was almost in reach, and he had his hand out clutching the brown envelope.

Lucas called to the boy to stop, but he couldn't hear above the beat in his ears.

Three feet, two feet.

Lucas lunged at the letter and slapped it out of the boy's grasp.

He jumped out of his skin and tore the headphones from his head.

'What the fuck!' he screeched, leaping away from the madman in front of him. 'What are you doing?' People looked over at the commotion.

Lucas searched for something to say. Nothing came. He looked at the letter face down on the floor.

'I'm sorry, I thought you were going to put it into a dead mailbox.'

The boy screwed his face up.

'A dead what?'

'I did the same thing the other day. I put a letter into this box and it was no longer in use. I had to get the mail guys to come open it up to get it back.'

'You had to what?'

'Sorry I startled you, I didn't want you to make the same mistake. It looks like it's in service now.'

The boy went to pick up the letter but Lucas moved first. The boy stepped back.

'You're crazy, man. You can't go round knocking things out of people's hands like that.'

'I'm sorry,' Lucas said handing him the letter. 'I thought—'

'You are one crazy person.' The boy approached Lucas with his arm outstretched as if he was feeding a wild animal and snatched the envelope out of his hand.

He stuffed it into his bag and scurried away to find another mailbox, preferably not one being guarded by a madman.

Lucas let out a huge sigh and pulled a pen from his jacket. He rolled up his sleeve and scribbled on the inside of his forearm. He retraced his route back to Maple Crescent with two thoughts in his head: where was Harper and who the hell was Mark Jameson?

* * *

Moran was about to start day two of her three-day promise to Harper. Her previous evening with Mills had been worse than expected. He talked non-stop about himself and insisted on buying the drinks. It felt like a disastrous date, but it achieved the objective.

Mills had been a happy bunny sitting opposite Moran with a beer in one hand and a fistful of corn chips in the other, waxing lyrical about how he could have played for the NFL when he left college. Moran had faked interest and nodded in all the right places. To be honest, she was more surprised about Mills having gone to college than about the NFL lie.

She had struggled to keep her mind focused and kept drifting off into the horror that was the Shamon situation. She didn't know if Lucas and Harper had made any progress or, if they had, if it would do any good. All she knew was Harper had her by the short and curlies and if the plot to capture Mechanic ever got into the open she was well and truly screwed.

Mills had rounded off the evening by walking her back to her tram stop. He said goodnight and for a heart-stopping moment it looked like he was about to move in for a kiss. Thankfully for him he didn't, if he had she would have decked him.

Moran arrived in the office early to figure out the best way to fake a problem with the Shamon account. She contacted the bank to make an appointment and by 9.15am it was time for the morning briefing.

Mills was unbearably chipper. He flashed a special good morning smile in Moran's direction as she took her seat.

'Morning everyone,' he kicked off. 'Going round the table, what do we have?'

Each officer reported on their slice of the case and Mills took notes. When it came to Moran she reported the issue with the Shamon account, indicating that she would be sorting it out with the bank today. She was acutely aware that she had to find another twenty-four hours of delay, and her latest pretend problem was not going to carry her through. But this was one step at a time.

Mills didn't challenge her, he accepted what she said and thanked her with another smile. Moran looked away hoping no one saw. The meeting wrapped up and she picked up a coffee on her way to the bank.

* * *

Lucas threw open the door to find Harper dozing in the chair.

'Good to see you're on red alert.'

'I was resting my eyes.'

'Looked like you were pushing out zeds.'

'No, no. Anyway we had the wrong guy. I caught up with him but he turned out to be a little shit who steals the takeaway food flyers.'

Lucas shook his head.

'He steals what?'

'Never mind. Where the hell have you been?'

'Catching the right one.'

'What? How did that happen?'

'Shortly after you ran off, another kid appeared and took the mail.'

'And?'

'Just as we thought, he redirected it.' Lucas rolled up his sleeve and showed Harper the name and address scribbled onto his inner arm.

'How did you get it?'

'By making myself look like a dick.'

'What do you mean, look like?'

Lucas ignored his remark.

'Get your ass in gear,' he barked at Harper.

'Where we going?'

'We have a new friend to call upon, Mark Jameson.'

Chapter 17

Mechanic stood in the shower and allowed the hot water to cascade over her head. She had been home just long enough to boil the kettle and down a cup of sweet black coffee. She was exhausted.

The images of the last seventeen hours played out in her head like a low budget S&M movie. They had planned to discuss business at some time during the evening but the pleasure side got in the way.

She pictured Jameson doing the very same thing, standing in his shower, wincing as the water flowed over his battered body. A session with Jameson always satisfied Mechanic's three basic needs: sex, whisky and violence. The harder she beat him, the harder he fucked her. And the more they drank, the more he could take.

They had collapsed into bed at 2.40am. He was asleep as soon as he hit the sheets and she had cradled his head against her breast, his breathing erratic and heavy. Through the thin drapes the streetlights had illuminated the room with a sepia glow. She had looked down at him lying next to her. His face, neck, hands and arms were unmarked, but the rest of his body was a morass of bruises, abrasions and scratches.

She had beaten him for six hours.

The game was always the same. She beat him until Jameson had an erection hard enough to poke a hole in the wall. Then they would screw each other's brains out. When he was about to come, they would stop, allow things to cool down, and drink Wild Turkey. Then the beatings would start again. The cycle repeated over and over until either he lost control and came, or physically he couldn't continue. This time his self-control was immaculate.

She had slipped into a dreamless sleep holding him in her arms. The alarm was set for 6am when the beating would resume, checkout was at 11am.

Mechanic stepped from the shower and wrapped herself in a bathrobe. She wasn't sure how much pain Jameson was in this morning but she was decidedly sore, and decidedly happy.

She fished an envelope from the behind the wardrobe and spilled its contents on the table. The photo statted picture of Elaine Cooper stared up at her.

The phone rang.

'Hello.'

'It's me, can you talk?' It was Jameson calling from the hotel.

'Yes, what's up, you okay?'

'I'm still trying to find that road truck that ran over me last night but other than that I'm fine thanks.'

'Yes, it was quite a night. You home yet?'

'No, still at the hotel. I called the organisers of that conference we are due to attend in San Francisco.'

It took Mechanic a second for her brain to get in gear and decode the sentence.

'Is there a problem?'

'No, but they've had to move things forward by a week, something to do with a mix-up at the venue.'

'When is it scheduled?'

'They want to hold it the day after tomorrow and asked if we could still attend. I said I'd get back to them.'

'That should be fine. Can you get the merchandise delivered in time?'

'No problem. We need to run through the agenda and make sure we have the presentation worked out. But I guess we can do that en-route to Frisco.'

'That's fine with me, is there a change in time?'

'No, all the arrangements are as previously agreed, it's simply a change in the date.'

'We can make that work. I'm looking forward to it. I will call you from the airport.'

'Have a safe flight, speak to you later.'

Mechanic replaced the receiver then picked it up again. She needed to book some tickets.

* * *

Jameson got out of the cab, paid the driver, and walked, or rather limped, across the road to his two-up two-down town house in the trendy Ocean Bay area of San Diego.

He dragged his roll-along bag behind him. It contained his shredded suit, two halves of a shirt and enough sex toys to run a brothel. He was an ex-Navy Seal and physically fit, but this morning he struggled to tow behind him a twelve-pound bag on wheels.

He opened his front door, dumped the bag in the hall and headed for the bathroom. He clunked around in the medicine cabinet and knocked back a handful of painkillers and anti-inflammatories. He needed a bath and some sleep. Mechanic had promised him an extra special night and boy had she delivered. Everything hurt.

Jameson went to the kitchen, rummaged in a cupboard, returned to the bathroom and turned on the taps. Hot water flooded into the bath and steam rose into the air. He unbuttoned his shirt with shaking fingers and peeled the material away from his body. It stuck to him where the blood had seeped through the fabric and congealed. The shirt dropped to the floor, he removed his jeans and underwear. Standing naked in front of the mirror the full extent of his injuries became clear.

His chest was pockmarked with what looked like purple bullet wounds where her heels had stamped holes in his flesh and his cock and balls were a kaleidoscope of colours. His stomach and ribs were a patchwork of blue and yellow, as the bruises spread under his skin. He half-turned. His ass, back and legs were criss-crossed with angry welts from the bite of her crop, and deep red tramlines ran down his body where her nails had raked away the top layer of skin.

Jameson turned off the taps and swirled a handful of salt into the water. He lowered himself into the bath and slid down until the water lapped against his chin, wincing as the salt got to work on his wounds. After twenty minutes the pain eased and the hot water soothed his battered body.

He closed his eyes and melted into sleep.

Outside, Lucas and Harper sat in their rental car.

'I figure that was our guy,' Harper said.

'Unless he takes in lodgers.'

'I'm not sure what he does for a living but he looked like shit.'

'We got to hustle. You stay here, I need to find a phone.'

Chapter 18

Lucas walked a quarter of a mile back towards town and found what he was looking for. To the side of a bus stop was a bank of payphones. He stood at the first one and punched in the digits. He fed a coin into the slot, spoke briefly, then hung up.

After a few minutes the phone rang.

'Hi,' he said.

'I can talk now.' It was Moran. 'Where's your attack dog today?'

'I'm sorry about that, I had no idea.'

'You two come as a pair, so excuse me if I don't believe you.'

'I didn't, I swear. I found out about the photographs a couple of days ago.'

'It came as a shock. I didn't expect anything different from a dinosaur like Harper, but you, Lucas, I thought we had a connection.'

'Is that why you told me to fuck off when I needed your help?'

She went quiet.

'I haven't told you that today. What do you want?'

'The good news is we've located Vickers.'

'That was fast. What I gave you was sketchy at best.'

'The bad news is Gerry Vickers turns out to be a ghost. He's a cover for a man called Mark Jameson, he's the one behind Sheldon Chemicals and Helix Holdings.'

'That's impressive work, shame you retired.'

Lucas delivered his punch line. 'We believe he's also the one who supplied Mechanic with the equipment to kill my wife.'

'Shit. How did you—'

Lucas interrupted. 'That doesn't matter. What matters is we need to move fast.'

Moran thought for a minute.

'You sure it's him?'

'As sure as we can be without a positive I.D. We could do with more background on Mark Jameson and a recent mug shot. He lives here in San Diego at 102 Waterfront Place, Imperial Beach.'

'Just a minute.' Moran scrabbled for a pen and paper. 'I'll see what comes up and fax it to your new number. What else?'

'Jameson has a direct line to Mechanic, and the plan is to use him to draw her out into the open. She trusts him and the likelihood is the hit on Darlene wasn't the first time they worked together. It's vital that Jameson remains untouched. He's no good to us if the cops start sniffing around. You have to lose the Shamon account transactions.'

'You gotta be kidding. Do you have any idea how much shit is flying around here? I'm already stretching it as far as I can, and I'm not sure how much longer I can hold out. You got maybe twelve hours at most.'

'That account information could cost us the only link we have to Mechanic.'

'I can't, Lucas. The guy running the investigation is sweet on me and I'm pushing my luck as far as it will go. You know how much scrutiny is applied in a murder investigation. If I turn up a blank it's bound to come out somewhere else.'

'Don't you want her dead?' This stopped Moran in her tracks. 'Don't you want to be the one who finally takes down Mechanic?'

'I do. I mean I did. But that was a long time ago and we got burned. I got burned.'

'You're at risk of getting torched again. If they arrest Jameson, the next stop is Mechanic and then they get you too.'

Moran went quiet.

Lucas continued, 'We need Jameson in the clear for this to work. All I can ask is you think about it.'

'Okay, okay. I'll get the details to you as fast as I can.'

'Oh, Moran, there's one more thing.'

'This has to be the last, I gotta go.'

'Can you think of someone in Mechanic's recent past that crossed her? Someone she would hold a grudge against?'

Lucas could hear the sound of a pen tapping rhythmically on a table.

'There's one that jumps out of the pack straightaway.'

* * *

Lucas replaced the receiver and pulled a small dog-eared book from his jacket pocket. He thumbed through the handwritten pages. He lifted the receiver again, dialled the numbers, and waited for it to connect.

'Hi, is that Fabiano Bassano? ... Yes, hi, this is Ed Lucas ... I'm fine thank you ... I want to take you up on that offer.'

* * *

Moran fed the printout into the fax machine and hit send. It cranked and whirred as the sheets spooled through the rollers. Mark Jameson, or Captain Mark Jameson to give him his correct title, was an interesting guy. Not from what the records said about him, rather what they didn't say. It said his date of birth, it said he was well educated, it said he owned and drove a car and lived in San Diego. It said he joined the navy at the age of twenty-one, and then it said absolutely nothing.

Moran fed the printout into the shredder and returned to work.

Earlier that morning her meeting at the Wells Fargo bank had gone well. Moran had shared with the bank official her concerns that the account records had been corrupted, and the bank official had confirmed that wasn't the case. Moran thanked her for the clarification and left. Easy and straightforward.

The important point for Moran was the meeting had taken place. The bank official had a record in her calendar and would no doubt be able to recall discussing the account of Nassra Shamon. For anyone who cared to check, that was all that mattered, and the precise content of the discussion was irrelevant.

It would buy her enough time to get through to the briefing tomorrow when she would be forced to declare the transfer of money to Helix Holdings. Then the whole investigative apparatus would descend and the race for who got to Jameson first would be in full flight.

Moran was seated at her desk when Mills appeared.

'Hey, how did you get on at—'

She interrupted him fast. 'What are you doing when you get off work tonight?'

Mills looked around at the empty office and shrugged his shoulders.

'Dunno, got nothing planned. Why, what were you thinking?'

'I thought we might grab a beer.' She put her head to one side and smiled.

'Yeah, that would be great. I'm not staying late, so how about six o'clock. Maybe catch a bite to eat?'

'Can't do food but a beer would be good.'

'See you at six.'

He sauntered out of the office as if he'd just found a hundred dollar bill in the pocket of an old suit.

Moran shuffled paper around trying to look busy. She didn't want a beer and she wanted one even less sitting across from Mills spouting his schoolboy chat. But most of all she didn't want him to finish his question and ask her how she got on at the bank.

* * *

Moran lay in bed waiting for the alarm to go off. It was 5.57am and she'd been awake since three. What little sleep she'd had was filled with the prospect of what lay ahead of her today. She had tossed and turned, rehearsing in her head what she was going to say at the morning meeting with Mills. Each time she said it, she died a little inside. But saying it was her only option.

The after-work drink with Mills had been as bad as ever. He had once more played the gallant suitor and made a big song and dance about buying the beers, but Moran had insisted. She managed to buy one round but that was it. He'd taken her to the same bar as before and fortunately they were showing the ball game, which kept Mills pleasantly diverted.

To his credit, he had avoided the topic of work, which should have been a welcome change compared to the majority of dates she'd been on. But by the time they left at eight o'clock she almost wished he had talked over the murder investigation. At least that would have given her an adrenaline rush rather than the dead space she felt inside.

The alarm went off. The local radio station gave the six o'clock time check and cut to the news. Moran was a news addict and would watch, listen and read about it whenever the opportunity arose. This morning she wasn't interested and shuffled off to the shower to contemplate her day under jets of hot water.

She dressed in her signature black uniform and decided she needed to eat. She never ate breakfast and looked expectantly in the fridge. It was empty, apart from a two-week old carton of milk, a slice of pizza and an almost full bottle of wine with the cork stuffed back in the neck. She ignored the wine, despite the fact it was by far the best option, and picked up the pizza. She peeled away the plastic wrap and inspected the thin crust, salami topped, something or another. She couldn't recall the last time she ate pizza at home, so threw it in the trash. The cupboard proved more fruitful and she gathered up her car keys and banged her front door shut with four cookies in her hand.

The journey into work passed by in a blur. She sat at her desk with an empty cup of coffee that she could not remember buying and for some reason seemed to be covered in crumbs. Moran unpacked her files and pulled out the one marked Nassra Shamon. She opened it and retrieved the printout showing the account transactions. Circled in fat blue ink were the three money transfers to Helix Holdings, and beneath it was a line entry saying Account Closed.

Moran played with the cardboard cup in front of her, spinning it on its base. Her hand shook slightly. She checked her watch, forty minutes to go to the morning briefing.

Mills breezed in.

'Morning,' he said in a voice too cheerful even for a breakfast TV presenter. He marched up to her desk, hunched over her and whispered, 'How are you today?'

'Feeling a bit off,' Moran said conscious that she might not be looking her best.

'Maybe you didn't drink enough.'

'Maybe.'

Mills turned on his heels and breezed out.

The office filled with people pulling folders and notepads out of filing cabinets and drawers. This was not the way days started. Where was the usual dribble of half-asleep bodies drifting to their desks in search of tea and coffee.

'Right. Shall we make a start?' Mills bellowed from across the corridor.

Everyone trooped off to the incident room.

A man leaned over Moran as he passed and said, 'He called it half an hour early today. Didn't you get the memo?'

She had been so preoccupied over what to do with the Shamon evidence it had completely passed her by. She scrabbled her files together dropping paperwork onto the floor, and trooped on behind.

'Let's go around the table. What do we have?' Mills said with his usual opener.

The man next to Moran piped up. He reported on the latest discussions with immigration and homeland security, and concluded there was nothing new to tell. Shamon had not left the country.

His report was over far too quickly.

Moran was conscious of the room falling silent. She looked up at Mills who was staring straight at her.

'Moran, what do you have?'

Shit, it was her turn.

Moran opened her file, consulted her notes and closed it again. She felt hot. Her face was burning up. Her stomach dropped to somewhere near her shoes. She clasped her hands together and they were clammy.

'You okay?' asked Mills.

'Er, yes. I just ...' The acrid taste of bile rose in her mouth, she swallowed it down.

Mills felt the need to prompt her. 'The Shamon money, you had a meeting with the bank?'

Moran looked at him and then panned around the table at twelve gawping faces all fixed on her. Her heart was thumping, pushing a torrent of blood around her head and it felt like a tourniquet was being wound tight across her chest. She leaned forward and placed both hands on top of the closed file.

Breathe, breathe.

'Yes, sorry. I went to the bank yesterday to clear up the erroneous data which had corrupted the account transactions. They sorted it out and nothing looked out place. Shamon lived a cash-only lifestyle, which is not uncommon for people visiting on a short-term visa. The month's down payment on the apartment was the largest sum of money and that was confirmed by the real-estate agency. Other than that, she made a series of cash withdrawals none of which raise any alarms.'

'Okay, so nothing to go on?'

'No, nothing.'

'Okay, what about the passenger manifests for flights leaving that day?' Mills was onto the next item on the check sheet.

Moran sat rigid with her eyes fixed on the file.

What the fuck was that? The words tumbled around in her head.

The room was spinning, the acrid taste of bile coated the inside of her mouth.

Moran bolted for the door.

'I'm sorry, please excuse me.'

She dashed from the room and down the corridor to the restrooms. She just made it to the cubicle as the vomit hit the toilet. The remnants of her breakfast splashed into the bowl. Moran coughed and gagged as the last of her cookies and coffee covered the porcelain. She recoiled, gasping for breath and reeled off a yard of toilet roll, holding it to her mouth. Her stomach knotted again and she retched clear liquid.

Moran steadied herself with one hand on the cubicle wall and the other on the seat, still clutching the toilet paper. She dabbed her mouth again, spitting into the water.

She sank on her heels and hit the flush. Backing out of the stall she ran cold water into the sink, leaned forward and splashed it onto her face. She straightened up and caught her reflection in the mirror. Her eyes were bloodshot and her skin looked thin and grey. She rested her hands against the sink and leaned forward with her head bowed. The deep breaths made her feel better and she raised her head.

'You lying bitch,' Moran said to no one.

She bumped her forehead against the mirror.

The restroom door opened. A woman who had been at the briefing came in.

'Are you okay?'

'Yes, it must be something I've eaten.'

'I put your file back on your desk. Can I get you anything?'

'No, I'll be fine. Thanks.'

Moran pulled a handful of paper towel from the dispenser. She patted her face and dried her hands.

'I didn't feel right when I got up this morning,' she said in an attempt to make things look normal.

The woman put her hand on Moran's shoulder. 'You sure I can't get you anything? You don't look so good.'

'I'll be fine now, I just need a couple of minutes.'

'Okay, take it easy.' The woman left.

Moran balled the towels up and tossed them in the bin. She ran her fingers through her hair and smoothed down her jacket.

She felt better.

The anxiety was gone. The sickness had gone. And the rushing in her head was silent.

But most of all she felt better because she had made her decision.

Chapter 19

Jameson was also feeling better. The tablets had kicked in and the salt bath had bathed his wounds clean. He was standing in his kitchen wrapping a length of crepe bandage around his torso and pinning it in place. He needed to keep the blood off his clothes. He also needed additional support for his ribs, which hurt like a bastard every time he coughed, sneezed or even breathed. He certainly felt better but his ribs needed a little more time.

While he ministered to himself he thought about Mechanic. He had received the usual message on his pager saying she was having a great time at the conference, which meant she was at the location and had picked up the gear.

The hit was on.

There was a sharp rap on the front door.

Jameson moved into the living room and parted the curtains. A middle-aged black guy stood outside holding a clipboard. His face looked familiar. Jameson dismissed it, all door-stepping salesmen looked the same. He let the curtains swing back and ignored him.

The man knocked again, this time a little harder. Jameson ignored it.

He knocked again.

Persistent or what? Jameson thought, pulling on his shirt and opening the door.

Lucas stood in the porch.

'Hello, Captain Jameson.'

'Do we know each other?' Jameson was taken aback by Lucas's personal approach.

'No, we've never met.'

'Look, buddy. I don't know what you're selling, or how you know my name, but I'm not interested.'

'I'm not selling, I'm buying.'

'Buying? Can you see a sign anywhere saying Yard Sale? You have me mixed up with someone else.'

'No, there's no sign, but I do want to buy from you.'

'Look, buddy, you're starting to tick me off. If you don't mind, I have things to attend to.' Jameson started to swing the door closed, but Lucas put his hand up to stop it.

Jameson's eyes went cold. 'Take your hand from my door before I rip your arm off, old man.'

'I want to buy your services.'

'I'm asking you nicely. If you're not off my property in three seconds, they will be taking you back to wherever you came from in a fucking ambulance.'

Lucas removed his hand but stood his ground.

'I want to hire the sniper who took out the target on the eighth floor of the Bakerville multi-storey in Tallahassee last year on 28 April at 8am.'

Jameson's aggression washed away in a heartbeat to be replaced with forced control. He stared at Lucas.

'I have no idea what you're talking about. You've been watching too many cop shows, old man.'

'I don't watch TV and neither does my client. But we do have an extensive network and extremely reliable sources.'

'You need to leave.'

'But this is business and you are a businessman. It's not good to turn away work.'

Jameson shook his head. 'You are barking up the wrong tree. I'm not a businessman.' He went to shut the door, and Lucas stopped it again with his hand.

'Okay, how about a game of word association?'

'How about I phone that ambulance now?'

'Gerry Vickers, Helix Holdings, Sheldon Chemicals, apartment forty-six Maple Crescent. How am I doing?'

Jameson's calm exterior was showing signs of stress.

Lucas continued, 'Lights on timers, a self-flushing toilet. All very ingenious. Precautions which are a little over the top for a simple captain who claims not to be a businessman. Do I need to go on?'

It was Jameson's turn to put his hand on the door to steady himself.

Lucas pressed home his advantage. 'In a little over twenty-four hours you will be raided at three in the morning by a SWAT team. If we can trace you through your business interests, so can they. If we can work out you have your mail redirected to this address, so can they. If I can turn up at your house unannounced, so can they.'

'Who are you?'

'I'm the person who can stop all that happening. We have someone on the inside who can make certain bank transactions disappear.' Lucas tried out his first lie of the day.

Jameson was so bewildered he bought it. Lucas could see him weighing up his options.

'Not here,' Jameson said. 'Meet me in the middle of Cabrillo Bridge on the south side at 2pm. It's at Balboa Park. Come alone.' Jameson pushed the door shut.

Lucas walked the two blocks to where Harper had parked his ass in a burger bar.

He slid alongside him in the booth and ordered coffee.

'Well?' asked Harper, stuffing the last third of a double cheeseburger into his mouth. His face looked like a hamster.

'He's shaken but wants to talk. He suggested a place in Balboa Park at two o'clock.'

'Is it safe?' Harper mangled the words through his partly eaten burger, spitting meat and bun on Lucas's sleeve.

'Is anything we do these days? He said come alone, so we'll drive there, and I'll go on foot.' His coffee arrived.

'Have a burger, they're great.'

'No thanks. I just had some.'

* * *

Jameson paced up and down his living room, it was 11.45am. Who the hell was that guy and how did he know so much? He picked up his car keys and slid a 9mm revolver into the back of his belt. Killing Lucas was not part of the plan, at least not for now. He had to get to grips with how much his mystery visitor knew and blowing a hole in him was not going to help.

He wanted to get to Cabrillo Bridge as early as possible to recce the place. In his experience, when people said they would come alone they invariably didn't.

As he pulled the door shut he heard the phone ring. He ignored it, got into his car and sped away.

The answer phone clicked in, Mechanic didn't leave a message.

* * *

Cabrillo Bridge runs west to east of the main entrance to Balboa Park. It was built in 1915 and spans Cabrillo Canyon, which cuts through the park. It has a two-lane roadway with a pedestrian access on either side and is modelled on an ancient aqueduct. It is one hundred and forty yards long. Jameson didn't give a shit about any of that, all he knew was that when he stood in the centre of the bridge he could spot someone coming from seventy yards away in each direction.

Harper drove over the bridge and passed through the main entrance. The tourist car park was on the right.

'You want me to tag along?' Harper said.

'No, it's best we keep this simple. Jameson is unlikely to turn nasty. I'm an unknown quantity and that's got to be burning a hole in him. I told him enough to make him piss his pants. He won't risk trying to take me out, he doesn't know what he's up against. You stay here.'

Lucas got out of the car and checked his watch, 1.45pm. He walked to the south side of the bridge and made his way along it.

There were groups of excited tourists taking advantage of the panoramic view of downtown San Diego. The sun was shining and cameras snapped away creating happy holiday pics, to be taken home, stuck in an album, and forgotten. Up ahead Lucas could see Jameson leaning with his hands against the anti-suicide fence which ran along the length of the bridge. The fence spoiled the view but had probably paid for itself many times over in reduced admin.

Jameson was staring at the high-rise buildings in the distance. He didn't acknowledge Lucas as he approached. Lucas adopted the same pose. Just two guys admiring the view.

'What do I call you?' Jameson broke the silence.

'You don't.'

'What do you want?'

'I told you. We want to hire the person who made the hit on the eighth floor of the Bakerville car park in Tallahassee on 28 April last year.'

'I don't know what you're talking about.'

'Stop playing games, Jameson. If that were the case you would not be here.'

'You know about my business activities. You know about my apartment. You know about Sheldon Chemicals and Helix Holdings. But that does not make me a hitman.'

'No, it doesn't, but you launder money and that's worth a long stretch in the big house. However, you are right, you're not the hitman, but you are the fixer. On 28 April you supplied the location, the rifle, the ammunition and the finger on the trigger. And that's all we want. We are not interested in making life difficult but you need to cooperate.'

Jameson's facade was cracking. *How much does this guy know?*

'Why go to the trouble of digging around in my personal affairs? If you wanted to hire someone, why not just ask?'

'You are a careful man, Captain Jameson, and you might have refused. We wanted to make sure you said yes.'

'And what if I don't?'

'We don't make the call and you get an early morning wakeup from the cops.'

'I don't like being strong-armed.'

'Don't look at it like that. I'm just making it easy for you to say yes. Look at it as a win-win situation. You get to avoid the close scrutiny of the law and my client gets what he wants.'

'You don't get to choose the one who pulls the trigger.'

'Oh, but we do, Captain Jameson, that's a deal breaker. My client has admired your work for some time and is insistent on that point, it has to be the same shooter.'

Jameson gritted his teeth, his mind doing backflips with the implications.

'Why?'

'That's our business. Let's say it's important to my client.'

'Is your man reliable – the one who can make the money trail disappear.'

'Yes.' The lies were tripping off his tongue.

Lucas watched as Jameson wrestled with his options.

'It's twenty-five grand up front and another twenty-five when the job is done.'

Lucas shook his head and whistled. 'That is way out of the ballpark. I tell you what, fifteen up front and fifteen after.'

'No way, the kit is state of the art and that costs. Plus my guy is the best, and for that you have to pay top dollar.'

'Okay twenty and twenty, that's the best I can do. And don't forget, you get the cops off your back thrown in for free.'

'Done,' Jameson said staring into the middle distance.

'How long will it take?'

'That's a "how long is a piece of string" question. It depends on the target and the location, the planning can take anything between a few days to a few months.'

'Let me ask the question in a different way. When will you know how long this will take?'

'I will have an initial estimate in the next few days. Who's the target?'

Lucas pulled a sealed envelope from his jacket and handed it to Jameson.

'There's one more thing.'

'What?'

'This is personal for my client and he wants to enjoy the ride. For his forty grand he wants to know how and when the hit will take place. He doesn't want a ringside seat, but he wants to know how it's going to go down.'

'Your client is your business. I don't want to know who he is.'

'You don't have to. You keep me informed and I can keep him informed. My client is a very detail-driven man and he loves to get his rocks off on the small print.'

Jameson thought for a few moments.

'I can make that happen.'

'Good.'

'How do I contact you?'

'You don't. I'll be in touch,' Lucas said.

They separated and walked in opposite directions.

* * *

Moran turned her key in the lock and almost fell into her hallway. She felt as if she'd been ripped open at the seams and the stuffing torn out. She dumped her bag on the coffee table and headed straight for the fridge.

The bottle of wine stood no chance as she grabbed it from the shelf and snatched a tumbler from the draining board. She lay on the couch, bit into the cork and yanked it free. She poured herself a measure big enough to lose someone their driving licence in an instant, and sank half of it in one go. The cold liquid felt good against the back of her throat, which was raw from retching. She slugged the rest back and topped up the glass.

After her unexpected visit to the ladies' room, she had returned to the office and worked a little longer. Then she told Mills she felt dreadful and went home.

'A few hours' sleep and I should be good to go in the morning,' she told him.

Mills was genuinely concerned and was being overly attentive. Normally when people were sick they were disregarded in a 'no time for weakness, we have criminals to catch' type of way, but not this time. He told her if she needed anything to give him a call. He had handed her a Post-it with his phone number scribbled on it. She of course accepted it with a weak smile.

She was also grateful that throwing up her breakfast meant there was no chance of her having to endure another evening of cold beer, corn chips and mind-numbing conversation. Her charm offensive had paid off and he now looked at her with puppy dog eyes whenever they were together. She needed him to be malleable and distracted, and he was certainly both.

Moran emptied her glass and filled it again. This bottle was way too small. It was half past two in the afternoon. She no longer felt as if she was going to vomit and no longer felt the need to collapse in a gibbering heap on the floor. On her journey home she told herself over and over that she'd made the right decision. If she told Mills about the account transactions she would have placed herself in the firing line.

Find Mechanic and they find me. The phrase buzzed around in her head. And besides, who did she have more faith in? Mills and his catastrophic approach to law enforcement or two retired police officers, one who was unable to run for a cab and the other who was unable to pass a bar. There was no competition, the two cops won hands down.

The inner turmoil she had felt for the last twenty-four hours was gone and she was enjoying the relief. The wine tasted good and Moran was at last feeling relaxed and thinking straight.

She lifted the phone off its base and dialled. The synthetic warble at the other end went on for ages. Eventually someone picked up.

'Can you put me through to Ed Lucas, he's staying with you.'

She could hear soft clicks as she was transferred to his room. The phone rang but no one answered.

'I'm sorry caller. Would you like to leave a message?'

'Yes, can you tell him I did the right thing. And can you pass on my number please.' She reeled off the digits and thanked the receptionist.

'Who shall I say called?'

'No name, just pass on the message.'

Moran drank what was left of the wine and settled into the soft cushions.

* * *

The phone burst into life. Moran jumped from the sofa and for a second couldn't work out where she was. She wiped the sleep from her eyes and looked at the clock, it was 6.25pm.

'Hello.'

'It's Lucas, I got your message.'

There was a pause, both of them conscious that a coded conversation was in order.

'I wanted to let you know I did what you asked.'

'That's good, because our fish has taken the bait.'

Moran didn't speak.

'You still there?' Lucas asked.

'Yes, I'm here. I want in on the fishing trip.'

'How do you mean?'

'I want to be in on what you two are planning. And that does not mean being on the end of the phone when you need something, it means I want to be properly involved. I want to know what's going down and when.'

'I think that's fine, we can do that. Why the change of heart?'

'That's for another time, for now I want to be in the loop.'

'I'll be in touch.'

Lucas hung up. To the trained ear it was probably the worst coded conversation in history.

Chapter 20

Mechanic parked her car across the street from the 24-hour mini-mart on a derelict piece of waste ground. The rain scythed down, bouncing off the road and hammering on the roof. The red digits on the dash said 9.15pm.

The store was small, with wraparound windows spilling shimmering cones of white light across the wet road. It was nestled between a pet shop and a carpet warehouse in a parade of shops, all of which boasted super savings and 70% discounts. This was a run-down area of San Francisco, but not so run-down that people didn't shop in the middle of the night. For groceries that is, rather than hookers and drugs. Mechanic could see the shop worker inside dressed in a red T-shirt and a cap with the company's logo sprayed on the front of both. He was busying himself with the tills and stocking the shelves.

Mechanic figured there had to be a gun somewhere on the premises. But with what she had in mind it would stay tucked away under the counter.

The car was a brand new Ford with less than a thousand miles on the clock. That new car smell filled the interior. It had been rented using cash that afternoon by a man with a fake driving licence. He had left it on top of the multi-storey three miles away, as instructed, with the keys on top of the front wheel. The ticket to get through the exit barrier was hidden in the sun visor.

In the trunk, buried beneath the spare wheel, was a hard black case containing a Glock 17 handgun, a cartridge with nine 19mm bullets and a silencer. Mechanic had the case next to her on the passenger seat. She snapped open the catches and lifted the weapon from the foam interior. She drew back the slide and checked the chamber. It was empty.

Mechanic pushed down the slide locks and the top of the gun lifted off to expose the barrel and the recoil spring. She removed them both and inspected them. With three swift movements she reassembled the weapon and examined the cartridge. From the weight she knew it was fully loaded. She checked the tension and alignment of the top bullet and snapped the cartridge into frame. Mechanic wound the suppressor onto the threaded barrel, pulled back the slide and the top shell entered the chamber. She was ready to go.

She thought about Jameson. How the hell he made things happen so smoothly was beyond her. All she knew was, when he said something would happen, it did, just like he said it would.

Mechanic hated walk-by hits, there were so many things that could go wrong. She played the scenario like a film in her head: Cooper would pull up outside the store in her Jeep Cherokee and bump the front wheels against the parking kerb. She would get out and enter the mini-mart saying 'Hi' to the guy behind the till. Grabbing a shopping cart she would do a mad dash between the aisles, filling the trolley with the same food she bought every week, and head for the checkout. That was the signal for Mechanic to make a move.

While Cooper was piling food into bags and chatting about the weather, Mechanic would head across the road to the far right of the carpet warehouse. Once there she would double back towards the store, keeping tight against the front wall. The first obstacle to overcome was the rotating CCTV camera set up on the front of the building.

Mechanic would stop short of the mini-mart to put two slugs into the camera and watch the red LED at the back go dim. Cooper would pay for her goods, say goodbye to the man and hurry from the store. She would flick open the tailgate of the truck and throw the bags into the back, spilling groceries over the floor as the rain stuck her hair to her head.

Mechanic would wait until she was in the driver's seat, shaking the water droplets from her hands and face. Then she would stroll over to the driver's window with her gun drawn and put a neat hole through Cooper's head. One shot, maybe two.

The side window would shatter, but given the noise of the rain the man in the store would never hear it.

Mechanic would continue walking across the road back to her car. Ten minutes later she'd retrieve another ticket from the barrier to the multi-storey and slide it into the sun visor. She would park the car in the same slot, put the Glock back in its case, hide it under the front seat and leave the keys under the driver's mat. She would swap into her rental car and drive out of town to the Holiday Inn next to the airport, get a few hours' sleep and be on the first flight back to San Diego in the morning.

With any luck the guy in the red T-shirt would only know something was wrong when he noticed his CCTV had gone blank or that Elaine Cooper had been sitting in her car for longer than usual. By which time Mechanic would be well gone.

Despite the mental rehearsal, Mechanic hated walk-bys, there were so many things that could go wrong.

The black and white patrol car pulled up outside the mini-mart. Two officers ran from the car into the store. They greeted red T-shirt guy and went over to the coffee station to get a well-earned caffeine injection.

'Shit,' Mechanic said to no one and slid down in her seat.

The clock said 10.17. It was still early and the cops would be long gone by the time Cooper arrived.

Mechanic was running the scenario in her head like a loop. She could visualise every detail, right down to the look on Elaine Cooper's face when she realised someone was standing next to her car holding a gun.

The clock said 11.34. The intel report said Cooper was a regular timekeeper and would arrive ten minutes either side of midnight. The cops had stayed twenty-seven minutes and had drunk enough coffee to make them pee for the rest of their shift. All was quiet and Mechanic was calm and relaxed. She pulled on a pair of black gloves.

Not long now.

The rain had eased but was still coming down fast. The sound of fat water droplets striking the roof no longer filled the car.

Mechanic was distracted by a noise to her left. She flashed a glance through the side window but saw nothing. The noise happened again but this time it came from the right. Mechanic drew the Glock and cracked open the door.

There it was again. A grating sound.

She stepped from the car and did a three-sixty. The waste ground was empty, the only noise was the rain hitting the ground. She got back into the car and placed the gun on the passenger seat.

There it was again. A dragging, grinding noise, as though furniture was being moved across a wooden floor.

She froze.

The sound was inside her head. Something heavy being dragged along the floor. It was growing louder.

Then a door slammed shut and she jumped.

No, this couldn't be happening, not now. Mechanic looked at the clock: 11.45.

The sound of voices echoed around her head. She balled her fists and punched the steering wheel.

'No!' she yelled.

Another door slammed and the voice was clearer now. She put her head in her hands and rocked back and forth.

'For fuck's sake,' she cried slamming her hands either side of her head.

The Jeep Cherokee pulled into the car park.

Mechanic fought to collect herself, breathing in through her nose and out through her mouth. The noises subsided as she watched Cooper bump her tyres into the parking kerb and jump from the truck. Mechanic's hands were shaking. She saw the guy in the red T-shirt wave hello as Cooper pulled a cart from the line.

Mechanic slowed her breathing and closed her eyes, focusing on the work in hand. The voices stopped. The minutes ticked by. She could see Cooper heading for the checkout. She stepped from the car, put the Glock in the waistband of her jeans and walked across the road ignoring the rain.

Mechanic reached the warehouse wall and could see the red glow from the back of the CCTV camera. Two dull mechanical spits and the LED went out.

Another door slammed shut in her head. Mechanic screwed her eyes shut and focused on Cooper. Should she abort the mission or plough on? She was so close now.

The plate-glass doors hissed open and Cooper bustled out into the night air with her bags. She scurried to the SUV dancing around the puddles. The Cherokee beeped, the indicators flashed and the tailgate opened. She flung the bags into the back and ran around to the driver's side.

Mechanic was rooted to the spot.

The voices were getting louder and she could hear the sound of heavy footsteps. She saw Cooper duck into the driver's seat and bang the door shut.

She had to move now.

The voices were loud. The footsteps were getting closer.

Mechanic lurched forward holding the Glock.

'What the fuck are you doing?' the voice boomed.

She stopped. Her feet nailed to the asphalt. Unable to move.

Cooper started the engine and slipped the shift into reverse. Mechanic saw the white reversing lights pierce the night.

'Kill the bitch.' Daddy's voice echoed off the walls in her head.

Mechanic tried to move her legs but she was paralysed.

Cooper looked in her side mirror and saw a figure silhouetted in black against the light of the store window. The figure was holding a gun.

She screamed and slammed her foot to the floor.

The truck wheels spun in the wet, then the tread bit into the road. It lurched backwards and accelerated hard across the car park.

'Kill the bitch!' Daddy's voice was deafening.

The jeep hurtled past Mechanic and smashed through the shop front. The plate glass burst upon impact. Red T-shirt guy dived for cover as shards of glass rained down and the back of the truck crashed its way through the store. The shelves buckled, sending tins, boxes and bags flying into the air. The vehicle juddered to a stop, its big diesel engine roaring, belching out exhaust fumes.

The collision threw Cooper backward then forward in her seat, cracking her head on the steering wheel. She yelped in pain. Red T-shirt guy scrambled to his feet, bleeding from an ugly gash on his left arm. He ran to the driver's door and yanked it open.

'Christ, what happened? You okay?' He reached in and turned off the engine.

Cooper was groggy but conscious. She slumped from behind the wheel and tumbled out of the cab. The shop guy caught her as she fell and sat her on the floor. He checked her over. Blood ran from a deep cut above her eye.

'I'll call an ambulance,' he said making a dash for the phone.

There was a spit and his head snapped back.

Mechanic was the other side of the truck with her arms outstretched across the hood. Red T-shirt guy keeled over backward and landed face down on top of Cooper. She screamed as he knocked her sideways. Cooper scrabbled to her knees, rolled him over and cradled him against her. She could see the ragged edges of bone sticking out from the right side of his head. His blood poured into her lap. She was unable to comprehend what was happening.

'Dave, Dave, wake up!' She was shaking his shoulders.

Blood ran down her jaw line and dripped onto his face.

Cooper looked up and saw Mechanic, the gun pointing directly at her.

'Kill her. Blow her face off. Do it. Do it,' Daddy snarled.

Mechanic closed her eyes and fought to regain control. The physical effort of standing shook her entire body. The whole room spun as she held onto the truck to stop herself collapsing.

She fired and missed.

Cooper screamed and snapped out of her daze. She scurried away on her hands and knees and darted up one of the aisles trying to get to her feet. Time after time she tripped and fell over the debris.

'No, no, no, no …' she cried as her feet slipped from under her.

Mechanic clawed her way around the front of the jeep. She stumbled against the end of the aisle and held on for balance.

Cooper's arms and legs pumped wildly as she tried to drag herself away. She tore items off the shelves to gain forward momentum but she slipped again and landed on all fours.

'No, no, no, no—'

The shell drilled a ridged hole in the nape of her neck, and then exploded out the front of her face. The force threw her forward. She landed with a splat, face down on the tiled floor with her arms at her sides, a halo of blood around her head.

'Taste it.' Daddy was gurgling with excitement.

Mechanic shook her head as the world swam in and out of focus. She staggered over to Cooper's body.

'Go on, taste it, I say.'

She bent down and trailed her fingers through the blood. It was warm and sticky.

'Taste it and be mine.'

She watched as scarlet droplets fell from her fingertips.

'Do as I say. Drink the fucking—'

Then there was silence.

The world stopped spinning and everything was quiet. Daddy was gone.

Mechanic took a moment to collect herself. She reached for a bottle of water, twisted off the top and poured it onto her face. The liquid splashed down her front and ran like clear tributaries in the dark red puddle.

Her head snapped back to the present. She had to work fast. Mechanic replaced the top on the bottle and stuffed it in her jacket, then worked her way around the truck to look behind the counter. Nothing there. She crashed her boot through the plywood door marked Private to find what she was looking for, and ripped the CCTV recorder from its mountings. She walked out of the store to her car waiting across the road.

Mechanic hated walk-by killings but this one had turned out to be worse than most.

Chapter 21

Moran woke up, but this time with a full three minutes to spare before the local radio station announced the time. She switched off the alarm without it sounding.

She felt as if a heavy weight had been lifted from her shoulders. She lay in bed thinking about the various plans Lucas and Harper could be hatching. It pained her to admit it but she had a grudging respect for Harper because deep down she knew, if the situation had been reversed, she would have done the same. But a grudging respect is different to liking someone. And she disliked him with a passion.

Moran was looking forward to the day, a novel feeling given what she had been through in the past week. She showered and drank a cup of strong black coffee as she dressed. The effects of a bottle of wine and no food had caused a little collateral damage as she examined her eyes in the mirror. Make-up was required, if she could remember how to apply it.

Moran arrived early and set about her day. She had been reassigned to help a colleague whose job it was to interrogate the flight manifests. His name was Johnno, he was in his late forties and wore a suit which probably fitted him when it was new ten years earlier. Moran had seen him around the office, but he always kept himself very much to himself.

The task was a soul-destroying job of cross-checking lists of people's names and their destinations against anything which looked like it could be Nassra Shamon. It was her first morning working on it and already she was climbing the walls.

The airlines were cooperative but not proactive, so if you needed something you had to ask. They didn't think to provide details of connecting flights or transfer schedules. You had to work it out and request it. It was clear to Moran that Johnno was in his element, he loved it. She was beginning to see why co-workers kept their distance.

Mills had stuck his head around the door and waved a good morning at her, obviously pleased she was back at work. She was fully expecting another invite for cold beer and corn chips.

Moran looked up and realised the office was full of people. It was 9.30am.

'What's happened to the morning prayers?' she asked Johnno.

'Not sure, maybe Mills has been pulled away on something else. He's fanatical about the morning briefing, so whatever it is must be important.' He buried his head into the mountain of paper and once again disappeared.

The morning ticked by and by 11.20am Moran was seeing double. The close layout on the VDU and the densely packed printouts were blurring into one. One flight was sounding very much like another and destinations were becoming interchangeable. She had tried to chat with Johnno about what he'd already found out but without success. She even tried to tempt him with coffee but was met with a shake of the head. No words were required.

From what Moran could gather the whole exercise was drawing a blank. There was no record of Shamon entering the country on a flight, though her visa said she had, and there was no record of her leaving the country or taking an internal flight. As far as this piece of the jigsaw was concerned, Shamon miraculously appeared one day in Las Vegas and had not left. Surely the obvious move was to check the car rental and public transport records out of Vegas in the days following the Ramirez killing. An obvious move but one Moran was not going to suggest. Ploughing through flight manifests was just fine.

She was so engrossed in her work that Moran failed to notice Mills standing next to her desk.

'Do you have a minute?'

'Sure, I could do with a break.'

'Let's go somewhere quiet.'

Moran was on full alert. An invite to talk somewhere quiet was Mills-speak for an invite to after-work drinks. Maybe he was plucking up courage to ask her out on a proper date, with food that didn't come out of a foil bag. She followed him across the corridor into a small office.

He sat at the desk and offered her the seat opposite.

'Can you close the door, please?'

'What's on your mind?' Moran asked.

'Yesterday, after you went home, I took a call from Miriam Took.'

The hairs on the back of Moran's neck stood to attention.

'She is an account manager for the Wells Fargo bank,' he continued.

Moran knew exactly who Miriam Took was.

'She called because she wanted to confirm that the account details she provided were okay. She said that during your meeting yesterday you were a little confused and she wanted to follow up to ensure everything was in order.'

Moran's heart was in her mouth.

'To be sure we had the correct information, she relayed the transactions over the phone. I couldn't tie up what she was saying with what you reported at the morning briefing. So I asked her to fax me the details.'

Mills slid a sheet of paper in front of her. Moran didn't need to look at it, she knew what it said.

'Who or what is Helix Holdings?'

Moran wanted to die.

'There are three sizeable payments to them around the time Ramirez was killed. And the day after his death the account is closed. You reported there was nothing unusual about the account.'

Moran said nothing. She was incapable of saying anything at all.

'Come on, Moran, I want to hear what the fuck you think you're playing at?'

The puppy dog eyes were no more, they were flashing anger.

'I can't explain, I just lost it yesterday.'

'Lost it, lost what? Lost your ability to spot an unusual payment on a bank statement?'

'You saw how sick I was yesterday, I wasn't thinking straight.' She was grasping at straws and sinking fast.

'Yes, you were sick, yes you may have been muddled in your thinking, but the meeting with the bank was the day before. Are you telling me you were unwell then?'

'No.'

'So when you had your meeting with Miriam Took what the hell did you talk about, the fucking shopping channel? Because it sure as hell wasn't Helix Holdings.'

'Yes, we talked about it but everything appeared okay.' She had her head well and truly below water.

'In what way does that look okay?' He stabbed a finger onto the sheet of paper in front of her. 'It sticks out like a cock on a Barbie doll.'

'I … I … don't know.' The words dried up in her mouth.

'This is serious shit. This is a murder inquiry. You are a detective, trained to look for things which could lead us to identifying individuals involved in crime. And you didn't think this was worthy of mention? The only conclusion I can make is you wilfully withheld information.'

'I'm sorry, I don't know what I was thinking.'

'No, and neither do I.'

He slid another piece of paper across the table.

'I'm suspending you from duty pending an investigation. You will be contacted in writing when the investigation is complete and you will be given a date to attend a meeting. If you so wish, you can choose to be accompanied by your union rep or a co-worker to support you. It's all set out in the letter.'

Moran picked up the paper and read it. It was in HR speak and basically said what Mills had told her. He'd rehearsed his lines well – she was screwed.

'You can pick up your things and I will escort you from the building.'

Moran got to her feet, still holding the letter.

'You need to surrender your badge and your weapon.'

She unclipped them both from her belt and laid them on the table.

'I can explain,' she said in one last-ditch effort.

'No, Rebecca, I don't think you can.'

Mills swept past her and held the door open.

She picked up her bag and her coat from the office and Mills walked behind her as she made her way from the building. She felt numb.

He followed her to the main door, turned, and left without another word.

Moran stood outside trying to comprehend what had happened. She was stunned and didn't move for a full five minutes. Then her head clicked into gear and she ran across the parking lot, she needed to get home.

Forty minutes later her front door clattered open and Moran made straight for the phone. She then pulled a small suitcase from her wardrobe and filled it with a selection of black clothes and toiletries. She piled other items into her handbag as a car horn blasted outside.

Moran left the house and jumped into the cab waiting at the kerb. The thirty-minute journey seemed to take forever as the traffic continued to build the nearer they got to the Vegas Strip. The cab swung into a drop-off zone and she shoved ten bucks into the driver's hand. While he was rooting around for change, she was gone.

Moran scanned the board and hurried to the Delta Airlines desk. She needed to catch a flight.

* * *

114

Mills returned to the incident room and dumped a file marked Nassra Shamon on Johnno's desk.

'Moran is off the case. Can you deal with this?'

'Yes, sure, boss,' Johnno replied looking up. It was his standard response to anything a senior person asked him, but it didn't mean he would do it. It was a response designed to ensure they would leave him alone.

Mills scuttled away to create confusion elsewhere. Johnno picked up the file and dumped it on top of the mound of computer printouts. Bank details were not as much fun as flight schedules.

Chapter 22

For the second time in two days Jameson stood in the centre of Cabrillo Bridge. He was doing his tourist act of admiring the high-rise view of downtown when he clocked Mechanic walking up the pedestrian way.

She stopped next to him, pulled out a camera and started taking snaps.

'What the hell happened, Jess?' Jameson said looking straight ahead.

Mechanic always felt weird when someone used her real name. She had spent so much of her adult life living with a false identity, it made it sound as though they were referring to someone else.

'She saw me and panicked and put the truck through the storefront. It got messy.'

'And the target?'

'The target was eliminated but I had to take out the shop worker as well.'

'That is messy.'

'Yeah, it sure is.'

'Where did you take her out?'

'Inside the store.'

'CCTV?'

'I disabled the one outside as per the plan but there were two cameras inside so I took the recorder.'

'Where is it now?'

'Busted up and deposited in six separate dumpsters. I burned the tape.'

'Good.'

'Sorry, it was a right cluster fuck.'

'Yes, but it sounds like you recovered the situation. And from what you've said, the cops will think it's a ram-raid robbery gone wrong, which is fine for us. It makes it look less like an execution.'

'Yeah, I suppose so. I feel like shit. I hate it when things screw up.'

'There are times when the best laid plans don't survive first contact and we have to react accordingly. It's the outcome that's important not how we got there.'

'I know, but this was a straightforward in-and-out job. The only collateral damage was supposed to be her driver's side window and a CCTV camera, not a whole fucking store, a truck and another dead body.'

'You dealt with the situation and made it work. Don't be hard on yourself. The client got the result he wanted, he's not going to care about the other stuff.'

'Thanks, I suppose I just needed to hear it.'

'Go look at your bank balance, that will make you feel better.'

Mechanic took the camera from her face and flashed him a sideways smile. Jameson flashed one back.

'How you doing?' Mechanic asked.

'I'm mending slowly. I'll be back in work tomorrow.'

'I was thinking another meeting would be good.'

Jameson's bruised cock twitched into life.

'You say when and I'll be there. But it's probably better if it's not for the next week or so.'

They allowed the moment to pass, both pretending to look at the skyline in the distance, each one picturing their favourite scene from the other night.

Mechanic broke the silence.

'Any more work in the pipeline?'

'We have one but it's too early to tell.'

'I need to disappear for a while. I'll be gone a few days.'

'Anywhere nice?'

'Not sure. I need you to do something.'

'What is it?'

'I want you to trace Lieutenant Commander Stewart Sells. I've lost touch and I don't know if he's dead or alive. If it's the latter, I want to know where he is, and if it's the former I want to know where he's buried.'

'Who is he?'

'My father.'

* * *

Moran got off the courtesy bus and made her way up the steps to the plane. The stewardess took her ticket stub and pointed out the correct aisle for her to find her seat. This was a flight of desperation, but it was her only remaining option if she wanted to stay a free woman. She took off forty-five minutes later.

Moran ate the in-flight food and listened to the piped music through cheap plastic headphones. She also downed three small bottles of wine, which had the desired effect. By the time the plane touched down in Atlanta she had been asleep for at least two hours.

The turnaround was mercifully short. After a quick bite to eat she was back in her seat on a different plane, ready to make the one hour and seven minute flight to Tallahassee.

The plane landed on time. In the arrivals hall she found the passenger information desk and used the house phones to call various hotels. Each hotel was advertised with a sunny picture and a speed dial button to contact them. On her third attempt she booked a room at the Days Inn for one night. The courtesy car picked her up outside and forty minutes later she was in bed. It was quarter to one in the morning.

She stared at the digits on the clock and reflected on a catastrophic day. She had gone from feeling good about life to lying in a strange bed in a different state and facing a disciplinary charge, all in the space of eighteen hours. Well, twenty-one hours if you count the time difference. And on that thought, exhausted, she went to sleep.

* * *

Moran had woken to a beautiful spring morning. After a shower and coffee she'd settled her bill with cash, hailed a cab and headed into the city. She was sitting at a bus stop, holding another coffee and looking at the front of the public records office. It was closed and wasn't due to open for another ten minutes. The morning commuters were also waiting at the stop, which provided her with cover.

Moran thought about the chain of events which must have happened after she left the office. Mills would have touched base with HR to inform them of her suspension and that she had been escorted from the premises. He would have reassigned her work to another person in the team, someone who already had the workload of two people. Even if Mills made it a top priority they wouldn't have analysed the bank records before today. So, given the time difference, she had three hours before whoever had the file would start making calls. That was ample time.

Moran had been on an early morning shopping trip and hated the results. She was dressed in a bright yellow puffer jacket, a bright red be any hat, which covered her head and most of her face, and thick-rimmed glasses. She hated the jacket, but it was the only item of clothing she could find at 8am which was at the other end of the colour spectrum to what she normally wore.

Through the frosted plate glass she saw the blurred outline of a figure unlocking the large doors. The public records office was open for business. Moran pulled her case along behind her and crossed the road. She pushed open the door and slipped inside. The building had the distinctive smell of polish and boredom. She approached the front desk.

'I'm looking for a company – it's called Herald Holdings.' Moran figured giving the real name was not a smart move and the name Herald would at least put her in the right area alphabetically.

'That's on the fourth floor. Come out of the elevator and turn right.'

Moran thanked the woman.

On the fourth floor she entered a huge hall crammed with shelves, each one stacked with files and ledgers. There were rows along both sides and two more down the centre. She scanned the interior looking for surveillance cameras. There was CCTV in reception and outside the elevators but she could see none in the hall. She made her way down the centre aisle looking for H.

She walked up and down reading off the company names. This was going to be more challenging than she expected.

A young guy with glasses hurried past.

'Are you alright, ma'am. Can I help?'

'I'm fine, thanks.' The guy went to walk on. 'On second thoughts, could you show me where to find Herald?'

The young man was delighted to be of service. Normally customers gave him the brush-off, so an opportunity to show off his encyclopaedic knowledge was rare.

'Of course, ma'am, it's down here.' He weaved his way through the maze and stopped against a wall of files. 'Which one were you looking for?'

'It's fine thanks, I can take it from here.'

'Okay, give me a shout if you need more help.' He walked away triumphant.

Moran waited until he had gone, pulled on a pair of gloves and ran her finger across the spines of the folders.

'Hartwell, Haskins, Haven.' She read the names under her breath as she shuffled down the aisle.

She heard someone enter the hall. She couldn't see who it was but she was no longer the only visitor.

'Hawshore, Healing, Helix. Got it. Helix Holdings.'

She could hear the quiet tones of a conversation. There was more than one new visitor.

Moran pulled the Helix Holdings folder from the stack and laid it on the floor. She knelt down, flipped it open and read through the documents looking for anything that said Sheldon Chemicals or Gerry Vickers.

The voices were getting closer. She stopped what she was doing and stood up. She eased her fingers between two large files and prized them apart, peering between them. A tall man in a grey suit was walking in her direction, accompanied by a uniformed police officer.

Shit! Her mind went into overdrive. Mills must have contacted the local precinct to sequester the file.

How the hell did they get here so fast? Mills never did anything that fast. No one did anything that fast. The words crashed around in her head.

She dropped to the floor and rummaged her way through the documents, there was so much paper. She could hear them clearly now as they got closer. They were coming down the central aisle to her left.

Moran furiously turned over page after page.

None of it said Sheldon.

None of it said Vickers.

She could hear their footsteps. She stood up and squinted through the files again, the men were almost on her.

Moran slammed the file shut and rammed it inside her jacket. She straightened out the remaining folders on the shelf and walked to the opposite end of the row. As the men entered the one side, she disappeared out the other.

What the hell was she going to do now? If the police suspected foul play they would lock down the building and that was not good news.

She walked casually out of the hall dragging her case behind her. She crossed the atrium, past the elevators and into the opposite hall. There she found a corner between two shelves, dropped to the floor and pulled the file from under her coat.

She spread the paperwork around her and frantically sifted through it. After much sorting and cursing she found a page relating to Sheldon Chemicals, then another and another. Then the documents relating to Gerry Vickers came thick and fast. Soon she had a wad of papers set to one side. She opened her bag and stuffed them in.

Moran checked the coast was clear and headed for the elevators, taking care to keep her back to the camera located in the corner. She pressed the down arrow and waited, her heart rate returning to normal. Seconds later the doors opened with a metallic ding. She stepped inside and hit level two. The doors trundled together, and were nearly closed when a fat hand darted between them, holding them open. They slid apart, and the cop and grey-suited man got in.

'Excuse me, ma'am,' the cop said when he saw Moran.

She nodded and stared at the floor.

The grey-suited guy was trying to minimise his embarrassment, explaining away the absence of the file. He hit level one.

'We'll get to the bottom of it, officer. It occasionally happens that files get misplaced. People don't always put them back in the correct location. We have a barcode system which identifies the file's last location. The boys downstairs will be able to help.'

Moran was at the back of the elevator and the men stood in front of her facing away. She could see the cop's face in profile. She recognised the look. He couldn't care less. His first job of the day was to respond to a request from another police force two thousand miles away. He had to secure a file relating to a company he knew nothing about, relating to a case he knew nothing about. He was warm, dry and about to be given coffee to compensate for being made to wait. He wasn't going to get too excited about a little admin mix-up. If this took all day, it was fine by him.

The elevator stopped at the second floor and the doors opened.

'Excuse me,' Moran said in a tiny voice. The two guys parted and she walked out. She entered the hall to her left, it was the same layout as the one above. She idled between the shelves pretending to locate a file. When she was sure no one was about, she pulled the file from under her coat and slid it amongst the others squeezed between Mountain Press Spirits and Montague Inc. That should take a while to find – barcode system, or no barcode system.

Chapter 23

The next day Lucas and Harper were having lunch at a bar on a corner in Old Town. The patio was decked out in brightly coloured mosaic tables with gas burners set in the middle, a warm luxury to be enjoyed when the sun went down.

'Did Jameson give a timescale?' Harper asked, slurping his margarita and wiping salt from his mouth.

'He said he would know in a few days. He also said he didn't know how long the hit would take to plan, it depended on the target and location.'

'What do we do in the meantime?'

'This, I suppose.' Lucas took a mouthful of margarita from his plastic cup. 'We drink and we wait.'

'What about the cash?'

'I have a call with Bassano's father later today. I'm not anticipating an issue, they are minted and the look on his face at the funeral said "name your price".'

'I figure it would be worthwhile keeping the occasional tail on Jameson. And that would be down to me, because he knows you.'

Lucas nodded as he took another gulp.

'You need a gun,' Harper said casually, like he was telling his friend to get a haircut.

Lucas grimaced at him over the top of his drink.

'When the time is right. You know I hate them.'

'They're a necessity. You need to get your head around it.'

'Get my head around it?' Lucas leaned in close and lowered his voice. 'That's rich coming from you. Let's not forget you shot me.'

'Not that again, when are you going to give it rest? That was …' Lucas paused and did some mental arithmetic. He failed. '… a long time ago.'

'Twenty-two months to be precise, which I think you'll find is not long for people who've been shot in the head.'

'It was an accident, stop whining. I visited you in hospital, didn't I?'

'Yes, but only so you could feed your face. People brought me fruit and chocolates and you ate them.'

'That's horseshit. You whine worse than any wife.'

That stopped the conversation dead in its tracks. Harper looked down at his drink. The reference to wives was a little close to the bone.

'Sorry, man. I didn't mean that.'

Lucas smiled and put his hand on his friend's shoulder.

'No you didn't. You're a jerk who shot me in the head by accident.' Lucas held up his plastic cup and Harper struck it with his.

'Cheers.'

'I saved your life, didn't I?' Harper said.

'Yes, you did that too.'

They chinked their cups together again as the food arrived.

* * *

The extra payment in kind, which almost hospitalised Jameson, must have worked wonders. He had the information Mechanic wanted by mid-morning on his first day back at work.

It was relatively straightforward to locate her father. He was alive and in the advanced stages of liver cancer. He lived in sheltered accommodation in Prescott, Arizona. What the hell he was doing there God only knew. It was exorbitantly expensive and the bulk of his military pension went towards the care bills, which was probably a good thing. If he had all the money to spend on himself, he would have drunk himself to death a long time ago.

After his wife died, he disappeared off grid for several years, which must have been when he decided to kill his liver. By the time he showed up in Prescott, he was well on his way to an early death. To start with he lived in a series of rented properties, until his health deteriorated to the point where he needed the daily attentions of a nurse. His doctor suggested Pavilion Park Homes, a sheltered housing project with care facilities on site. The amount of care you received depended on how much you needed, or that was what it said in the brochure. In reality the amount of care was governed by how much you were willing to pay.

Ex-Lieutenant Commander Stewart Sells had lived at Pavilion Park for three years and needed more care than a fifty-nine-year-old man ever should. He liked the place and had a string of ex-military guys to hang around with, each one damaged in his own way and each one older than him. This was where Stewart Sells planned to spend the last of his days. Arizona suited him, the weather was hot and dry, the liquor was hot and dry, and the women were, well, hot anyway.

He was happy. The only issue was how many days he had left, and every time he attended clinic they told him it was fewer than the time before. If only he would stop drinking and allow the drugs to do their work. But that didn't figure for him – what was the point if he couldn't indulge himself from time to time. The problem was that for Stewart Sells indulging himself meant drinking so much he fell down.

He didn't own a car on account that he was rarely sober enough to drive. On the occasions when he felt the urge to travel, he rented a vehicle from Alamo and drove the one hundred and one miles south on the I-17 to Phoenix. It was a journey of one hour and forty minutes on a good day. But then taking a trip to Phoenix was always a good day because there were far more hookers in the state capital.

Ex-Lieutenant Commander Stewart Sells was happy with his lot in life and didn't appear overly concerned about killing himself.

* * *

125

Mechanic was desperate, she had to do something. The latest psychotic attacks had shaken her to the core. It was strange to think that following the death of her sister the voices had stopped. The prospect of Daddy roaming around in her head again was terrifying.

The San Francisco job was a disaster, despite what Jameson had said. The hit would have been clean and executed with the minimum of fuss had she been functioning normally, if you can call blowing a stranger's face off normal.

She had to reach some sort of closure with her father. It was the only thing she could think of to silence the voices. She couldn't go back to the time when Daddy ruled her life, compelling her to destroy families, killing the father and children while leaving the mother barely alive. It was a desperate move for a desperate person, but after the events in San Francisco that word described her well.

Mechanic decided the safest route was to travel by car. Taking flights was always a risk because of her fake I.D. It was the best US military intelligence had to offer, but if there was an alternative method of travel, she would rather not push her luck.

At three hundred and seventy-two miles it was a day's drive via the I-8 and the I–10 East. There were plenty of places to stop on the way so it shouldn't be difficult. It was a three-day round trip, maybe four, depending on what she found when she got there.

Mechanic threw a bag in the back of the car and set off for Prescott as the concrete span of the Coronado Bridge was silhouetted against the early morning sun.

Chapter 24

Mechanic had no idea what to expect when she found her father and even less idea what to say when she did. She hoped the words would come. Words that would enable her to make peace with the man who had blighted her life for so long. The man who had sought solace in raping her when his adulterous wife left him. The man she allowed to abuse her to protect her twin sister Jo as she slept two doors away. The man who chose his drug-taking whore of a wife over his daughters. The man who compelled her to kill.

She had no idea what to say. But she would have to find the words in five minutes' time as Pavilion Park Homes came into view.

Mechanic drew up outside the entrance and stepped out. The place was a gated community of red-brick bungalows and manicured lawns. There was an intercom mounted on the wall, and she pushed the button.

'Can I help you?' the detached voice of a woman crackled from the speaker.

'Hi, I'm here to see Stewart Sells.'

'Is he expecting you?'

'No, I want to surprise him. I'm his daughter Jessica Sells.'

There was silence for a few seconds then an electric motor buzzed into action and the gate swung open. She walked up a block-paved path and into the reception hall.

'He's in the communal room.' Mechanic recognised the voice of the woman on the intercom. She poked her head above the semi-circular desk in the corner. 'Straight ahead, second on the left.'

As Mechanic made her way along the pristine white corridors he could hear the chatter of excited voices. Large double doors were pinned back and she entered the room. A card school was in full swing with four guys seated at a table and a cluster of men behind them jeering and catcalling.

She recognised her father in an instant. Or to be more accurate, she recognised his voice. It still had that curious mix of soft southern drawl and clipped military diction, and it still boomed with the authority of a man used to being in charge.

What Mechanic didn't recognise was the emaciated body and balding scalp. The ends of his fingers were white and thick, and his hands trembled as he held onto his cards. His arms were a patchwork of red scabs where he had raked them raw. The remaining skin on show was tainted a jaundiced yellow.

He looked up when she entered the room and his eyes registered a flicker of recognition, then he continued playing his hand.

Mechanic took a seat at the back of the room and watched the game. Her dad was the dominant character in the group, hurling insults and jokes around in equal measure. He looked up again, and Mechanic could see the cogs turning as he stared at the uninvited visitor.

He returned to his cards. Ten minutes later he threw his hand onto the table and blasphemed.

'Goddamit, Doug. Do you have a stack of aces up your sleeve?' he challenged the man sitting opposite.

'No, but you sure have a stack of them in your ass.'

The group burst into riotous laughter as they stood up and milled around.

Mechanic made her move. She weaved her way through the crowd and touched her dad on the shoulder.

'Dad, it's me.'

Steward Sells turned and regarded her as if she was a street beggar, his pale watery eyes searching her face. Then a light bulb went off in his head.

'Jo,' he shouted. 'Jo, how lovely to see you!' He took her hand. 'Hey, guys, this is my daughter Jo. Sorry – it's been so long, I didn't recognise you. Your hair is different and—'

'No, Dad, I'm Jess,' she interrupted.

He looked at her and screwed his eyes up, another light bulb going off in his head. He dropped her hand.

'You're not Jo?'

'No Dad, I'm Jess.'

He took a while to adjust to the new information.

'Hi, Jess, it's good to see you.' He couldn't have sounded less sincere if he tried. 'What brings you here?'

'I thought it was about time I came to visit.'

He nodded his head and forced a smile.

'You hungry?'

'Er, yes, I could eat something.'

'Let's go eat.' Stewart Sells marched out. The warm welcome for his long-lost daughter was over.

They walked out of the building in silence and across the street to a rib shack, him in front and Mechanic following behind. They were shown to a corner table and a waitress dressed in black with a pink and white gingham apron appeared with two glasses of water. The ice chinked as she set them down in front of them.

'Hey, Mr Sells, good to see you.'

'Hey, Janine, what's cooking today?' He gave her the warmest smile of the day so far.

'The smoked baby back ribs and the slow roast belly pork are flying out of the kitchen.'

'Two smoked ribs it is then.'

Mechanic watched the waitress disappear back to the kitchen with her unopened menus. Apparently she wanted ribs as well.

She and her father enthusiastically sipped their water so they didn't have to speak.

Mechanic broke the silence. 'How did you end up here? Why Prescott?'

'It was recommended by a naval officer buddy of mine who's also an addict. Prescott is the recovery destination of choice for people wanting to kick their dirty habits. The place is full of rehab centres, detox clinics, halfway houses, sober homes and care facilities. You name it, they got it. The locals say there's over a thousand people at any one time in some recovery programme or another, it's the biggest industry in town. I figured that sounded like the place for me.'

'Is it going well for you here?'

'I get the right medicine and the right care. I have friends and places to visit, so yes, I guess it's going well.'

Mechanic looked at her father and tried not to let her thoughts give her away. The sight of his deteriorating body would suggest things were as far from going well as you could get. A million questions crashed around her head. None of which she was able to ask.

They both returned to their water.

'Why are you here?' Stewart Sells asked.

'It's been a long time and I wanted to see you.'

'That sounds like a politician talking.'

'No, it's true. I wanted to find you because it's been a while.'

'Maybe it has, maybe it hasn't. How is Jo?'

She had prepared herself for this question but it didn't make it any easier to answer.

'I lost touch with her too. Have you had seen or heard from her?' Mechanic imagined her sister lying in a cemetery somewhere in Vegas.

'Nope, not seen or heard from her in a long time. I thought you girls had fallen off the end of the earth.'

'Yeah, sorry it's been so long. That's why I came.'

'Things change and shit happens. But anyway you're here now and I suppose we should enjoy our meal.'

Mechanic wasn't sure how to respond. So she didn't.

They sat in silence until the food arrived. When it did each plateful could have fed a family of four and the waitress struggled to manoeuvre the dishes onto the table.

'Wow,' Mechanic said. 'They sure make them big.'

'That's why I come here. It's enough food for at least two meals. What we don't eat we can take out in a box.'

They tucked into the mountain of food.

'You not married?' he asked.

'No, never had the time or the inclination. After the army I was so busy moving from place to place I never got the chance to put down roots.'

'Did Jo marry?'

Every question about her sister caused Mechanic to take a deep breath before answering. Her emotions were still running close to the surface and she couldn't let that show.

'As I said, we lost touch, so she might be. I don't know.'

'I always thought she had the makings of a great wife and mother so I'd be surprised if she didn't get hitched to some guy. I never thought you would though, you never struck me as the type.'

And what fucking type is that exactly? she wanted to scream in his face. But she scooped a forkful of pork into her mouth instead.

He continued. 'No, you were never the marrying kind and I could never see you with kids.'

That might have something to do with you fucking robbing me of my childhood and making me into a psycho bitch who kills for kicks. The words stayed in her head as she rammed in another forkful. If this had been a cowboy movie, tumbleweed would be blowing through the restaurant. The awkwardness was thicker than the gravy.

'How long you planning to stay in town?' he asked.

'A couple of days maybe. I thought we could do stuff together, if that's okay.'

'You picking up the tab for lunch?'

'Er, yes, sure.'

'Then it's okay with me – you keep paying the checks and you can stay as long as you want.'

He piled food into his face and waved his glass at the waitress for more water.

Mechanic looked at the prematurely dying man opposite and the memories of what made him a monster came crashing back.

The meal ended with no more conversation. Mechanic paid the check while he collected the takeaway boxes, and they left.

'I got things to do this afternoon,' Stewart Sells said as they strolled out into the bright sunlight.

'Okay, I need to find a place to stay, so can I see you later? We could have dinner.'

'You paying?'

'Yes, I suppose—'

'Then come by after six.'

'Which bungalow is yours, I'll come and pick you up.'

'See you at six.'

She reached out her hand, but all she touched was empty space as he turned and walked away.

Mechanic wasn't sure what she'd find in Prescott, but this didn't feel like a reconciliation, it felt more like a rekindling of abuse.

Chapter 25

Mechanic arrived at the red-brick village a little before six o'clock. Her heart was banging in her chest at the prospect of another meeting with her father but she was determined to make things right between them.

The night guard buzzed her through the front gate and she waited in reception. Her watch ticked past the hour and there was no sign of him.

'My dad said he'd meet me here at six,' she said to the man in the security uniform. 'I'm thinking he might have got confused with the time. His name is Stewart Sells, can you tell me where he lives?'

'No, ma'am, we can't divulge tenant information, I'm sorry. You'll have to wait here.'

Mechanic shook her head, but arguing would be a waste of time.

The minutes ticked by.

At 6.17pm the security guy slipped on his jacket and ambled out the back of reception to do his rounds. Mechanic saw her chance and headed off into the network of single-storey homes.

She wandered the paved walkways looking for something she recognised. One of the men she had seen at the card game came out of his house.

'Hey,' she said. 'I'm here to meet Stewart Sells but I've lost the slip of paper he gave me with his address. Do you know where he lives?'

The old man stopped at the top of his path.

'Sure, honey, I saw you earlier, you're his daughter, right?'

'Yeah, that's right, I saw you too. Quite a card school you have going there.'

The old guy laughed and his chest rattled.

'He's at Simpson Place, number twelve.'

'Thanks.'

'Not sure he's in though, haven't seen him since this morning.'

'Where does he go when he's not at home?'

'How would I know?' he said, his tone changing to one that said 'enough questions already'.

Mechanic thanked the old guy and set off to find Simpson Place.

She didn't have to go far, and he was right, there was no one at home. Mechanic peered through the living room window, the place was empty and the TV was off.

She retraced her steps back to reception and headed out the gates. After thirty minutes of walking the streets, she found her father. He was keeping a bar stool warm in a fleapit of a liquor joint. The bar was long and narrow, and decked out in dark wood panelling with a thirteen-inch portable television hanging from one wall. It stank of spilled beer and bad breath, and the blades of the ceiling fan did nothing but ensure the stale odours were evenly swirled around the room. A line of crumpled figures sat at the bar either staring into their glass or squinting at the flickering images on the screen. A crew of drinkers were crammed in behind them, propping themselves up with one hand against the bar and a drink in the other. This was not the place to come for a round-table discussion.

Mechanic pulled up a stool next to her father.

'Hello,' she said.

'Who? How did you …' He slurred his words and his breath could have taken the paint off a door.

'I came at six, but you weren't at home.'

'Jo, it's fantastic to see you.'

'No, Dad, it's Jess. We were going to meet and have dinner together.'

'Oh, yeah, that's right. You're Jess, aren't you?' He took an exaggerated sway to the right and bumped his shoulder into hers. Mechanic flinched from the contact, it felt like being hit by a plastic bag full of coat hangers.

'What time ish it now?'

'It's nearly seven o'clock.'

'No, is it?' He pulled up the sleeve on his left arm and checked the time on his non-existent watch. His yellowing parchment skin was tissue thin.

'Don't you want to eat? You need food.'

'How did you find me? Who told you I was here? The bastards are not supposed to say I'm here. Who was it?'

'No one told me.'

'Then how did you know?'

'Two things, it's obvious you drink and it's also obvious you can't walk far, so it had to be somewhere close to home.'

'I don't drink. I'm on medication.'

'Okay, whatever you say. Do you want to go for something to eat?'

'Not hungry.' He motioned to the barman and another drink arrived in a chipped, stubby glass. He flipped his thumb in her direction. 'She's paying.'

Mechanic nodded and ordered another whisky with ice.

'Where is Jo?' her father asked, draining his glass and rubbing his mouth with the back of his hand.

'I don't know, Dad. I told you, I've lost touch.' The whisky arrived in a replica glass, minus the chips. Special treatment for new visitors no doubt.

'I liked Jo, she was always good to me.'

'Yes, I liked her too, Dad.'

'She had class. She was always the one who would go far. She was the one who had something about her.' Mechanic could feel her stomach sink. She sipped her drink, she was going to need it. Her father continued. 'You know, when your mother left me for that douche bag, Jo was the one who kept me going, Jo was the one who got me through it.'

Mechanic's fingers turned white as they tightened around the glass.

'Yes, Dad, Jo is a great person to be around. Now let's go get some food.'

'She always made me proud.' He waved his hand and the barman poured dark liquid the consistency of sump oil into another chipped glass. 'She had the looks, she had the brains, she was the full package.'

He jabbed his thumb in Mechanic's direction. The universal sign for 'this one's paying'.

'Yes, okay, Dad, I get it. So can we go out for dinner as planned?'

'It's my one big regret that I lost touch with her. She would have looked after me. She would have made sure I was alright.'

Mechanic knocked back the liquor, the ice cold against her lips.

'You're drinking yourself to death, Dad. I'm not sure Jo would be able to help.'

'What do you know? I have medication every day and that keeps things in balance. I can have a few drinks because the meds counteract the booze.'

'If you want to stay alive, you have to stop drinking.'

'Don't talk stupid and anyway who the fuck are you to talk?' The low murmuring voices around them went silent.

'I'm your daughter and I care about you.'

Stewart Sells dropped his head forward and, with his chin resting on his chest, he gazed into his drink.

'You want to know something?'

'What?'

He lifted his head and leaned in close.

'You were a good fuck when you were younger but no man in his right mind would touch you now.'

The glass shattered in her hand.

'Shit!' Mechanic jumped back as shards cut into her flesh.

The bartender scuttled over with a handful of towels. He swept the pieces of glass from the bar and threw a filthy towel to Mechanic.

'If you want trouble, go somewhere else,' he said.

Mechanic wrapped her hand in the cloth. *How about I vault this bar and shove your head up your ass?* She kept her mouth closed.

'I'm sorry, it was an accident. There's no trouble here.'

Her father carried on as if nothing had happened.

'I mean, look at you.' Stewart Sells was poking his finger into her shoulder. 'No wonder you're not married, talk about damaged goods. You were only good for one thing back then and I doubt you can do that now.'

Mechanic balled her bloodied hand in the towel.

'Now Jo on the other hand, she was class. While you, you were nothing but a fuck bag.'

He sank what remained of his drink and motioned to the bartender, who shook his head as he polished glasses with a stinking rag.

'No more,' he said.

Stewart Sells grunted and slid from the stool. He steadied himself on Mechanic's arm and staggered through the guys at the bar towards the exit.

'The bitch is paying,' he said over his shoulder.

Tears fell onto the cracked veneer as Mechanic stared at the blood seeping through the towel. The barman tore a slip of paper from the till, stuffed it in a glass and slid it along the counter top. It came to rest in front of her.

She hadn't bargained on paying such a high price for the trip, and the cost had nothing to do with the ten bucks she left under the glass.

Chapter 26

The needle on the speedometer hugged fifty-five as Lucas drove along the I-8 East away from San Diego. He was heading for Bonds Corner, a small unincorporated community in Imperial County, a journey of one hundred and thirty miles. It was in the middle of nowhere, its only claim to fame its location close to the Calexico US port of entry for trucks crossing the US-Mexican border. Lucas had to be there by 9.30pm.

The traffic was light and he made good time. The miles flew by and in under two hours he hung a right and hit the CA-111 travelling south. The road was slower, with trucks of every description trundling their way to the border. After a while he came to the intersection with the CA-98, turned left and drove parallel to the state line. Eight miles further on Lucas saw the sign saying Bonds Corner.

He swung the nose of the rental car off the road and onto the makeshift hard-core parking lot. He killed the engine. Cassandra's Café was a thirty-foot trailer set back from the road in a deserted dustbowl. Lucas knew he was in the right place because the name was painted in four-foot-high red letters across the side, he couldn't miss it. He pulled the car around the back and got out. There were arc lamps poking out of the roof, leaving the trailer sitting in its own oasis of light, while outside the hard-core area the rest of the landscape was pitch black. But no amount of blinding white lamps could disguise the fact that it was a shit-hole.

Lucas walked up the three steps to the wrought-iron security gate and yanked it open. It swung towards him and he pushed against the screen door.

The inside was clean and airy with a long counter running down the one side with a line of red leather bar stools stacked against it. On the opposite side were six booth seats, also decked out in red leather, each one set against a window. The place was completely at odds with the exterior decor.

Lucas strode in and slid into a booth facing the door. Two men sat at the counter. One was a road-worn trucker with an empty plate in front of him and a mug of coffee big enough to drown a small horse. The second was an older man, a biker, with expensive leathers and a glossy helmet. He was reading a local paper, sipping iced water.

Lucas stared out at the blackness.

A middle-aged woman ambled over to him wearing a blue dress and a white apron.

'What would you like to drink, sweetie?'

Lucas looked up. She had a mop of tightly permed brown hair and wore half-moon glasses perched on the end of her nose. She smiled but the look on her face said 'It's late, I'm tired'. Her name badge said Marge, she didn't look like a Cassandra.

'I'm ready to order,' Lucas said.

'Okay, sweetie, what'll it be?'

'I'll have waffles with French toast and a side order of bacon please.'

The woman stared at him over the rim of her glasses.

'You know we have a dinner menu, right?'

'Yes, that's fine thanks.'

'You haven't looked at the menu. Shall I give you a couple of extra minutes, sweetie.'

'No, no, I'm fine. Waffles, French toast and bacon please.'

The trucker stopped drinking his bath of coffee and snorted.

'Okay, sweetie, anything to drink with that?'

'Regular coffee please.'

The trucker looked over, shook his head and snorted again. Lucas imagined that in the world of truckers, real men didn't drink regular, they drank frigging enormous.

Marge went behind the counter and spoke to the man working in the kitchen. Lucas could make out snippets of the conversation.

'Well, I don't know, Earl, maybe he can't tell the difference between nine twenty at night and nine twenty in the morning.' Marge was defending his waffle order.

Lucas gazed at his reflection in the window and kept glancing over to the door. He checked his watch and played with the packets of sugar in the bowl. He pulled out his car keys and placed them on the table.

The biker guy jumped down from his stool and picked up his helmet. 'Cheerio now,' he said in a British accent.

Maybe a tourist but more likely an ex-pat, Lucas thought. He watched as the screen door clanked shut, followed minutes later by a roar as a big Honda motorbike with British plates chugged across the car park. The guy checked both ways and blasted off into the night.

Lucas was still mulling over the 'he must have been an ex-pat' deduction, when Marge appeared beside him.

'Coffee, sweetie.'

She placed the steaming mug in front of him. It was very different from the sludge he was used to drinking in the worst café in Florida. It was excellent coffee, strong and bitter.

The screen door opened again and a short man walked in carrying a black Puma sports bag. He was not old, but not young either. However, he was old enough to know you don't go out dressed like that.

His jeans were torn at the knees and he wore a pair of greasy work boots. His tatty denim jacket was threadbare and his elbows stuck through holes in the sleeves. His hair was long and lank, and he didn't look like he owned a comb or a razor. This guy didn't just need a bath, he needed a trip through a car wash.

Marge clocked him with a disapproving glance, the expression on her face now saying 'dirty hobo'. He shuffled in and took up a place at the counter across the way from Lucas. He dumped the bag at his feet and eased himself onto the stool. The truck driver didn't flinch, he was obviously more comfortable with the hobo than he was with Lucas.

The food arrived. Marge arranged the plates in front of Lucas.

'Need a refill, sweetie?'

'No thanks, I'm fine.'

'Enjoy your food.'

Marge went back behind the counter to serve the hobo.

'Enjoy your breakfast more like.' The truck driver sank the last of his enormous coffee and threw ten bucks onto the counter. He scowled at Lucas as he left.

Lucas tucked into the waffles, they were light and fluffy, really good. Or they would have been at seven thirty in the morning. But at half past nine at night they were a proving a struggle. Lucas persevered, pretending to enjoy his sugary dinner.

The hobo ordered coffee. Marge was much less chatty and didn't once call him sweetie.

Lucas shovelled slabs of waffle into his mouth and crunched on the bacon. This was a seriously tasty breakfast.

The hobo drained his coffee, jammed his hand in his pocket and spilled a bunch of change onto the bar. He dropped from the stool, turned and stood directly in front of Lucas. He moved in close and Lucas could smell engine oil.

'You got a light, buddy?' he said taking a pack out of his pocket.

'No, sorry, I don't smoke.'

Lucas noticed the hobo's hands were soft and clean, his nails neatly trimmed. He shot an unlit cigarette in his mouth and walked away. Lucas watched him leave and the trailer door slammed behind him.

He looked down. His keys were gone.

Lucas continued to munch his way through the food and finished off his coffee. His belly told him it was time to stop. He looked at his plate, there was more than half of it left.

Marge came over.

'You want a top-up, sweetie,' she said holding a pot of freshly brewed coffee.

'No thanks, that was great. Can I have the check, please.'

'You didn't like it, sweetie?' Marge eyed his plate, like a mother eyeing the unfinished plate of her wilful child.

Lucas felt compelled to respond. 'It was real tasty, but I can't finish it, can I have it in a box to go?'

'I suppose so, sweetie.'

Lucas could hear the latest exchange between Marge and Earl.

'Well, I don't know, Earl, maybe he'll eat the rest for breakfast. I mean breakfast for real, not ….'

Lucas was eager to leave. He saw the tail-lights of a beaten-up Ford on the hard-core. The front wheels bumped onto the road and sped away.

Marge showed up with a Styrofoam box and the check.

'I put some plastic cutlery in there as well, sweetie. Enjoy the rest of your night.'

Lucas picked up the box and left notes and a handful of change on the table. He waved a silent goodbye and walked down the steps to where he'd parked his car.

He crouched down at the driver's side and ran his hand under the front wheel arch. He felt along the top of the tyre and retrieved his keys. He unlocked the car, moved around to the back and popped open the trunk. The small courtesy light cut through the interior gloom. He banged the lid shut, got in the car and drove away.

* * *

The roads were clear and in a little over two hours Lucas was back in San Diego sitting in his apartment. The speedometer had hugged a number much bigger than fifty-five on the way back.

'How did it go?' Harper asked.

'Like clockwork.'

'Any problems?'

'A trucker wanted to rip my head off for ordering waffles, French toast and bacon. But other than that it went fine.'

'That was an unusual way to identify yourself. Whatever happened to wearing a red rose and carrying a newspaper.'

'That's what they said to do, so that's what I did. I figured they must think no one orders breakfast at that time of day.' He tossed Harper the takeout box. He opened it and set about the congealed mess with the plastic fork.

'What was the guy like?'

'Real scruffy. He'd have made a convincing hobo if it wasn't for his one-hundred-dollar manicure.'

Harper stifled a laugh.

'Is that it?' Harper asked casting his eyes down to the floor. Sitting in the middle of the room was the black Puma sports bag.

'Yup.'

'You checked it?'

'Didn't see the point. What am I going to do at ten o'clock at night on the side of the road in the middle of nowhere if it's wrong?'

Harper put away the box of food and sat down next to the bag. He drew back the zip and opened it up.

The first thing that struck them was the smell of newly issued bank notes. Harper reached inside and pulled out a brick of money. He upended the bag and bundles of tightly wrapped cash spilled onto the carpet.

'Jesus,' he whistled under his breath. He stacked them into piles of five and began to count.

He looked like a kid playing with a set of very expensive building blocks.

'Forty thousand dollars,' he said once he'd finished stacking.

There was a rapid knock at the door.

'Shit, who's that?' Lucas said.

'Room service,' said a voice on the other side.

Harper looked at Lucas and mouthed the words, 'I didn't order room service.' He jumped up, ran to the bedroom and returned with his gun.

Lucas scrabbled around on the floor throwing the money into the bag.

Another knock.

'Room service.'

Lucas zipped the bag shut and shoved it behind the couch. Harper was by the door, his gun pointing to the ceiling.

'Who is it?' Lucas asked.

'Room service.'

Lucas pulled back the lock. He twisted the handle and cracked open the door. He peered through the gap.

It was Rebecca Moran.

Chapter 27

'What the—' Lucas stepped back. Moran shoved the door open and forced herself inside.

Harper levelled his weapon, unsure what the hell was going on.

Moran walked to the centre of the room and dumped her bags. She saw the gun.

'Really, Harper? Put it away, cowboy.'

Harper slid the gun in his waistband and skulked off to the bathroom.

'What are you doing here?' Lucas asked.

'It's a long story.'

'Are you on your own?'

'Oh yes, I'm very much on my own.' She slumped into an armchair.

'How did you find us?'

'I faxed you the information on Jameson, remember, and I am a detective after all. Or was until thirty-six hours ago.'

'How did you get past the man on reception? Are you booked in?'

'No, the hotel was full. Getting in was easy, I think he thought I was a hooker.'

'Fucking unlikely.' Harper returned and sat opposite Moran.

Moran wasn't sure if that was a compliment or an insult. She plumped for insult.

'Come on, Moran,' said Harper. 'Put us out of our misery, why are you here?'

'I've been suspended from duty.'

Harper let out a belly laugh.

'How come?' asked Lucas.

'I did what you asked. I said there were no unusual transactions on the Shamon account and it came back to bite me. The guy running the investigation discovered the truth and I was out.'

'What exactly do the cops know?' asked Harper.

'They know about the monies transferred to Helix Holdings and they know they came from Nassra Shamon.'

'And you figure this Shamon woman is Mechanic,' said Lucas.

'Yup.'

'So we're screwed,' said Harper, getting out of his chair and waving his arms around.

'Not necessarily,' said Moran.

'Of course we are. When I told you to bury the account details, I didn't just mean lie about them. I meant delete them. Get rid of the evidence. Bury them. You stupid woman!'

'Wow,' said Lucas. 'Let's all calm down.'

'Calm down, my ass. We are now facing the prospect of the cops pulling Jameson when we are closing in on a deal that will lead to us to Mechanic.'

'Deal, what deal?' asked Moran.

'This fucking deal.' Harper went behind the sofa and pulled out the sports bag. He opened it and shook the contents onto the floor.

'Jesus Christ.' Moran's eyes were the size of saucers.

'But it doesn't matter now because we're fucked. You fucked us over.'

'No I haven't.'

'That's enough, Harper,' Lucas said.

'I can't fucking believe it. All that work, all that planning, and you've screwed it up by being sloppy. You get suspended and think you can walk in here to lend a hand. That's it, isn't it?'

Harper lunged across the room and put both hands on the arms of Moran's chair his face inches from hers.

'You stupid little schoolgirl!'

Moran reached around and pulled the gun from his waistband. She jammed the muzzle under his chin.

'You touch me and I swear I'll fucking kill you.'

Everybody froze.

'Moran, don't be ridiculous, put the gun down,' Lucas said.

Harper inched back as he felt the cold metal boring into his flesh. He lifted his hands off the chair in a sign of surrender.

Moran got up, the gun digging hard into his throat.

'Do you hear me?' she asked, forcing him to retreat.

She drove Harper all the way across the room and back into his chair.

'Moran, put the gun down,' Lucas said.

'I said, do you hear me?' Moran hissed the words in Harper's face.

Harper nodded.

'I want to hear you say it. Do you hear me?'

'Yes, I hear you.'

'Good.' She strode over to her bags and opened one up. She rooted inside and produced a fistful of papers. She walked back to Harper and threw them in his lap.

'We are not fucked, because these are the documents relating to Sheldon Chemicals and Gerry Vickers. I took them from the Helix file and hid the rest in the records office. I doubt if they will find it for some time.'

'You went to the records office in Tallahassee?' asked Lucas.

'Yes, powered flight is a wonderful thing.' She put the gun on a side table. 'So you see the cops won't be looking for Jameson, because they don't know he exists. They will unravel it eventually, but until then we proceed as planned.'

Harper looked sheepish, and a little shaken at by being taken out by a schoolgirl.

Chapter 28

Mechanic booked herself into The Kings Motel just off the main drag, about two miles east of town. It was low-end accommodation that bordered on being a dump. The rooms were small and the plumbing banged in protest every time someone flushed the toilet. She slept on top of the quilt with a blanket thrown over her to avoid the wildlife living between the sheets.

The Kings did however have a few redeeming features. The man behind reception didn't ask for ID, so Amy Cheshire was now the new guest staying in a double room, for single occupancy, for two nights. He accepted cash for the booking and most important of all, the car park had no CCTV.

* * *

Mechanic had a bad night tossing and turning thinking about her father and their conversation in the bar. Eventually, as the digits on the radio alarm flicked over to 3am, she got up and switched on the TV. There were only four channels and each one was showing a crap programme. But the numbing effect worked well and she drifted off to sleep with the TV on in the background.

When the morning light burst through the thin drapes, Mechanic felt better. In the shower she had managed to convince herself that it was the booze talking and she should give her father another chance. She handed her key into reception and headed into town.

She parked up opposite Pavilion Park Homes and walked to her father's place. She rapped on the door. There was the sound of frantic scrabbling coming from inside and the door sprung open. In the pale glow of the early morning sun Stewart Sells looked even more yellow than usual, especially when dressed in pyjama bottoms with no top. Mechanic looked at his body: skin and bones with not much else.

'Oh, hi,' he said.

'Hi, how are you this morning?'

'Pretty good, how about yourself?'

'Yeah, I'm okay, but I'm hungry. Have you had breakfast?'

'Er, no, and I could eat right now. Come in while I get ready.'

She entered the small bungalow and closed the door. The place was brightly decorated and carpeted throughout. Mechanic could see a bedroom and bathroom and a small kitchen through an arch in the wall. There was a faint smell of fresh paint. It was pleasant enough.

Unfortunately, the lounge was littered with unwashed plates and the two-seater sofa and armchair looked like they'd been sat on by an elephant. The kitchen was no better, with not an inch of worktop visible due to the food wrappers and takeout boxes strewn across it. A mound of dirty laundry was piled into one corner of the bedroom. Red emergency cords hung from the ceiling in every room. Mechanic figured the maintenance of the building was the responsibility of the home, while the rest was the responsibility of her father.

He busied himself in the bathroom and emerged fully clothed. Mechanic wondered if there was another pile of dirty clothes in the bathroom and he had dressed himself from that. It looked as though he had.

'Ready,' he said.

They walked out of the complex and across the street to the rib shack. They were greeted by the same waitress as the previous day who ushered them to the same table. Mechanic seized her chance and grabbed a menu.

'I'll be back to take your order in a minute,' said the waitress.

They both sat in silence deciding what to eat.

'How was your evening?' Stewart Sells had a gift for saying the unexpected.

'Not good, now you ask. We had a fight, don't you remember? I called to take you to dinner and I found you in a bar.'

Mechanic tried to make light of the situation and present it as a hilarious mix-up.

'Oh yeah, right. It's my meds, they make me a little crazy. No harm meant, no harm done.'

Mechanic thought about the cocktail of drugs he must be taking: sorafenib, morphine, alprazolam, diuretics. None of them had the side effect of making a person bat-shit crazy. And anyway, drugs or no drugs, what was said last night was meant to cause maximum harm. She tore herself away from her train of thought.

It was the whisky talking, that's all. Mechanic kept trying to convince herself.

'Let's put it behind us,' she said. 'What would you like?'

'You picking up the check?'

Mechanic paused. 'As always.'

'Then it's gotta be steak and eggs,' he said triumphantly.

The waitress arrived and Mechanic ordered an omelette and coffee. As the waitress was about to leave, Stewart beckoned for her to lean forward. He whispered in her ear. She nodded and disappeared into the kitchen.

'What you got planned today?' Mechanic asked.

'Not a lot, I thought we might hang out together.'

'That would be great. What do you want to do?'

'Oh, I don't know. How about if we take things on the fly. Do what we please.'

'Yes, okay, that sounds good.' This was much better.

The waitress appeared carrying a tray with two glasses on it. She placed them on the table. Mechanic stared at the drinks, picked one up and sniffed it. It was whisky. Two double shots.

'Excuse me.' Mechanic held up her hand, but the waitress was gone.

'I thought a little livener would set us up for the day.'

'I'm not drinking at nine thirty in the morning.'

'They're not for you.' He picked up a glass and drained it down in one. The second one quickly followed.

'Don't you think it's a bit early for that?'

'Nonsense, I take my meds first thing in the morning and no one tells me it's too early to do that.'

The waitress returned to their table with fresh cutlery, coffee and two more glasses of whisky. She arranged the knives and forks in front of them and straightened out the napkins.

'Dad,' Mechanic said. 'Steady on.'

'It's gonna be a good day, I can tell.' The four shots of liquor met the same swift ending as the others.

Mechanic watched her father sink the whisky and rearranged the cutlery and napkins. Unnecessarily.

The waitress showed up again, cleared away the glasses and replaced them with two more. Mechanic said nothing.

'Do you hear anything from Jo?' He put the glass to his lips.

Mechanic said nothing.

'Do you hear from Jo?' He banged the empty glass down on the table and grabbed the other one.

'No, Dad, I keep telling you. We've lost touch.'

'That's a shame. Me too. I miss Jo.' He tipped the liquid into his mouth and knocked his head back. It ran down his throat with all the after effects of drinking cola. He wiped his mouth with the back of his hand.

'Oh good, here comes our food,' was all Mechanic could think to say.

The waitress served up the plates and left two more glasses on the table.

He went to pick one up and Mechanic put her hand on his.

'How about we eat?'

He stared at her for a second and removed his hand.

'Yes, okay, they're not going anywhere, are they?' He snatched the knife and fork and tore into his steak.

Mechanic observed her father as though it was feeding time at the zoo. He sawed away at the meat and slashed at the eggs. She watched his right hand shake under the pressure of cutting through the steak with a heavy serrated knife.

A knife like that could take a man's head off, she thought.

He folded a forkful of meat into his mouth.

'I was thinking,' he said treating Mechanic to a full view of the meat as he chewed it around in his mouth. 'How do you fancy spending more time here?'

Mechanic tried to avoid looking at the macerated food.

'You mean stay longer?'

'Yes, it would be good for us to get to know each other better, don't you think?'

These were the words Mechanic had been waiting to hear.

'Yes, of course. I have some time owing to me at work and could book more nights at the motel if that's what you want.'

He downed a whisky and shovelled in more egg.

'I was thinking we could, you know, do things together.'

'I want to spend time with you, Dad. There are issues that need sorting out and they could take time. We have to talk them through.' Mechanic was so overcome she ignored the next drink as it disappeared down his neck.

'That's settled then. We'll start today.'

'Yes, that would be great.' Waves of emotion swept over her.

They both ate in silence. Mechanic was bursting with the excitement of a new start. A new chapter. Finally a chance to lay to rest the demons of the past.

Two more whiskies arrived. Mechanic motioned for the waitress to take them away but her father raised his hand.

'I'll make these the last.' His speech was slurred.

Mechanic finished her breakfast and nursed her coffee. Her father was still hacking away at the rare meat swimming in runny egg yolk.

'Where are you staying?' he said through another mouthful of food.

'At a place called The Kings Motel. It's not great but it was cheap.'

'I know it. We could take a ride down there after. You can show me around.'

'There's a park and a lake, we could take a walk.'

'How about you take me to the hotel and we chill out there for a while.'

'Er, yes, okay.'

He slurped another whisky down.

'I'm done,' he said throwing his cutlery onto his plate. He was swaying in his chair and suddenly lurched forward putting both hands out towards her on the table. 'So what do you say? How about we spend some time together at the motel?'

'Yes, that would be nice.'

Mechanic felt something brush against her leg. Like a cat was walking under the table. It touched her again. She looked down to see her father rubbing his foot up and down her leg.

She was paralysed.

He leaned back in his chair and drank the last glass dry. He was smiling at her.

She watched as his foot stroked up and down. She tried to move her leg away, but it wouldn't budge.

'Shall we go?' His voice slurred out the words as he fixed her with a lopsided grin.

Mechanic was fixated by the movement of his foot. She felt numb. She stared at the knife.

A knife like that could take a man's head off. The words rattled around in her head.

Her father leaned forward and linked his fingers together under his chin.

'You ready?'

A knife like that could take a man's head off.

Boiling rage erupted through Mechanic's body. She sprang to her feet, her hands shaking, desperately trying to control herself.

A knife like that could take a man's head off.

Mechanic lunged forward and seized the knife.

Stewart Sells jumped back in his chair, his eyes bulging and his mouth wide open.

A knife like that could take a man's head off.

The blade flashed in an arc.

The woman on the next table shrieked and cowered beneath her napkin.

The serrated edge slammed into wood as Mechanic plunged it into the table. The crockery bounced around and shattered on the floor.

Mechanic ran from the restaurant and out into the street. She bent forward, covered her head with her hands, and let out an agonising scream. It was a terrifying sound.

The knife was sticking straight up, the carved handle vibrating back and forth with the point buried deep in the table.

Stewart Sells sat rigid in his chair. All eyes were on him as the whisky swam around in his brain.

'What the fuck's got into her?' he said to no one in particular.

He remained seated as the manager rushed over.

'Are you alright, sir?'

Stewart Sells considered the question carefully. No, he wasn't alright. He had a large check to settle and was now too drunk to rent a damn car to drive to Phoenix.

Chapter 29

Mills was bouncing off the walls. It had been two days, and by now he should have the Helix Holdings file in his sweaty hands. But so far he had received nothing. This was the second morning he had got up at 4am to call his counterpart in Florida PD as soon as he got into work.

He had bombarded them with calls requesting immediate updates. And every time he received the standard response.

'I can assure you we are working hard on this, but if the file isn't there I can't send it to you.'

Mills had threatened to take things further up the line, which hadn't gone down well. This had made Mills as popular in Florida as he was in Vegas. All he could do was wait, and make nuisance calls.

* * *

Jameson had also been hard at work finishing the initial planning phase of the job. He had pulled an all-nighter, which was not unusual for him. He often survived on two hours sleep and functioned perfectly well the next day.

He switched off his computer, shuffled papers into a large manila envelope and sealed it shut. He scribbled on the front and stuck a stamp in the corner. Tomorrow morning it would be sitting in P.O. Box 508 waiting to be collected.

The planning had taken less time than expected. The target had come to Jameson's attention in the recent past when he had provided an intel report on the same man. Jameson's men on the ground had done their homework and the intel was still current, so with a few minor amendments they were good to go.

Jameson had remembered the previous job as a summary execution, a killing that would send a message to others that said 'I'm the new boss'. It would appear that things had not gone to plan. The target was obviously alive and well, and continuing to piss people off, and the previous client had not been seen again.

It was time for a shower and to head off to work.

Jameson threw the envelope onto the passenger seat and started the engine. In his mirror he could see a car parked on the other side of the road. The driver had his window down and was staring at him.

It was Lucas.

Jameson reversed from his drive and drew up next to Lucas. He nodded and pulled away. Lucas cruised in behind and followed. They drove out of the estate and onto the freeway. Four lanes rammed with morning commuter traffic, everyone in a rush, everyone in the wrong lane, everyone getting their day off to a bad start.

Lucas stayed well back. Jameson signalled and eased over to the nearside lane. Lucas followed suit. A junction came up and both cars ran down the exit ramp to join an old beat-up single lane road. As they travelled along it for about three miles, the road surface got progressively worse with sections of the asphalt crumbling way. Lucas could feel the suspension bottoming out as they crunched along. He noticed there were no other cars in sight.

Jameson pulled off the track and came to rest on a piece of waste ground under a railway bridge. Lucas swung his rental car around and parked next to him, facing the opposite direction. Both men buzzed down their windows.

'Don't do that,' Jameson said.

'Do what?'

'Don't turn up at my house like that.'

'I like the personal touch. Do you have news for me?'

Jameson wanted to press the point but let it drop.

'Yes, it's done. It will be with my guy tomorrow.'

'That's fast.'

'Let's just say we got a lucky break.'

'What happens next?'

'I talk it through with my man and we agree the finer details.'

'I'm impressed,' said Lucas. 'My client will also be impressed. But then you did come highly recommended.'

'Do you have something for me?'

'I do.' Lucas handed Jameson a brown paper bag through the window. He looked inside. Twenty paper bricks, each containing a thousand dollars.

'When will it take place?' asked Lucas.

'I will provide you with the details, as requested, when I have a confirmed plan with my guy.'

'Sounds fair enough. Do you know when that will be?'

'Tomorrow, maybe the next day. It depends.'

'Okay, Jameson. I will be in touch.'

'Don't turn up at my house.'

It was too late. Lucas had buzzed his window closed, rolled out from under the bridge and rejoined the road. He would have liked a swift getaway but instead he had to trundle along trying not to burst his tyres. He was pleased with his performance but was full of nagging anxiety. The money drop had meant he had to leave Harper and Moran to their own devices, and he was worried that when he got back there would only be one of them left.

Jameson let him go. The money smelled good. He watched Lucas disappear into the distance. There was no point getting too close when there was no need. He waited ten minutes then swung his car onto the road.

He was already late for work but first he had to stop off at a post office.

* * *

Mechanic drove back with her hands clenched so tight around the steering wheel her knuckles were white. *What the fuck was I thinking?* It was madness to assume her father would behave any differently. He had always been a pig, and that's what she got. What was she thinking?

She stared through the windshield with vacant eyes. Towns, road signs and traffic flew by but she saw none of them. She was numb.

Where do I go from here?

What impact does this have on the voices in my head?

The questions tumbled around her along with the picture of that knife as it slammed into the table.

At the one hundred mile mark she'd loosened her grip on the wheel and was paying attention to the road. By one hundred and fifty miles she had pulled over to fill up with fuel and get an extra strong coffee. She emptied the entire contents of the sugar dispenser into the mug. The massive rush of caffeine and sugar ensured she was buzzing for the next two hours. She began to feel human again.

At three hundred miles her mind was wandering onto other things.

I wonder who the target is on the latest job?

Where's it going to take place?

By ten miles from home she was thinking more clearly. She had been stupid to believe the trip would resolve anything. Her father was a monster who was never going to change. He would soon be dead and she would raise a glass on the day. Until then she had to draw a line under it and move on.

Mechanic marched through her front door. She ached from the journey and was hungry. She dumped her bags and headed into the kitchen, opening the refrigerator. She took out a piece of cooked chicken and a carton of fruit juice and ate standing up. The red indicator on her phone was blinking – she had a message.

Mechanic pushed the button and a voice said, 'Hey, Jess, wondered if you fancied a beer tomorrow. Call me back. Bye.'

The voice was light and cheery. It was Jameson. It meant she had mail to collect tomorrow morning.

She checked the time, four thirty.

She finished off the chicken and the juice and went into the bedroom to change. She decided to do what she always did when she wanted to blow away the cobwebs, she reached for her running shoes. Fifteen minutes later she was pounding down Sixth Avenue towards the harbour. This time she was taking it easy. The six-hour journey had sent her muscles to sleep and the run was waking them up nicely.

Mechanic crossed into Marina Park South and followed her usual route. The view across the bay to Coronado Island was spectacular. It wasn't a real island, it was connected to the mainland by a spit of land which ran south to Imperial Beach. Coronado was one of Mechanic's favourite places to go to chill out. The beach was amazing.

She left the park behind her and ran north parallel to the water until she reached Seaport Village, a bustling collection of tourist shops and restaurants. The sun was dipping in the sky and felt warm on her face as she chewed up the miles. She felt relaxed, endorphins coursing around her body.

Mechanic had chosen one of her longer routes, a distance of about eight miles. She would be back before six, in time for a long hot soak in the bath followed by a healthy dinner and an early night. She would sleep better tonight.

Moran's jaw dropped open as Mechanic ran past.

Chapter 30

'I'm telling you, it was her,' Moran said, her hands held out in front of her with her palms turned up, exasperated by her constant need to repeat herself.

'Are you sure?' Lucas asked again, pacing around the room.

'For fuck's sake, I was as close to her as I am to you now.'

Following his morning meeting with Jameson, Lucas had arrived back at the hotel to find that despite his worse fears Moran and Harper both appeared to be in one piece. However, they were not both in one place. There were two notes left on the table. One said *Gone to find a bar*, the other said *Gone out*. Neither was signed but it was clear which one was which. Harper had returned a few hours later stinking of beer, and fell asleep in the chair. Lucas wiled away the time watching TV, planning and speculating on what Jameson was doing. Moran had taken off into the city to calm down and find a different place to stay. She was still angry at Harper and wanted to give herself space. She had even done a little shopping, which was not like her at all.

After losing Mechanic, Moran had got back to Lucas and Harper as fast as she could. She'd burst into the room and blurted out what she had seen. The revelation knocked them sideways. It also had the effect of disarming the tension between herself and Harper. An uneasy truce had broken out between the pair of them.

Lucas paced around the room and the questions continued thick and fast.

'What did she look like?' asked Harper.

'She looked like Mechanic. She had short dark hair. She was tanned and was wearing running gear. It looked like expensive kit.'

'How short? How short was her hair?'

'You know short, like a pixie cut. With a side parting.' Moran fiddled with her own hair to mimic the style.

'Could it have been someone who looked like her?' Lucas said.

'Yes, it could have been, but it wasn't. It was her, one hundred percent.'

'Did she see you?' said Harper.

'No, I don't think so, anyway she doesn't know who I am. I must have looked like any another tourist.'

'Okay, what happened next?'

'I was drinking wine outside a bar in Seaport Village taking in the view when she ran by. It took a second for it to register. But when it did, I left my shopping at the bar and took off after her. There was no way I could keep up. I followed for the next minute or so, but that was it. She was gone.'

'You chased after her?'

'I tried to, without giving myself away, but she burned the ground like an Olympian. I had no chance. She was really fast.'

'Could you have got a cab and followed that way?' Harper asked.

'Give me a break, it's a pedestrianised area, there are no cabs.'

'What then?'

'I went back to the bar and asked the waiters if any of them had seen the woman who just ran by. They all said the same thing, that loads of runners use this route, and none of them had noticed anyone in particular.'

All three sat in silence.

'Okay, what do we think?' Lucas said.

'She could be resident here or passing through. We've given Jameson a job, so she could have flown in to discuss it with him,' said Harper.

'You said the kit looked expensive.'

'Yes, I would say so.'

'Would you take expensive gear with you when you're travelling? Or would you take old stuff?' Lucas asked.

'Under normal circumstances, old kit, but maybe she only buys the best.'

'We know she's a runner. What else would she do?' asked Harper.

'Go to the gym,' said Moran.

'Yes, that's what I figure. She keeps herself in shape, and we know she's strong, so she must work out somewhere.'

'How about we check out the gyms within a three-mile radius of Seaport Village, and if that throws up nothing extend the search,' said Moran.

'Back it up a while,' said Lucas. 'We have a sound plan to use Jameson to get to Mechanic. If we go blundering around asking questions, one of two things is going to happen. One: she will disappear, or two: she will kill us.'

'I'm not saying we ditch the plan with Jameson. We carry that through, this gives us a second opportunity. We have to use this to our advantage. And you're right we have to be extra vigilant when we're out. You both need to cover up,' said Moran.

'It's a dangerous game,' said Lucas.

'Like playing with Jameson isn't?' replied Moran.

'There is another alternative,' said Harper.

'What's that?'

'Pick up Jameson and beat it out of him. Get him to tell us where Mechanic is living.'

'Jameson is an ex-Navy Seal. Look at us, I don't think that's going to happen, do you? And if we try to blackmail him he will disappear along with Mechanic. He has a ton of money, remember?'

'So what do we do? We can't do nothing,' said Harper.

'I could go back to Seaport Village first thing tomorrow. There's a chance she might train in the morning and use the same route. I have running gear with me, which would make it easier,' said Moran.

'I could make enquiries at the gyms,' said Lucas. 'I don't have a picture or a name, but I can give a good description. See what falls out.'

'That's worth a try, I can do that with you,' said Harper.

'No, I have a different job for you.'

Lucas walked to the bedroom and returned with the Puma sports bag. He unzipped it and threw two bundles of cash to Harper.

'We need to plan ahead. Which means we need gear.'

'Does that include guns?' Harper said with a twinkle in his eye.

'Unfortunately, yes,' said Lucas.

Chapter 31

All three rose early the next morning. They had agreed the most effective way to keep in touch was to leave messages with hotel reception. It would probably piss off the staff but it was the best they could do. If anyone encountered Mechanic, they were to follow at a distance and wait for the others. That is unless she was running, then it was a case of forget it.

Moran had found a different hotel on Second Avenue a short distance from where Lucas and Harper were staying. She ran out of the main entrance along Market Street towards the marina dressed in running gear. She arrived at Seaport Village and found the spot where she had seen Mechanic. The bar was closed, as were most of the shops. Some restaurants were open offering breakfast. The place was alive with runners. Her watch said 7am.

She perched on a low wall and watched the procession of sweaty T-shirts and Lycra. Moran needed to conserve her energy, because if Mechanic ran by it would take every ounce she had.

* * *

Lucas trawled through the telephone directory in the hotel and, armed with a map, located ten gyms within a three-mile radius of Seaport Village. He mapped out his route and set off. The first one was across the street but first he had to go shopping.

Thirty minutes later he was standing outside the first gym on the list. The metal sign above the door said Marty's Gym and underneath was a picture of a dumbbell with the words 'The Ironmongers' written across it. Lucas climbed the stairs. He was wearing a broad-brimmed hat and thick-rimmed spectacles –even by his own admission he looked weird.

Behind reception was a man with the face of a twelve-year-old boy, his muscles bursting out of his vest which was two sizes too small. He looked up as Lucas shuffled through the door at the top of the stairs.

'Can I help you?' he said trying to mask his disbelief.

'I'm looking for someone, a woman, about five feet ten inches tall, short dark hair. She probably trains a lot. Do you have anyone like that?'

'The boy shook his head. No, sir, it's mainly men who train here. It's not really a ladies' gym. You might want to try Pure Fitness, it's two blocks further down.'

Lucas consulted his map. Pure fitness was next on the list.

* * *

Harper was having a much more productive morning. He had bought all the local newspapers he could find, taken them to the nearest café, and ordered coffee.

He skimmed through the pages looking for the classified ads sections. Two coffees later he had marked three gun shops on the map provided by the hotel. He set off to find Guns and Tackle, situated just off Broadway and Union Street.

He found the store but didn't bother going inside.

It was big, bright and prosperous, selling everything you needed for a camping and hunting holiday. Rifles, crossbows, tents, sleeping bags, the place had the lot. It was staffed by eager college kids wearing green shirts with the company logo on the back.

The second store was no better. It was called The Sport and Liquor Store and was the size of a small Wal-Mart. The store showcased hundreds of handguns and rifles, along with wall upon wall of bottled booze.

Alcohol and guns, now there's a sensible mix, thought Harper.

He carried on walking.

The last on the list was a cab ride away near Cambridge Square. He read out the address to the driver. After fifteen minutes they swung left off First Avenue onto Quince Street. Harper paid the guy and stepped out.

He looked around. There were no gun shops to be seen. Harper checked the address in the paper. Sure enough, he was in the right place. He walked east to the junction with Second Avenue and saw what he was looking for, sitting on its own down a narrow side street.

The rusted sign said Guns 'n Ammo.

The storefront had a hundred years of grime baked into it and the windows were brown and opaque. Harper swung open the door and a bell chimed.

The interior was tiny in comparison to the other stores, crammed with glass-topped cabinets stacked full of handguns. Against one wall was a rack of rifles, an iron bar clamping them in place. A lone man stood behind the counter. He was in his late forties with a stubble face and the remnants of his dinner on his shirt. He was over two hundred and thirty pounds with little piggy eyes staring out of his puffy face. Under his belly Harper could see a gun hanging from his belt.

Harper felt at home.

The man nodded to Harper, who nodded back.

Harper walked up and down the display cabinets looking at the handguns.

'Can I help you?' the man said.

'I'm looking to buy.'

'That's good,' cause we're a store.'

Harper smiled as he perused the parade of handguns and hunting knives.

'What are you looking for?'

'A handgun and ammo.'

'What sort?'

'Something semi-automatic, 9mm, good stopping power.'

'Good stopping power, eh?'

'Yeah, something like a Glock, or a Colt, or a Browning.'

'We have those.'

The man walked behind the glass display cases and selected three guns. He returned to the counter and put them on the top.

Harper checked each one over. Popping out the magazines, pulling back the slides, feeling the weight.

'How much?'

'The Glock is three fifty, the Colt is three hundred and the Browning is three twenty-five. You like what you see?'

'I do, but I don't want these.'

'But you said you wanted something like this.' The man looked edgy.

'I do, but not these.'

The man placed both hands on the counter top and leaned forward.

'Are you here to play games?'

'No, I'm here to buy.'

Harper opened up his jacket and reached into the top pocket.

The man's hand moved to his gun.

Harper eased out the wad of bank notes. The man's piggy eyes widened when he saw the flash of green peeking above the lining.

'I'm looking for something a little less visible, if you get my drift?'

The man stared at Harper.

'You're not a cop?'

'No, I'm not.'

The man stroked his chin. He picked up the guns and replaced them under the glass.

He made eye contact with Harper and glanced up at the ceiling. Harper knew what he was doing. The man was pointing out the CCTV camera in the corner.

'These guns are not for you, sir, but I might have a better selection in the back.'

The man walked from behind the counter and turned the lock on the front door, flipping over the sign to say Closed.

Harper followed him into the back.

It was small and dingy. There was an office with a rickety old desk, and a sitting room with a kettle and a sink. The place smelled of old socks and gun oil. The sound of Harper's boots resonated against the wooden floor. There was a window at the back which was as dirty as those at the front. The man drew the drapes, flicked on a lamp and pulled a flat-edged screwdriver from the desk drawer. He pushed the sofa to one side, knelt down and levered the flat edge between the floorboards. He lifted up a square of flooring.

He fished his hand around under the floorboards and brought out a slim briefcase, then another and another. There were four cases in total. He cleared the desk and laid them down, popping open the clasps.

He lifted the lids to show the guns.

'May I?' Harper said.

The man stepped to one side and Harper went through the same inspection routine as before.

'How many do you need?'

'Two.'

Harper turned the guns over in his hand. The serial numbers had been filed away.

'Can these be traced?'

'No, they've not been used, they are brand new.'

Harper nodded approvingly.

'How much?'

'A grand a piece.'

'Fifteen for the two.'

'Seventeen fifty.'

'And you throw in a box of ammo for each?'

'Yes, okay.'

Harper selected the Browning and the Berretta. The man put both guns into one case and retrieved two boxes of Parabellum 9mm shells from the hole in the floor.

Harper peeled off the money from his wad of notes and gave it to the man.

The man held the notes up to the dim lighting.

'They are fine,' said Harper.

'They are,' he replied.

The man closed the lid, snapped the catches shut and handed the black hard-topped case to Harper.

'Better that you leave this way,' he said.

The man ushered Harper further into the back of the store and out through a door. It opened onto a narrow back lane.

'Great doing business with you,' Harper said as he stepped outside.

The guy shut the door and Harper could hear the sound of bolts being thrown across.

Harper had a big grin plastered on his face. Not because he was pleased with his purchases but because he still had the knack of sniffing out a bent business.

* * *

Mechanic arrived home after her run to the post office. She had pushed the pace and was breathing heavily. She tossed the padded envelope from Jameson onto the kitchen worktop and opened the refrigerator. A cold bottle of mineral water and a long, hot shower was in order.

She twisted the top and the gas fizzed.

'It's time to play.' Daddy's voice came out of nowhere.

Mechanic spun around to see where he was, but the apartment was empty.

'Time to play!' the voice yelled.

Mechanic stopped in her tracks. The voice was inside her head.

'The family a few streets down. You saw them yesterday. Kill them.' The voice was snarling.

Mechanic was frozen to the spot.

She broke from her paralysis and rummaged in the kitchen drawer for the skewer. The flame from the gas ring burned blue as she held the metal in the flame and tore off her vest.

'No, no, no,' she chanted over and over.

'They would make a nice addition to the collection. Kill them. Get your gun and let's go play.'

'No, no, no!' Mechanic screamed the mantra, trying to drown out the voice.

'Get your gun and let's go out to play.'

She could feel the room swimming around her.

She held the skewer and watched it turn black in the heat. The image faded in and out of focus. Her hand trembled. A creeping numbness moved through her body.

She dropped the skewer and it rolled away from the flame.

She fumbled around to pick it up but her hands wouldn't work.

She swayed. Her legs gave way.

Mechanic slumped to the floor with her back against the kitchen cabinet.

'Get your gun and let's go.'

She tried to grab the hot metal, but it was out of reach.

She pushed with her legs but they crumpled beneath her.

There was a rushing in her ears. She could feel her peripheral vision closing in.

'Get your gun and let's go play.'

Mechanic gritted her teeth and once more lunged for the handle of the skewer.

She fell back and everything went black.

Chapter 32

Mechanic's eyelids flickered. Through the watery slits she could make out a blurred white light. She felt woozy.

Her eyes half-opened, and the light came into focus. It was a large circular globe set into the ceiling. She realised she must be lying on her back looking up. Her mouth was dry. Her eyelids weighed a ton and they closed again. Her brain slowly engaged.

Mechanic opened them again. Above her head was an inch-wide aluminium tramline that looped its way across the whitewashed ceiling. She tilted her head down to lower her gaze and saw two beds opposite, both with yellow curtains draped either side.

Her eyes closed and she processed the images. After an eternity her brain came back with an answer – she was lying in a hospital.

She looked around. Her head felt as if it was floating in mid-air.

Sure enough there was a person lying in the bed in the corner with an IV line running under the bedcover. The other two beds were empty. Mechanic could see through a set of open doors into a corridor with medical staff rushing about.

Lazily her brain sent a signal.

What the fuck am I doing in hospital?

Mechanic closed her eyes and tried to catch up. She moved her fingers and toes, they were fine. She moved her arms and legs, they were fine too. She wasn't in any pain.

What the hell am I doing in hospital? The thought played through her head again.

Mechanic looked down to see herself covered in a thin blue sheet. She lifted the top cover to see underneath, she was clothed in a white nightgown. The skin on her left hand was grazed and she had a bruise on her elbow. She brought her hand up and felt the contours of her face. Everything was fine.

She lay there and picked through the debris in her mind, trying to piece together what happened.

She could remember being at the post office, collecting the package and leaving it on the worktop. She could remember feeling thirsty and the hiss of the gas escaping from the bottle, then taking a hot shower.

The picture of the skewer changing colour in the blue gas flame filled her mind.

'Fuck,' she said under her breath. The realisation jolted her body.

She could remember Daddy's voice booming in her head telling her to kill the family who lived on her street. She could remember the gun.

Shit. she could remember the gun.

She had it in her hand when she left the apartment.

'Fuck,' she said again.

She snapped her eyes open and looked around. A cop was talking to two female medical staff outside in the corridor. The urge to fight or flight surged through her. Mechanic tried to raise herself up but her limbs felt like lead. She needed to get away.

Then her brain kicked in.

The cop is not here for me.

If I had been caught with a gun, or worse, I would be in a room on my own, handcuffed to the bed. The uniformed officer would be in the room with me not flirting with the nurses.

A nurse passing the door clocked that Mechanic was awake and bustled into the room. She was small and pretty, dressed in green scrubs. She had the bubbly air of someone who had not worked in the healthcare profession for long.

'Hello, my name is Sara.'

Mechanic nodded in return.

'How are you feeling?'

'A little groggy.'

Sara picked the chart from the bottom of the bed and scribbled on it.

'Do you hurt anywhere?'

'No, I'm in no pain.'

'What's your name?'

Mechanic stopped. It was a strange question to ask. She knew cognitive questions were used when patients had suffered a head injury, questions such as what day is it, what year is it, or who is the president? But never what is your name?

She toyed with the question.

Maybe she's asking because they don't know my name. If I didn't have ID with me when I was brought in, how would they know?

'I don't know,' answered Mechanic.

Sara scribbled more onto the chart.

'Are you a diabetic?'

'No.' Mechanic kicked herself for answering quickly.

'Are you on any medication?'

'I don't think so.'

Sara made more notes. Mechanic remained silent hoping it would prompt Sara into filling in the gaps.

'You're in Fairfield Memorial Hospital. A man found you unconscious in a car park and called 911. They brought you in and you've been out cold for six hours. You have a graze on your left hand, probably from when you fell, but other than that you have no other injuries as far as we can tell. Do you remember anything?'

Mechanic shrugged her shoulders.

Sara walked around the bed and poured water into a plastic cup. She handed it to Mechanic who took a sip.

'Do you have a history of blackouts?' Sara continued.

Mechanic shook her head.

'We noticed burn marks on your stomach. Do you recall how they got there?'

Mechanic shrugged her shoulders.

'So, you know you are not a diabetic, you don't suffer from blackouts, but you don't remember your own name?'

Mechanic shook her head. Sara looked sceptical.

'Okay, I will inform the doctor you're awake, he will want to see you.'

Mechanic watched her leave.

What the fuck happened to the gun? The thought raced around in her head.

What did I do to the family?

Mechanic had to get out of there fast.

She hoisted herself up on her elbows and turned on her side. From there she swung her feet off the bed and onto the floor. The room melted away into a spinning soup and she gripped the bed frame. Slowly the room stopped moving and came to a halt.

Mechanic looked down at the locker beside her bed to find her clothes in a plastic bag. She pulled on the jeans and wrestled the sweatshirt over her head.

When the hell had I got changed into these?

Mechanic slid her feet into her shoes and checked the top drawer of the cabinet. It was empty, she had no personal effects. She staggered around the foot of the bed pulling the chart from its holder.

She took a deep breath and wandered out. As she passed through the doorway into the corridor she held the paperwork up to her face and walked past the cop. She scanned around for exit signs, found one and headed for the elevators. Ten minutes later she was outside hailing a cab.

'Can you take me home, please. I have no money on me because I came in the ambulance with my son. I can pay you when I reach home.'

'Sure thing, lady. You wouldn't believe how many times I get asked that.'

She folded herself deep into the seat in the back of the taxi and tried to think.

The guy found her in a parking lot, no the nurse said car park. Which car park and what the hell was she doing there?

The only one she knew was where she parked her own car. It was a private space, beneath the apartment block, for tenants only.

Maybe I went to the car to get something.

Then realisation dawned on her.

I needed my car to drive to the family's house.

Shit, did I collapse on the way there or the way back?

They arrived at her home and Mechanic let herself in with a spare key she left with the neighbours. The gas ring was still hissing away, the air in the apartment was hot and dry. She switched it off and returned to pay the driver. She waited for him to leave then ran to the underground car park. Her car was in its allocated space. Mechanic scouted on her hands and knees, looking under the car. Sure enough behind the front wheel was the gun and against the fence were her keys. They must have spilled onto the floor when she fell. She retrieved the gun and checked the magazine, it was full.

Thank God.

Mechanic went back to her apartment, made coffee and fixed herself a sandwich. She was feeling more lucid and her body was returning to normal. The padded envelope lay on the worktop, unopened.

It would have to wait.

Mechanic took a shower and changed. She threw a few clothes into a backpack and looped it over her shoulder. She checked the gun and slid it into the front pocket. The car keys were in her hand as she slammed the front door behind her.

She was heading to Prescott.

Chapter 33

Mechanic got out of the car, it was a little after 10pm. The journey had taken forever because she kept having to stop. Her stomach churned at the thought of seeing her father again but she had no choice.

She parked two blocks away and walked to Pavilion Park. The warmth had gone from the day and the night air was cool. The sky was clear with the half-moon throwing silver light onto the red-brick houses. She skirted around the wrought-iron gates and turned left along the road circling the complex. After fifty yards the high brick wall gave way to a wooden fence with bushes growing at its base. Mechanic kept walking.

The plot of land stretched back for another two hundred yards, and then the fence ran out. The back to the estate was wide open. The only security was three bands of galvanised wire strung between posts driven into the ground. The land leading up to the properties was an obstacle course of rubble, mounds of earth and scattered pallets of building materials. Either there hadn't been enough money to complete the development or the projected demand was nothing like what had been forecast. Mechanic lightly tapped the wire to see if it had an electric current running through it. She slipped through the gap and headed towards the bungalows.

She figured that after their last encounter her father wouldn't agree to see her. At this time he was probably out, so a different approach was in order.

She found Simpson Place and scouted around the back of the properties. Each one had a small open-plan garden at the rear, with a paved area and a tiny piece of grass, a line of low bushes marking out the perimeter. Stewart Sells' bungalow was the one at the end. It was in darkness, as was the rest of the street.

Mechanic walked up to the patio door, pulled on a pair of gloves and tried the handle. It was locked. She peered across and allowed herself a brief smile. The living room window was on the latch. She rifled through her bag and brought out a hunting knife. The thick blade made short work of lifting the catch and Mechanic was in.

The smell of fresh paint had been replaced with the smell of dirty clothes and stale food. She checked the rooms, Stewart Sells was not at home. Mechanic sat on the sofa in the dark and waited. The churning in her stomach had gone, replaced with cold resolve.

On the stroke of eleven she heard a movement outside. There was lots of cursing and the noise of scuffling feet, and then the sound of a key being inserted into the lock. After much scraping of metal on metal her father fell into the house, his hand still holding onto the key. Or to be more accurate, he had one foot planted in the living room with the other stuck on the front path. He swayed back and forth suspended from his front door trying to regain his balance.

'Fucking lock,' he scowled, tugging at the key.

With a herculean effort, he took an enormous stride forward and launched himself into the house. He slammed the door shut with the keys still jangling in the lock. He turned back and reached for the light switch, his index finger prodding and stabbing at the wall until it hit the button.

He turned and jumped out of his sagging yellow skin.

'What the f—'

'Hello, Dad.'

'How did you … When did you … What the …' The whisky had robbed him of his ability to complete a sentence.

'We need to talk.'

'But how did you …' He swivelled at the hips and pointed at the door, toppling back against the wall.

'You left it open, so I let myself in.'

He stomped through to the kitchen and pulled a mug from the pile of dirty crockery in the sink.

'You want to talk?' he called over his shoulder as he dragged items from the cupboards onto the floor. 'What do you want to talk about?'

He moved into the bathroom and Mechanic could again hear the sound of cupboards being ransacked.

'Fuck it,' he said returning to the living room. He banged the empty cup on the table and flopped into the armchair.

'We need to talk.'

'You said that already.'

'I need to talk about what you did.'

'What did I do?'

'When I was young. I need to talk about what you did when I was young.'

'What did I do?'

'What do you mean, what did you do?' Mechanic's cold resolve was starting to melt.

'You come in here uninvited and say you want to talk about what I did? What about what you did?'

'Dad, this is about you.'

'The fuck it is. If it's about anything it's about you stabbing a knife into a table. That's what it's about.'

'No, this is about you and what you did to me.'

'Go on then. What did I do?'

'You abused me when I was young and it's damaged me all my life.'

'Damaged? What damage? You wanted for nothing. You ungrateful bitch.'

Tears welled in Mechanic's eyes and her bottom lip trembled.

'You starved us. We had no food in the house. I went to school in dirty clothes.'

'I did the best I could.'

Mechanic leaned forward and clasped her hands in front of her as though she was praying.

'No, you didn't. I want you to acknowledge what you did to me. I want you to take responsibility.'

'Take responsibility for what?'

She slid from the sofa and knelt in front of him.

'You raped me. I was a child, for God's sake.'

'Don't give me that shit. You wanted it every bit as much as me. There you were, with your furtive looks, and your special smiles, and your skirts hanging way up to here.' He grabbed his crotch with his hand.

'No, it wasn't like that.' She threw her hands in the air.

'That's exactly what it was like. It was the same when I was stationed in the Far East. Those child whores. They would come around all bobby socks and pigtails, little pictures of innocence. Next they would be giving you the come-on, asking "you want fucky-fucky, mister? I blow you good, mister, ten bucks, mister". They even wore their school uniforms, the little whores.'

Mechanic stared at her father, her mouth gaping open.

'You made me wear my school uniform,' she said in a whisper.

'You were the same as them.'

'I wasn't the same as them, I'm your daughter.'

He leaned forward, she could smell liquor on his breath. Her senses catapulted her back to when she was twelve years old. The same stench on his breath as he pawed and penetrated her body.

'Did you fight me off? Did you go to the police? No, and that was for one reason and one reason only. You were gagging for it.'

'I did it so you would leave Jo alone.'

'Jo? Jo? She had class, she wasn't a child whore like you. I would never touch Jo, I'm her father.'

'You're my father too!'

'Yes, but with you I'm the father of a child whore. And by the looks of it you grew up to be nothing more than an adult whore.'

He came out of his chair and grabbed her.

'Child whore, child whore!' he shouted as he grappled with her shoulders. She raised her hands and fended him off.

Child whore, child whore. The words echoed around the room.

He was doing his best to overpower her. It was like being attacked by a six-year-old boy. She held his arms to stop him. They were thin and sinewy. His skin felt like it wasn't attached to the flesh underneath.

Child whore, child whore. The words tore holes in her brain. She looked at her father snarling with exertion. The words weren't coming from him.

Child whore, child whore. The words were coming from inside her head. Daddy was back.

'I'm gonna give you a good fucking to teach you a lesson.' She could see her father mouthing the words in front of her.

'Stop!' she yelled as she fought him off.

I'm gonna give you a good fucking, teach you a lesson. The phrase burst in her head. Her father wheezed and blew saliva in the air.

The room spun.

Daddy's voice was blasting away inside her head, while her father fought to take her down. *A right good fucking is what you need,* the voice rasped away inside her.

Mechanic screwed her eyes shut.

She could no longer figure out what was in her head and what was real.

Child whore, child whore.

'Be quiet!' she yelled, releasing him and clutching both hands to her ears.

He forced her back and she tumbled onto the sofa, he shoved his hand between her legs.

'Be quiet!' she screamed again as the voices shredded through her mind.

He was on top of her.

Mauling at her breast with one hand and trying to undo her jeans with the other.

'Quiet!' Her hands were clamped either side of her head trying to crush the noise.

She could feel his mouth slavering over her neck as he forced down the zip on her jeans.

She screamed to blank out the voices.

Child whore, child whore.

He slid his hand into her underwear and tore at her shirt. She felt his fingernails scraping at her skin.

Mechanic seized his shoulders and flipped him around, onto his back. His arms and legs flailed in the air like an upturned beetle.

'Don't you ...' he said as she grabbed his chin with one hand and the back of his head with the other.

'You fucking child whore,' he said writhing around, trying to right himself.

Crack!

She rotated her hands in opposite directions and the vertebrae in his neck snapped.

There was silence.

He went limp.

Mechanic lay there for several seconds listening for any sign of breathing. She shoved him to the side. Stewart Sells fell to the floor, dead.

Mechanic got up. She looked down at her father who stared back, his mouth gaping open.

She took hold of the low table and dragged it near the sofa. Then she went on a hunt. It was unlikely her father was looking for cleaning products when he came back, there had to be whisky hidden somewhere. She turned over the furniture and scoured the cupboards and drawers. Nothing. In the bedroom she spied the pile of dirty laundry spilling out of the basket and onto the floor. She dug around inside and her hand hit something hard. She pulled out a bottle of cheap liquor two thirds full.

Mechanic went to the kitchen, picked a mug out of the sink and returned to the living room. She filled it with whisky and placed the cup on the table.

She stood astride her father, put her hands under his arms and lifted him up. His head lolled back. She positioned his body over the table then slammed him down onto the edge. His head cracked open on the corner. The cup bounced onto the carpet spilling liquor over his chest. He landed with his face buried against the sofa an ugly gash at the base of his skull.

The room was quiet. Inside Mechanic's head was quiet.

* * *

Mechanic wasn't sure how to feel. Her father was dead. She had killed him with her bare hands. She was expecting feelings of desperation, grief and panic. With that in mind, the feelings of pure elation were completely unexpected.

The drive back should have been exhausting and tiresome, instead Mechanic had the radio blaring out country tunes while she howled along to the ones she knew, and the ones she didn't. She stopped to refuel and get a bite to eat. The guy at the gas station was thrown by her cheery manner and smiling face at 3am. She even caught herself flirting with him at one point. She had not slept in twenty hours but she was buzzing. The six hour journey home flew by.

* * *

She pushed open her front door and headed straight for the refrigerator, making fresh brewed coffee and a cocktail of fresh fruit. The sun was peeking over the horizon and a cool orange glow washed through the apartment. The coffee tasted amazing and the fruit zinged on her tongue.

Mechanic took a knife, cut away the flap from the envelope lying on the table and spread the contents on the worktop. She spooned mango into her mouth and swallowed hard before she choked. This was a tough decision, she was torn.

The job would mean going back to Vegas, which made it a definite no. The mug shot was of Alfonso Bonelli, which made it a definite yes.

Chapter 34

'Alonso Bonelli. Are you out of your fucking mind?' Harper jumped up from his seat. 'Do I have to remind you that Bonelli was the man who skimmed a bullet past my head in a fake execution. He let his goons rip my arms from their sockets by dangling me from a forklift, and then he tells them to bury me in the desert. You mean that Alonso Bonelli?'

Up to that point the day had been going well.

Lucas, Harper and Moran were in Moran's hotel room briefing each other on the day's events.

Moran had repeated her stakeout of Seaport Village, with the same degree of success as the day before. Which was nothing. She had found that her pretence of being a fitness bunny was wearing thin. People were giving her suspicious glances. Her idea of a workout consisted of sitting on a wall in her running gear, drinking coffee and then wandering about.

By 10am she had decided to abandon Seaport Village to try her luck at the various parks the city had to offer. She couldn't stay there any longer for fear of someone calling the cops.

Harper was still basking in the glory of yesterday's purchases. And, as of this morning, Lucas and Moran were the proud owners of brand new illegal firearms, ammo, binoculars, and walkie-talkies with a two-mile range. Harper had spent today pounding the streets checking out the list of gyms. He had met with two types of response: either, 'Sorry, sir, I don't know anyone fitting that description', or, 'Sir, that describes half the women who come here'. The day had been a waste of time.

Lucas had paid Jameson a surprise visit at 7am. To reinforce his dominance, he had ignored Jameson's previous warnings and turned up outside his house. The man was not happy.

And it was when he reported on the conversation that followed that Harper had blown a gasket.

'Shit, Lucas. It never occurred to me to ask who the target was, because it never occurred to me you could be so stupid. Start from the beginning and run it past me again.'

'Okay, I'll go through it word for word,' Lucas said. 'I met with Jameson and he told me the initial plans were complete and he was awaiting confirmation from his shooter. I told him I needed to know the details. He refused. I reminded him of the deal and told him that our client was growing impatient. He refused again. I stressed to him that in the same way we had made the financial transactions disappear, we could just as easily make them reappear. He finally gave in and said that Bonelli holds a weekly meeting with his troops at a hotel on Fremont Street in downtown Las Vegas. It's held at ten thirty every Friday, a chance for Bonelli to eyeball his lieutenants and discuss the performance of his drugs and racketeering empire. Bonelli arrives at 10am sharp. The hotel is heavily guarded but it has one weak point. Bonelli always arrives by car and parks in a private space at the back. He enters the hotel through a side door and uses the service elevator to reach the executive lounge at the top. He's escorted by a small army at all times.'

'The thinking behind the security routine is sound,' Moran interrupted. 'By entering the building via the service route they have a much smaller space to control than if they took him through the gaming floor.'

Lucas nodded. 'Exactly. Jameson said the weak point is the ten feet of tarmac between the car and the side door. Bonelli is out in the open for five seconds tops, but it's perfect for a sniper's bullet.'

'Did he say where the shooter would be?' Moran asked.

'He said there is a low-rise motel a few blocks away. It's an ideal vantage point from which to blow a hole in Bonelli's head.'

'And far enough away to pack up and disappear before anyone comes calling,' said Moran.

'Okay, okay, I get all that,' said Harper. 'But of all the bad guys in Vegas, why the hell did you choose Bonelli as the target. You could have chosen anyone. Bonelli wants us both dead. You do remember he has mug shots of you and me? He probably has them pinned to his toilet wall so every time he takes a crap he can think of new ways to kill us.'

'Yes, I know that. But it had to be someone Mechanic would go for. When I first met Jameson he told me that he discusses the hit with his shooter to confirm the plan. That would suggest that if Mechanic doesn't like it, she can say no. And we had to ensure she said yes.'

'She has a massive grudge against Bonelli,' said Moran. 'If I'm right, Bonelli killed her boss and held her hostage for days. She eventually escaped by killing the guard along with Bonelli's brother Enzo. She would want to finish the job by taking out Alfonso as well.'

'This is a huge risk. That's all I'm saying. It's been just over a year since Alfonso Bonelli thrust the photographs of you and me under my nose and threatened to blow my head off. He didn't strike me as the type of man who would forget about that in the space of thirteen months.' Harper returned to his chair.

'Your points are noted. If I could have guaranteed Mechanic would take the bait with anyone else, I would have done it differently. It means we have to be extra vigilant but it's worth the risk.'

Harper snorted. He knew Lucas was right.

'We have the bones of Jameson's plan. We can work with that to identify where this place is.'

'Did he say which Friday?' asked Harper.

'No.'

'Today is Tuesday, I guess we need to go to Vegas.'

* * *

Across the other side of the city Mechanic was staring at the photograph of Bonelli. The contract troubled her, was she taking it for the right reason? This should be a cold, clinical decision based upon the likelihood of success and the size of the payout. But with Bonelli there was a personal element which was clouding her judgement. She would be walking into the lion's den.

Thirteen months may have passed, but Bonelli would like nothing better than to slice bits off her while she was still alive and feed them to his dogs.

The hit was straightforward. The exit plan was uncomplicated. It was the perfect job.

The phone rang. It was Jameson.

.

Chapter 35

The journey to Vegas was long. They had hit the road by 7am with Lucas and Harper in the rental car and Moran driving her own vehicle. They travelled in convoy along Interstate 15, a three hundred and thirty mile route passing through Victorville, Barstow and Baker, and crossing the Nevada state line at Primm. With the scorched Mojave mountains behind them, it was a long slow descent into Vegas. They crested the summit and the Strip looked less than a foot long as it shimmered in the distance thirty-five miles further north.

They headed straight for Moran's place. She let them in, it was good to be home. Moran checked her mail, there was nothing from Mills.

Lucas opened and closed every cupboard in the kitchen trying to fix coffee, while she found tourist maps that she had acquired when she first moved in. She spread the map of downtown on the table.

'Jameson told you that Bonelli used a hotel on Fremont Street and the weak point was a ten foot slice of tarmac running between the car and the service entrance.'

'That's right,' said Lucas. 'He said the hit would come from a low-rise motel a few blocks away.'

Lucas handed her a coffee.

'He also said something about it being a private parking space,' said Harper.

Moran circled a line on the map with her finger.

'This is downtown and this is Fremont Street. The main hotels and casinos start here, at the Union Plaza hotel, and run east to west for four blocks. I figure this must be the location Jameson was referring to.' She switched maps to an artist's impression of the delights of downtown. Each hotel, casino and bar was depicted by a small caricature.

'If we focus on this area, we have maybe ten places we need to check out.'

'Jameson said a hotel. Some of these are gambling halls. We should start with the hotels and widen the search afterwards if we draw a blank,' Harper said.

'Agreed. Let's take two each.'

* * *

Lucas looked at his watch as he stepped out of the car onto Fremont Street. They walked the short distance to the junction with Fourth Street. It was 3.15pm.

'Let's split up and meet up at Sassy Sally's at five thirty. Do we all know what we're looking for?' he said.

Moran and Harper nodded. They went their separate ways.

Lucas had the Golden Nugget and the Four Queens, two of the biggest casinos in the centre of downtown. The buildings stood either side of Second Avenue and sprawled onto the sidewalk to greet tourists as they passed by, hoping their sheer glitz would suck them in. Lucas passed the Sundance on his left and saw Harper disappear inside, and a block further on he came to the Four Queens.

The sound of chiming bells and falling change filled the air. He dodged between the people strolling along the sidewalk beneath the elaborate canopy of gold lights stretching out above their heads. Two showgirls wearing ostrich feathers and not much else strutted up and down on six-inch heels. Lucas tried to keep his mind on the job while bumping into the man in front.

He turned left and strolled down the side of the building. The car park was at the back. In fact, everything that was necessary to run a busy hotel and casino took place at the back. Alcohol and food deliveries, laundry, trash, staff arriving and leaving work, it all happened out of sight of the punters.

The frontage along Fremont Street was glamorous and exciting, but away from the Strip the transition into ugly and drab was ruthlessly sudden. The backs of the hotels were grey, dirty and functional. Lucas continued walking until the chain link fence ran out and he stepped onto the lot.

It was vast with enough spaces for a thousand cars. Each space was marked in flaking white paint. He made his way to the hotel. There were fancy doors leading through to reception and there were service doors marked Private, some with warnings plastered across them saying Caution – Alarmed. He skirted the perimeter and checked every corner and recess, but none of it looked right.

Lucas moved on. He didn't bother returning to the front, but instead he scurried to the other side of Fourth Street to the derelict expanse of concrete next door, the Golden Nugget.

It was the same story. The parking lot butted up to the building but nothing matched Jameson's description. He paced out every contour of the hotel.

Nothing.

* * *

Harper was closing in on his second parking lot of the day. Fremont Street made him smile. Whether it was the sight of the forty-foot-high plaid-shirted neon cowboy Vegas Vic, who waved his arm with a cigarette hanging from his mouth and said howdy to the folks below, or the Stetson-wearing cowgirl Vegas Vickie sitting in a flouncy dress kicking a shapely leg at old Vic from the opposite side of the street. It confirmed to Harper what he suspected all along. This place was crazy.

Harper almost ricked his neck while walking past the Golden Goose and Glitter Gulch, a couple of strip joints with a fearsome reputation. All of which contributed to his wide grin. He cut down Main Street and circled around to the back of the Las Vegas Club. It was much like the other sprawling parking lot. He found nothing.

* * *

Moran wandered past the Horseshoe. It clanged and chattered as people fed coins and tokens into machines promising double jackpots. The smell of smoke and cheap perfume wafted out onto the sidewalk. It had a frontier-land feel, with its low ceilings and red velvet wallpaper. Moran wrinkled her nose and gave it a wide berth.

The building merged seamlessly into the Mint. The hotel-casino had a futuristic look with a huge pink canopy of lights that swept across the front of the building in a wave and shot fifty feet into the air at the far left. It stood out from the other hotel facades on the street.

She reached the junction with First Avenue, turned right and found the parking lot. After thirty minutes of mooching around and poking her nose into the nooks and crannies, she left. She needed a drink.

By five thirty Lucas was already seated in the upstairs bar of Sassy Sally's sipping a cold beer. A long bar ran down the left-hand side with black leather bar stools sitting underneath. He had completed his tour of the parking lots in double quick time and was already on his second drink, courtesy of the eagle-eyed waitress in the short mini dress.

Moran and Harper arrived and the waitress descended on them in a flash. The drinks were on their way.

'Nothing,' said Harper. 'Nothing matched the description from Jameson.'

'Same here,' said Moran. 'I scoured every service entrance and every inch of concrete, and none of it came close.'

'I saw a parking space next to a side door, but it was well undercover. It was hidden away from any sniper shot.'

The drinks arrived. The waitress handed them out and placed another beer in front of Lucas. Next to the one he already had.

'Do we widen the search?' asked Harper.

'We could, but Jameson was very specific. We must be missing something,' said Lucas.

'Maybe, but what?' replied Moran.

'I don't know, but what I do know is, we haven't found it.'

'How about we take a look at the bars and clubs as well. It's a narrower search area and it might throw up something new,' Harper said.

'It's worth a go. Shall we meet back here at, say, seven thirty?'

'Yes, and we can get a bite to eat then as well.'

Moran and Harper emptied their glasses, then waited for Lucas, who had to chug his down.

'I'll take the Golden Goose and the Glitter Gulch,' said Harper, a little too quickly.

* * *

Seven thirty came around fast and they were all back at Sassy Sally's sitting at the same table. They had already been there for twenty minutes and the conversation had dried up. There are only so many ways of saying 'Nothing doing'.

'This is frustrating,' Lucas said, stating the obvious.

'It's pissing me off,' said Harper slurping his beer.

'I'm off to the little girl's room,' said Moran.

Harper waited until Moran was out of earshot. 'What do you think?' he asked.

'I'm as pissed off as you.'

'No, not about that. About having little miss Girl Scout with us.'

'She's a good cop and she's a sharp operator. I'm glad she's on the team.'

Harper clammed up. Perhaps sharing his views was not a good idea.

They drank their beer in silence.

Moran dried her hands and came out of the restrooms into the bar. There was a small window set into the wall to her left providing a view out to the back. Moran stopped and stared out across the vast grey expanse of never-ending parking lots and part-finished developments. She watched security lights flare into life as the sun disappeared.

Over to her right was the Mint, the hotel-casino she had checked out earlier. From her vantage point she could see the roofs of row upon row of neatly packed cars. The flash of an argon light cutting through the dusk caught her eye. It came from above a doorway tucked away at the side of the hotel. The cone of white light beamed across a triangular space with a wall running down the one side and a six-foot high metal partition at the end. The metal barrier segregated it from the rest of the lot.

She moved close to the window, cupped her hands to her face and peered down. She couldn't see if there were lines painted on the floor. But she could see the words PRIVATE PARKING written in bold black letters on the wall.

A few minutes later all three of them were taking turns to stare into the brightly lit triangle of tarmac next door.

'That must be a ten foot walk,' Harper said.

'Maybe more, depends how far down they park the car.'

'I didn't see it because of that metal wall at the end.' Moran felt the need to justify herself.

'Well, you've seen it now,' Lucas said.

'I can see something else.' Harper scanned the middle distance, away from the Mint. 'I might be wrong, but beyond the top of those warehouses, I can see the windows of a hotel.'

Chapter 36

The three of them spilled out into Fremont Street, the neon signs exploding with vivid colours against the fading light. They hustled to the back and crossed over into the parking lot.

'I'll go, three of us wandering around is going to raise the alarm,' Moran said. 'You two wait here.' Lucas and Harper nodded and stayed on the street.

Moran sauntered across the hard concrete standing and reached the metal partition. It was painted battleship grey, made of thick galvanised steel, and mounted on a stand. The whole thing was on wheels. She gave it a shove and it moved. She heaved some more and it trundled across the floor banging and clanging as it went. She forced open a two-foot gap and slipped inside.

She had the hotel wall to her left and a rendered block wall to her right. The block wall was about seven foot high and connected with the hotel about thirty feet further on. At the apex was a door. Moran estimated the floor space – there was enough room to swallow up a large car and from the back passenger seat to the door was at least twelve feet.

She walked towards the door.

'Can I help you, ma'am?' A man was craning his neck around the metal wall. 'This is off-limits to guests.'

Moran went into Oscar-winning mode.

'I'm sorry,' she said in a thick mid-western accent. 'I was here last night, well, not here exactly, I was the other side of that metal wall, and I spilled my purse on the ground. Now I can't find things and I thought they might have rolled under here. Can you help, honey?'

The man gripped the steel with a beefy hand and shoved it aside. He was dressed in a security uniform with a baton, pepper spray and handcuffs hanging from his belt. He had no gun.

Moran had her Browning in her bag.

'You're a long way from the parking lot, ma'am. Are you sure you dropped it here?'

'You know, honey, that's the problem. I was a little drunk and I might have got a little lost. But I'm sure I was here. I think.'

The guard stepped past the partition and looked around. 'I can't see anything, ma'am, maybe you dropped it somewhere else.'

'Yes, maybe I did, honey. Is this the Pioneer?'

'No, ma'am, it's the Mint. The Pioneer is a couple of blocks away on the other side of the street.'

'You know, I might not have been here after all.'

'That's okay, ma'am, it's pretty confusing.'

'Thank you for helping me look, honey.' Moran slinked past the man as he shook his head.

She waved her hand and walked away. She could hear the sound of metal wheels trundling over uneven ground.

She circled left and met Lucas and Harper.

'That's got to be the place.'

Harper took out his field glasses and scanned the horizon. The top windows came into focus.

'And that has to be where the shooter will be.'

* * *

They arrived at the Jackpot motel. It looked everything its name said it wasn't. Nobody staying there would ever think they had hit the jackpot.

The place was long and thin, one room wide and four storeys high. Reception was located in a separate building to the left. The front of the motel was covered in fading blue paint with fading white doors. A network of wooden walkways ran around the outside on each floor with a stairwell in the middle and one at either end. They nosed the car across the parking lot.

'CCTV at the back but none at the side,' Moran said looking out of the car window. They came around again and parked at the side.

'I'll distract the person on reception, you find a way onto the roof,' she said.

They piled out of the car and went their separate ways.

Lucas and Harper kept tight to the wall and looped around the back. There was a metal ladder bolted to the wall with a semi-circular cage build around it.

Lucas looked at the height and wished it were him creating the diversion and Moran climbing to the roof.

Moran was getting on famously with the young guy behind the counter. He was all bouffant hair and gleaming smiles, she was all coy and pretty.

'Are you full at the moment?' She had dropped the mid-west drawl.

'No, we have plenty of rooms, would you like to see one?'

You don't waste any time, Moran thought.

'No it's fine thanks. How much for a night?'

'We have discounted rates for the weekend. When were you planning to stay?'

The conversation rambled on. Moran maintained eye contact and feigned interest.

The young man was falling over himself with good intentions. She was more interested in the CCTV images on the TV in the corner. The more she batted her eyelashes, the more he was distracted.

After much heaving and puffing Lucas and Harper were standing on the roof. Lucas was blowing like a twenty-dollar hooker and rubbing his injured leg. The place was cluttered with air-conditioning units, cable trays and switchgear. They were both leaning with their elbows on the front wall looking through binoculars. Two hundred and fifty yards away, over the top of the warehouses, was the Mint. In the dark they could make out the oblong shape of the grey metal partition.

'It's a perfect shot,' Harper said. 'Bonelli would be walking away from the shooter in a dead straight line. Excuse the pun. No need to pan to the right, or to the left. Just line it up and bang.'

Lucas shuddered. He wondered if it had been the same with Darlene. Did Mechanic have to pan the rifle, or was it a simple case of lining up the shot and bang. He shook the thought from his mind.

'This is the place,' said Lucas.

'There is one slight problem. This building is high enough to take the shot from the room below.'

'Yes, but it's unlikely. The walkway passes in front of the windows, so the line of sight could get blocked. The shooter has five seconds and then Bonelli disappears. Also, the maid is going to be turning down rooms at 10am. It's too much of a risk.'

'Agreed. You would take the shot from here.'

'Let's go.'

They climbed down the ladder and headed to the car. Moran was already there. Lucas struggled to get in.

'Well?' she said.

'That's the place. The shooter would have a great shot.'

'What did you find?'

'Apart from à teenager with raging hormones, there is a CCTV monitor behind the desk. As expected, it covers the back but not the side. They aren't busy, we can park up here and be out of sight.'

'We need to get back, we got planning to do.'

Chapter 37

The likelihood of the hit taking place the next day was slim. Only a few days ago Jameson had said the time was yet to be decided. If it was going down this week, he would have said so. But tomorrow was Friday and they couldn't take the chance.

The three of them had built a childlike model of the motel with food boxes, crockery and cushions. Each part was represented by something from Moran's apartment.

The plan was to take Mechanic when she was on the roof. That way she had limited escape options and her attention would be focused on the twelve-foot piece of concrete lying between the back door of the car and the side entrance.

It is the Achilles heel for any sniper. You are so focused on what is happening at the dangerous end of the barrel you are oblivious to what's happening behind you.

The plan was simple. Two people on the roof, one person on the ground keeping watch. The two on the roof would hide amongst the air conditioners and switchgear. When Mechanic was zoned out and focused on the hit, they would strike.

There would be no big speeches, no long recitals telling Mechanic that this was payback time, no watching her squirm as they told her this was justice for all those she had murdered, no looking deep into her eyes and saying this was revenge for killing Darlene. That kind of stuff only happened in the movies. In real life, it was shoot on sight and shoot to kill.

Tactically they had a decision to take. Who was going to pull the trigger? Lucas was the natural choice but the hike up the ladder had proved a challenge with his injured leg. Moran had made the point that he was at risk of doing himself even more damage and that was the last thing they needed. Lucas had to accept the practical common sense of the situation and agreed to stay on the ground.

The communication would be done with series of squelches. Squelches happen when the talk button is pressed on a walkie-talkie. The person on the ground would squelch once when Mechanic was spotted, telling those up top to expect her arrival.

The issue of timing was difficult. Mechanic would not want to arrive too early for fear of being discovered. They, on the other hand, had to arrive in plenty of time to be ready. They opted for 8am, two hours before the hit was scheduled and when the reception boy would be busy with checkouts.

Lucas and Harper retired to their hotel and ate dinner in their room. Moran cooked a pizza from the freezer. All three got an early night but didn't sleep a wink.

* * *

The next morning Moran ate breakfast as she got ready to leave. It was 7am and she had arranged to meet Lucas and Harper near the motel at seven thirty to run through last minute details. It was unusual for her to eat anything in the morning but given the potential for holy shit to be let loose today, breakfast was a sound idea.

She put the gun into her backpack along with the box of shells, the walkie-talkie and the binoculars. She gave herself one last look in the mirror and puffed up her hair. It sank back immediately. She shrugged and opened the door.

Mills was standing on her doorstep.

'Jesus.' Moran stepped back. 'You scared me.'

'Sorry, I didn't mean to.'

She heard the words but his face said the opposite.

'What are you doing here?' Moran eased the bag from her shoulder and pushed it out of sight with her foot.

'This is not a social call,' Mills said.

'I thought you were going to write to me when you'd concluded your investigation. Did you send me something? Have I missed it?'

'No, this is about a different matter, but it is connected.'

Moran screwed her face up.

'I want you to come to the station to answer a few questions.'

Fuck, this is not good.

'Answer a few questions about what?'

'We can talk about that at the station.'

'Can't we do this another time?'

'No.'

'Am I under arrest?'

'Have I read you your rights?'

Moran shook her head and followed Mills down the path. She made for her car.

'No, it would be better if you came with me.'

She shrugged and climbed into the passenger seat.

Mills pulled away and headed for the station.

'What is this about?' asked Moran.

'I'll tell you at the station.' Mills stared straight ahead.

Her outward demeanour was of someone mildly inconvenienced, in her head she was screaming blue murder.

They travelled the rest of the way in silence.

* * *

Lucas and Harper nosed the car into a side street and pulled over. Neither of them was in the mood for chatting. The gravity of the situation was weighing heavily on them both. It was unlikely they would see any action but that sensible piece of deduction did not remove the chance that they might come face to face with a vicious serial killer this morning.

The clock on the dashboard ticked past the half-hour mark.

'She's late,' Harper said.

'Give her a few minutes, she's probably stuck in traffic.'

'We weren't stuck in traffic and we use the same route.'

'Give her a few more minutes.'

The silence returned. Harper toyed with his gun.

The clock said 7.40am.

'We need to make a move,' said Harper. 'She knows the drill, she can catch us up.'

Harper climbed onto the roof and pressed himself against one of the metal cabinets covered with yellow lightning flashes warning of electricity. He figured Mechanic would position herself along the front wall where she had the best line of sight to the target. It would be directly in line with the door and Bonelli's head. He found the ideal spot, the electrical cabinet was twenty feet away to the right. The switchgear inside hummed in the still morning air.

Lucas was off to the left of the motel grounds watching the back. He could see the ladders leading up to the roof at either side of the building. He had the walkie-talkie in his hand.

They waited.

Where the hell is Moran? They both had the same thought.

* * *

At the station Mills ushered Moran into an interview room.

'Wait here,' he said and left.

Moran picked at her fingernails. She checked her watch every five minutes. She needed to get back home, grab her bag and get to the motel fast. What the hell was Mills playing at.

Moran's patience ran out and she had her hand on the door handle ready to leave when Mills returned carrying an envelope. She sat down again and he shut the door.

'Will this take long?' she asked.

'That depends on what you have to say.'

'Come on, Mills, spit it out.'

'We located the Helix Holdings file held at the public records office in Tallahassee. We believe it had been deliberately misfiled. The file had been tampered with and documents removed – the forensic accountants are working on it now to piece together what's missing.'

'That's all interesting stuff, Mills, but why have you brought me in here to tell me that. I'm no longer on the case so what's it got to do with me?'

Mills removed a photograph from an envelope and set it in front of her. The picture showed the back of a person waiting outside an elevator with a suitcase. They were wearing a knitted hat and a hideous canary yellow jacket. Moran gazed at the image and steeled every muscle in her body not to flinch.

She looked at Mills.

'So, what am I looking at?'

'Well, if I'm right, it's you.'

'Ha, dressed in that get-up. I don't think so.'

She slouched back in her chair and pushed the photo back to Mills. Her head went into overdrive.

Shit, this must be taken from the surveillance camera at the public records office. Mills can't have a picture showing my face, or right now he would be ramming it down my throat.

Mills returned the favour and pushed the photo back to her.

'It's your height, your build. I think you went to Tallahassee to cover your tracks.'

'Oh yes, that's exactly what I did. I left here and went straight to the airport, jumped on a plane, flew two thousand miles and hid the file in a place where it was bound to be found. Yes, that's a really smart move.'

'I think that's precisely what you did, and I will prove it. We are dusting the file for prints, and when we identify yours I will be in touch. Tampering with public records is a serious offence. The removal and destruction of public records is a serious offence. They carry with them a jail term of up to three years. Adding that to withholding critical information in a murder case makes it quite a rap sheet.'

'Is that it?'

Mills nodded his head.

Moran looked at the print. The white skin of her hand was clearly visible, poking out of the sleeve of the jacket. What Mills could not see was the gloves balled up and stuffed into the pocket.

Dust away, she thought.

Dust away.

* * *

At the motel, time ticked by. Lucas was hopping from one foot to the other trying to control his nerves. Harper spent his time checking his weapon over and over again. He was afraid to walk about in case Mechanic saw him on her approach to the motel. He was calm and collected.

His watch said 9.20.

* * *

Moran was finally on the move. She raced home, picked up her bag and screeched her car up the road heading for the motel. Lucas and Harper must have put an amended plan in place. She had to be careful on her approach, the operation could be underway by the time she got there. She couldn't screw it up.

The motel came into view and she pulled over. She tracked the remaining one hundred yards on foot. Her walkie-talkie made a squelch sound.

Harper had depressed the button sending a single squelch to the other unit. He was asking Lucas if he could see Mechanic. Lucas responded with two squelches – no. If Mechanic appeared, Lucas would give three squelches to signal she was on the ground.

Harper checked his watch, it was 9.55. He craned his head around the cabinet. The coast was clear.

He made his way to the front wall and lifted the binoculars to his eyes. He could see the metal partition. A few minutes later he saw the door open and a big man in a dark suit walked out. He crossed the triangle and heaved the metal wall to the side.

A black SUV swung into the parking lot and headed over to the man waiting in the gap. The vehicle eased inside and the man opened the rear door. Harper recognised Bonelli immediately as he got out of the car.

Harper counted in his head.

One.

The man acknowledged Bonelli with a nod of his head and closed the door.

Two.

The front doors opened and two men got out.

Three.

Bonelli walked along the side of the SUV.

Four.

The entourage marched to the apex of the triangle.

Five.

One man opened the service door and moved to the side.

Six.

Bonelli stepped through the gap and was gone.

Today was not the day, Harper thought.

He edged his way down the ladder and met up with Lucas. Moran was standing beside him.

'Where the hell did you get to?' he asked.

'It's a long story.'

Harper shook his head and tutted loudly. They walked back to their cars.

'Today was not the day,' Harper said, out loud this time.

'Looks that way,' replied Lucas.

'When you realised Mechanic was a no-show did you take a look at Bonelli?' Moran asked.

'Yup, and at 10am sharp he pulls up in a big limo, a load of heavies get out and escort him through the side door. If I'd had a long gun, his brains would be all over the whitewash.'

'What's our next move?' asked Moran.

Lucas jumped into his rental car.

'You two can stay here and keep a low profile while I go back to San Diego and piss someone off by parking outside his house.'

Chapter 38

Bonelli was sitting in the private lounge on the twenty-first floor of the Mint. It looked like an English old boys' club with high back wing chairs, gaudy wallpaper and walnut tables. Crystal chandeliers hung from the vaulted ceiling and purple velvet drapes were looped back either side of the windows.

Bonelli was holding court. His men were clustered around him in a semi-circle, each one swallowed up by their easy chair, each one with a glass beside them. A waiter dressed in black tie was in attendance, bringing more drinks on a silver tray.

It was easy to see who was in charge. Bonelli was seated in the biggest chair, with the most flared wings and the highest back. He looked like a Disney villain.

Since Mechanic had killed his brother, Alfonso Bonelli had done well with the business. The word on the street said he was too much of a knucklehead to make it work. His brother had been the smooth, suave, sophisticated one, with the gravitas of a corporate executive. Alfonso was the enforcer.

Rival gangs had tried to move in on his turf following his brother's death. His murder was seen as a sign of weakness and they smelled blood. Unfortunately, the blood they smelled was their own and Alfonso ruthlessly crushed them. Once that was done, life returned to business as usual – supplying class A drugs, prostitution and a new line in extortion. Alfonso Bonelli had proved his critics wrong, and there were now fewer of them to doubt him.

He liked the routine of getting his men together once a week. It was a good discipline he had read about in a self-help book about running a successful company. It gave him the opportunity to bond with his team and hold them accountable for their performance, or that's what the book said. For Bonelli it was an opportunity to look into the whites of their eyes to tell if they were lying.

The meeting was drawing to a close and each person had reported on their activities for the week. Most importantly they had reported on how much money they had made.

'Has anyone got anything else they want to raise?' Bonelli said.

'Yes, Boss, I got something.'

Bonelli nodded at the forty-year-old man, with a shaved head, bursting out of his suit.

'Do you recall a while back we were looking for two men, one white and one black. They were connected with Harry Silverton. We circulated mug shots of them both, remember?'

Bonelli leaned forward from his chair.

'Turns out, one of my guys thinks he saw them yesterday.'

* * *

Lucas drummed his fingers on the steering wheel while he watched the front of the two-up two-down town house in the trendy Ocean Bay area. It was 7am.

Jameson clocked him as he closed his front door and got into his car. Lucas followed him. They pulled onto the highway, bound for the dirt road leading to the piece of waste ground under the railway bridge.

The surface of the road seemed to have deteriorated since Lucas last drove it. The suspension complained every time the wheels sank into a pothole. This was killing his car, or, more precisely, the rental company's car.

They swung around on the waste ground and Jameson jumped out. Lucas did the same.

'I told you not to do that,' he barked.

'Save it,' Lucas said. 'My client was delighted by the progress and ecstatic with the details you provided.'

'That's good. I am flexible towards my client's needs.'

'Yes, you are, and it is appreciated, I can assure you.'

'I aim to please.'

'Do you have an update?'

'I do. I have a finalised date. Tell your guy that the job will go down next Friday.'

'How will I know when it's done?'

'You strike me as a well-informed man. I don't think it will be necessary for me to tell you.'

'That's a good point, we will probably know before Bonelli.'

Jameson cracked a smile.

'How do you want the balance of the money paid?'

'Cabrillo Bridge. Be there at 3pm on Friday. That will give me time to get confirmation.'

'That's good. By then I will also have confirmation. We can compare notes.'

There was nothing more to be said.

Lucas bounced down the road wrecking the shock absorbers on the rental car, not looking forward to the long drive back to Vegas.

* * *

Bonelli catapulted out of his chair. The forty-year-old guy bulging out of his suit thought he was a dead man.

'When? Why the fuck didn't you tell me?'

'But I'm telling you now, Boss.'

'When did he see them?'

'It was yesterday. A woman was nosing around the back of the Mint and said something about looking for her purse. One of our men talked to her, she got confused and left.'

'And? Where do the two guys come into it?'

'She walked off the parking lot and met up with them. The two men from the mug shots. It was them.'

'Is he certain?'

'Yes, he's a reliable guy. If he says it was them, I'd put money on it.'

Everyone else was welded to their seats.

'Why the fucking hell didn't you think to bring this to me yesterday?' Bonelli flung his arms in the air and slapped them onto the arms of the chair.

'I knew we were getting together today, so I assumed it would be okay to tell you now.'

'You assumed, you assumed?' Bonelli was turning red.

'Sorry, Boss. I thought it would be okay.'

Bonelli jumped up and marched around the room.

'Let me get this straight. Yesterday one of your men spots the white guy who killed two of our men. You know they are linked to the death of my brother, right? And you think it's okay to tell me about it today?' His voice rattled the chandeliers.

'Sorry, Boss.'

'Sorry!' Bonelli drew his gun and pointed it at the man quivering in his chair. He walked up to him and drove the muzzle into his forehead.

'Sorry?' Bonelli said, his hand shaking.

The man cowered with his head between his knees.

'Sorry, sorry, sorry …' His snivelling voice filled the room.

Bonelli jammed the gun into the back of his head.

The man pissed himself.

Chapter 39

Harper wasn't too sure what Lucas meant when he told him to keep a low profile while he was in San Diego. He interpreted it to mean 'stay in your hotel and don't be an idiot'.

He had been holed up for most of the day and so far so good. But now Harper was restless and thirsty, with almost twenty thousand dollars in a sports bag stuffed in a closet. It was not the ideal set of circumstances to ensure a low profile.

He hailed a cab, jumped in the back and leaned forward over the front seat.

'Fremont Street, please.'

Harper sat back with a token of Fabiano Bassano's appreciation tucked away in his wallet.

The driver dropped him off outside the Horseshoe, and Harper made a beeline for the bar. The first ice-cold beer didn't touch the sides as he chugged it down. Before the barman had a chance to return with his change he needed another. Keeping a low profile was thirsty business.

The place was a cacophony of noise with slot machines chiming out honky-tonk tunes and spewing coins into metal trays, while guys in denim shirts huddled around the gaming tables hollering and whooping. It was built-in entertainment.

Harper was especially entertained by the casino waitresses in their low-cut mini-dresses with a split up one thigh. They served the punters gambling away their hard-earned cash. It almost made Harper wish he were a gambler, but gambling wasn't one of his numerous vices. However, ogling the women as they weaved their way through the throng, balancing their trays high in the air, definitely was.

After three more rapid beers the effect of the mini-dresses and low-cut tops was getting to him. He left the Horseshoe and turned right. He could see the neon signs of the Golden Goose and Glitter Gulch up ahead.

* * *

There was a soft tap on the front door. Moran opened it to find Mills standing on the step.

'Have you come to arrest me this time?'

'No, but I do have more questions.'

'Look, Mills, it's late. I don't have the patience to come down to the station to look at pictures of random strangers in yellow jackets. Can't this wait till tomorrow?'

'We don't have to do this at the station. It won't take long.'

Moran moved over and Mills stepped inside.

She perched on the edge on the sofa and he settled into the chair.

'What is it this time?' she said.

Mills pulled two mug shots from his pocket and handed them to Moran.

'How do you know these men?'

Moran nearly fell on the floor. Staring back at her from the two four-by-six prints were Harper and Lucas. She froze everything trying not to react.

Moran pursed her lips and shook her head.

'Am I supposed to know them?'

'You were with them the other night.'

'I was? Where the hell was that?'

'You were with them in Fremont Street, at the back of the Mint.'

Moran's head felt like it was about to explode.

Where in hell's name was this going? she thought looking at the photos.

'I've never seen these guys before, who are they?'

'I need to ask the questions. How do you know them?'

'We've done that one already. The straight answer is, I don't. What is this about?'

'You were seen at the back of the Mint, where you met with these two men.'

Sparks of realisation started popping in her head. The guard. The guard must have seen her chatting to Lucas and Harper. But what would that have to do with Mills?

'I was at the back of the Mint the other night, although what the hell that has to do with the police is beyond me. I had dropped my purse and a security guy helped me look for it.'

'That's right, and when you left the parking lot you were with these two men.'

'Look, I am getting bored of saying this. I was not with them.'

'The guard says you were.'

Moran had a burst of clarity which stunned her into silence. This was not a police matter – if it was she would be answering questions at the station. This had to be about something else.

The explanation chilled Moran to the bone.

The security guard had to be on Bonelli's payroll and recognised Lucas and Harper from the manhunt a year ago. He reported it up the chain of command and Bonelli had squeezed his network to get information and find them. Mills must be part of that network. The back of the Mint was plastered with surveillance cameras, her face must have been circulated, Mills knew exactly where to start.

The realisation hit her full on. Mills was not only a useless cop, he was bent as well.

Moran found her acting skills.

'Wait a moment. After I looked for my purse, two men asked me for directions. I don't know who was more drunk, me or them.'

'You were drunk?'

'Yeah, I was drunk. Here's a newsflash for you, Mills, it's been a fucking stressful time.'

Mills flinched at the rebuke.

'And these were the men you spoke to?'

'They might have been. I spoke to a ton of people that night.'

Mills reached out and took the photographs from her hand.

'I still don't understand. What does this have to do with me?' Moran asked.

'We want to speak to them. Did they say where they were going?'

'Look, Mills, I can hardly recall talking to them.'

Mills stood up. The conversation was over. He headed for the front door.

'If you run into them again, give me a call.'

'Are they dangerous?'

'We need to ask them a few questions.'

Moran opened the door and showed him out. She leaned on the doorframe and watched him go. She had to find Harper fast.

Chapter 40

Harper sauntered past the Mint and ducked inside the first strip joint he came to. The man on the door was the size of a family wardrobe. He nodded as Harper made his way inside. The wall of music hit him as he pushed against the inner door.

The ceiling was packed with glitter balls, while spinning spotlights cascaded a starburst of red, purple and blue around the room. Speakers hung in the corners, thumping out the beat like giant metronomes. The bar was to the left and a black raised runway ran down the centre. Above the runway a carpet of lights spilled a patchwork of colour onto the stage. A row of chairs ran down either side, occupied by glassy eyed men with their tongues hanging out.

Women strutted up and down the runway in their underwear, making eye contact with the men and gyrating in front of them. When a punter stuck a bill into her panties the woman was his for the next three minutes. Around the walls were signs saying No Touching.

Harper went to the bar, ordered a beer and took in the sights around him. There were booth seats against the far wall occupied by groups of men. Women wearing next to nothing flitted around to ensure the guys were having a good time and had a drink in their hand.

The beers flowed and Harper found himself drawn to the runway. One woman kept crooking her finger to beckon him over. The first few times, he waved his hand and looked away. She was absolutely gorgeous and Harper was finding it difficult to say no.

She rotated her hips and stuck out her ass. Harper caved in.

He picked up his drink, moseyed over to where she was dancing and plonked himself on a chair. She dropped down in front of him, licked her finger and drew it up the centre of her body. He reached in his pocket for money. He found a five dollar bill. She turned and bent over, Harper slipped the note into her panties. She started grinding away.

But Harper wasn't looking at her. His attention was drawn to the wardrobe-sized man ushering two men into the club. They were dressed in double-breasted suits and stuck out from the rest of the punters like a sore thumb. They scanned the room paying no attention to the women. They were looking for someone.

Harper ducked down so his chin was almost level with the top of the runway. The dancer took this as a sign for her to get down and dirty. She sank to the floor and spread her legs wide. She was totally bemused when Harper slid from his chair and used a passing waitress to shield him from view as he scurried to the back. He could feel the gun tucked into the back of his belt. It gave him a small swell of comfort, but a fire fight in a crowded bar was not a good idea.

The men in suits split up and paced either side of the runway.

Harper reached the back of the club and found the restrooms. He dashed into the ladies' room and banged open each of the stalls. The one at the end had a window set into the outside wall.

He went inside, locked the door and climbed onto the seat. The latch on the window was welded shut with paint, and try as he might he couldn't free it. Harper removed his jacket and wrapped it around his gun. He smashed it into the glass. The window shattered.

* * *

Moran flung the car against the kerb and jumped out. She was met by a wall of tourists clogging up the sidewalk. One question hammered away at her. Where would Harper go?

The answer was straightforward and she headed up Fremont Street to the nearest strip club. The wardrobe-sized doorman gave her a quizzical look as she arrived at the entrance. She darted back to the kerb and looked around. Shit, there were so many clubs. Which one? Moran thought hard. The answer was obvious: the first one he came to.

She was about to go in when she heard the faint sound of glass shattering. The doorman heard nothing over the noise in the club.

Moran darted to her right and ran down First Street.

* * *

The men in suits were working their way through the room, checking everyone out. They moved in unison to the back of the club and came to the restrooms. They burst open the door to the men's room.

Harper could hear the thumping noise of doors slamming next door. He covered the window ledge with his jacket and squeezed through the gap. Shards of glass buried in the window frame tore at his shirt and bloodied his skin. He rolled out onto the single-storey sloping roof.

Harper slid down the tiles and tumbled off the edge. He hit the concrete hard and his gun spun from his hand. Above him he could hear the sound of raised voices.

Moran ran across the back of the strip joints looking for a way in. She could see the window with the glass missing – two men in suits were forcing themselves through the gap.

Harper was dazed from his fall. Pain shot up his legs as he sat on the ground.

Where the hell is my gun?

He scrambled to his feet. He could hear the men sliding down the roof. He spun left and hobbled down a narrow alley at the side of the building. His path was blocked by a brick wall. He was trapped.

Harper looked around, the walls on either side were too high to scale. He hid behind a bin which was spilling over with empty bottles. The sound of metal-heeled shoes striking concrete filled the yard.

Moran tried a door in the back wall but it was locked. She tried another, that was locked. The third one opened. She cracked it ajar to see the men in suits. They had their backs to her and were poking around, their guns on show.

Moran drew her weapon.

Harper could hear the men talking in low tones as they searched the yard.

'Hey, look,' one of them said picking Harper's handgun off the floor.

Harper pushed himself tight against the wall. He could hear their footsteps getting closer. They rounded the corner and headed down the alley.

Moran slipped through the door and crabbed her way across the yard. The men were in front of her, edging closer to Harper.

They spotted him.

'On your feet,' one of them said, levelling his gun at Harper's head. 'Keep your hands where I can see them.'

Harper shuffled to his feet.

The other man pulled a dog-eared photograph from his pocket.

'It's him,' he said.

'Okay, old-timer, we are going to take a walk, nice and gentle. If you feel like being a hero, we can carry you out of here if you prefer.'

Moran crept around the corner.

Harper saw her but kept his eyes glued to the man in front.

Moran stepped closer and held up three fingers on her left hand.

She counted them down.

'Come on, old man, move it.'

Three, two, one.

Harper darted to his left and the men sprang forward.

Moran slammed the Berretta into the back of the first guy's skull. His legs buckled and he slumped down.

The second man hesitated. He had to stop Harper from running but there was something happening behind him. The split second of indecision was all she needed.

Moran pivoted on her left leg and smashed the instep of her right foot into his face. His nose burst into a bloody pulp and his cheekbone shattered. He keeled over sideways and smacked into the wall, sliding to the floor in a heap.

The first man was groaning. He had heaved himself onto all fours with blood running down his neck onto his shirt. Moran stepped back and lashed out with her boot. It caught the guy behind the ear. He hit the ground with a splat.

Moran grabbed Harper by the arm.

'Come on,' she said as they hurried for the door. Harper was limping. He stopped to retrieve his gun.

They walked along the back road and cut through onto Second Street, where Moran's car was waiting.

They piled in and pulled away.

'Thank you,' Harper said. 'You saved my life.'

'Yes, I did.'

'How did you know I was there? And how did you know I was in trouble?'

'I'll tell you later, but right now we gotta get out of here.'

Chapter 41

Harper squirmed in the passenger seat trying to get comfortable while Moran powered through the streets to get home.

'You were really something back there,' he said.

'Yeah, I've picked up a few tricks along the way.'

'It would have been simplest to use your gun and start popping away.'

'Yes, and that would have brought the whole of the LVPD down on our heads. And we were having enough trouble with two of Bonelli's boys. We didn't need more.'

'Yeah, that's easy to say. But when you're faced with a situation like that it takes balls not to use it.'

'I don't have balls.'

'Yes, you do.'

Moran continued to fill Harper in on her theory that Mills was bent. They had to get a message to Lucas fast to stop him travelling back to Vegas.

Moran opened her front door and scurried to the bedroom to fill a bag with clothes and toiletries. Harper called the apartment they had stayed in while at the Gaslamp District. Lucas was staying there but was out. Harper left an urgent message with the switchboard telling Lucas to stay put.

Their strategy was simple. Vegas was too dangerous and they needed to move out fast. The logical place to go was San Diego. At least there they had the opportunity to continue to track down Mechanic, even if that had proved unsuccessful the last time.

'Ready,' Moran said appearing in the hallway with two bags.

They had one more stop to make before heading south. A small matter of collecting twenty thousand dollars in a black Puma sports bag.

* * *

While in San Diego, Lucas, Harper and Moran spent their time scouting for Mechanic. Harper and Lucas trawled the gyms and Moran ran around the parks and boardwalks like a mad woman. Despite their best efforts, Mechanic eluded them. Not surprising, as she was three hundred and thirty miles away in Vegas, finalising preparations. Things were going well.

The days passed quickly.

They practised the operation to take out Mechanic until they saw it in their sleep. A local park was the ideal location to test out the radios, though they ran the gauntlet of a thousand disapproving glances from parents playing with their children, concerned at the spectacle of three adults playing games with walkie-talkies.

They discussed what to do with Mechanic's body and reached the unanimous conclusion that leaving it on the roof for the police to find was the best option. A lone sniper shot through the head on a rooftop had the all hallmarks of a gangland killing. A useful diversion.

Harper cruised by Jameson's place on numerous occasions to check it out, but each time the house was deserted. He was tempted to stop and take a closer look, but there was nothing to be gained by spooking Jameson and maybe getting his ass kicked in the process.

Moran decided the best approach was for them all to stop over in Henderson the night before, the second biggest city in Nevada. It lay sixteen miles southeast of Vegas within easy striking distance of the Jackpot motel, and more importantly was outside of Bonelli's jurisdiction. They were less likely to run into any of his guys there.

Moran booked three rooms for one night.

* * *

It was 9am, Thursday.

They checked their equipment for the hundredth time, hauled their gear into the cars and set off. Harper fished around in his jacket pocket and pulled out an oblong package.

'I bought you a present,' he said placing it on the dashboard.

Lucas had one eye on the road and the other on the gift. It was in a brown paper bag and wound with packing tape, Harper's version of gift wrapping. Lucas grabbed it.

'What is it?'

'Open it and find out.'

Lucas put it in his lap and tore at the paper with one hand while steering with the other. He struggled, but after much scraping and cursing he got it open.

'It's a camera?' Lucas said holding it up.

'Yes, one of those Polaroid things.'

Lucas looked across at Harper and frowned.

'You said you wanted to videotape the life draining from Mechanic's eyes, so you could watch it over and over again.'

'I remember.'

'Well, a video camera was too big to wrap. So I got you this.'

* * *

7.30am, Friday.

Lucas, Moran and Harper drove to the Jackpot motel in two cars. The traffic was heavy but moving as the rush hour took hold. They travelled bumper to bumper away from Henderson on the 508 until they hit Las Vegas Boulevard. A sharp right brought them to the junction with Bonanza Road. The motel was further along on the left.

Moran pulled into a slot at the side of the building, while Lucas nosed his car into a residential side street a hundred yards away. None of them had woken early that morning because none of them had slept a wink.

Harper checked his kit. It was all in order. He pulled the door handle, Lucas placed his hand on his arm.

'Good luck.'

Harper smiled and stepped out, closing the door. Lucas watched him turn the corner and walk out of sight.

Lucas waited ten minutes then followed him. Thirty yards to the left of reception was a small green area with ornamental trees and bushes. Lucas settled himself amongst them and pulled out his binoculars. From his position he had the perfect angle to watch the back of the motel and also keep an eye on the traffic entering and leaving the lot.

He could see Moran disappear over the lip of the building onto the roof. Harper was halfway up the ladder.

Five minutes later Lucas heard a squelch on his intercom. They were in position. Now it was a waiting game.

Harper and Moran sat on the floor behind separate electrical cabinets. Moran had her gun beside her and was staring into space, blocking everything from her brain. Harper fiddled with his gun and ate chocolate.

The morning was brightening up as the sun rose. It was clear with a slight breath of wind. Mechanic's preparation time would be minimal. No cross wind to adjust for, just set it up and bang.

Lucas watched as people left the motel and headed for their cars with suitcases and bags. New staff arrived dressed in blue coveralls. A truck delivered fresh laundry in wire cages and took away the dirty stuff. A small van dropped off cases of bottled water.

Lucas looked at his watch. It was nine thirty.

He saw the white roof of a van drift into the parking lot. The rest of the vehicle was obscured by cars. It parked up and the driver's door opened. Lucas saw a head emerge wearing a blue baseball cap. The head moved around the van and slid open the side door.

The person disappeared for a second then rattled the door across and walked to the front. Lucas stared through his binoculars and held his breath.

Shit! It was Mechanic.

Even with the peak pulled down, Lucas was in no doubt. It was her.

Lucas felt a shudder run through his body.

Mechanic wore a tight green fleece and khaki pants, she had a long thin black backpack slung over one shoulder. She looked around and walked to the back of the building.

Lucas pressed the talk button.

Moran and Harper jumped as their radios emitted a squelch. *Fuck, this is it.*

They both gripped their guns, got up from their sitting positions and crouched down, their heart rates climbing rapidly.

Moran strained to hear the ladder creak as Mechanic made her way up, but all she could hear was the soft breeze. Harper had his back pressed against the metal, fighting the temptation to take a look over the top.

The minutes ticked by.

Harper looked at his watch, nine forty.

Moran was shifting her weight from one leg to the other.

The minutes ticked by.

What the hell was keeping her? Harper thought.

His watch said nine forty-seven. There was still no sign of her.

This was not allowing enough time for Mechanic to set up her rifle, calm her breathing, lower her heart rate and get in the zone.

Something was wrong.

He peeked around the metal box and broke cover. He ran to where Moran was hiding.

'I think she must be in one of the rooms beneath us.'

'She's not here, that's for sure. It's the only other place.'

They both left the security of the switchgear cabinet and ran to the edge.

Moran jerked her weapon over the side and pointed it down the ladder. It was clear. She stepped over the wall and started to climb down, closely followed by Harper.

They reached the bottom.

It was nine fifty-one.

Moran took the left-hand side and Harper took the right. They ran up the stairs to the outside walkway on the third floor. Moran could see Harper looking into every window with his gun levelled as he traversed towards her. A woman came out of a room dragging a heavy case.

Shit, that was close!

Harper and Moran held their guns behind their backs and kept moving. Harper passed the woman and walked on.

Some rooms had their curtains closed while others were wide open.

Moran and Harper kept checking.

They met in the middle.

'Nothing.' Moran looked at her watch: 9.58.

Harper took out his field glasses and trained them on the back of the Mint. The grey metal partition was pulled across to the side and the black SUV was already easing its way into the slot.

'Bonelli is in place.'

'Where the fuck is she?' Moran said.

Bonelli's head appeared.

Moran ran past Harper looking through the motel windows.

Harper counted down.

One.

The man acknowledged Bonelli with a nod of his head and closed the door.

Two.

The front doors opened and two men got out.

Three.

Bonelli walked along the side of the SUV.

Four.

The entourage marched to the apex of the triangle.

Five.

One man opened the service door and moved to the side.

Six.

Bonelli stepped through the gap and was gone.

'Fuck,' Harper said.

'What the hell just happened?'

Harper pressed the button on his walkie-talkie.

'She is a no-show. Repeat, she is a no-show.'

They marched across the front of the motel, down the central stairwell and over to reception.

Moran was half-expecting to see Lucas walking towards them, but he wasn't. They were ten yards away from the place where he had been hiding but they couldn't see him.

Harper broke into a run and reached the small green area. The grass was pressed flat to the ground where he had been sitting, but there was no Lucas.

'Lucas, come in please,' Moran said into her radio.

They heard the crackling sound of her voice coming back at them. Harper swung around and switched his radio off.

'Do it again.'

'Lucas, can you come in please.'

The metallic voice was emanating from a set of bushes six feet away.

Harper stomped around and found the radio lying in the grass.

Moran joined him.

'What in hell's name are these?' she asked.

She picked up a handful of small white paper squares.

Harper stared at them. His eyes filled up.

'They're sugar packets. Mechanic has taken Lucas.'

Chapter 42

'Fuck, fuck, fuck.' Harper stomped around in the bushes.

'Stop it, Harper. Think, man, think,' replied Moran.

'She must have been here, right? Lucas buzzed us to say she was here.' He continued stomping.

'But then we heard nothing.'

'He must have had eyes on Mechanic. How the fuck could she walk nearly thirty yards towards him without Lucas raising the alarm?'

'She must have grabbed him. He should have shot her, that's what he should have done.'

'Maybe it wasn't her,' said Harper.

'If anyone would be able to positively ID Mechanic it was Lucas. It was her alright.'

'No, I mean maybe it wasn't her that took Lucas.'

'What are you getting at?'

'Lucas spots Mechanic and buzzes us to say she's here. Then while he has his eyes focused on her, someone whacks him and takes him away.'

'You wait in my car.' Moran tossed Harper the keys and ran in the direction of the reception block.

Moran burst through the doors.

The young man with his hormones on fire looked up.

'Hi, good to see you again.'

'I need you to help me.'

'Why of course, ma'am, what is it?'

'I've got a delicate situation.'

The guy's eyes widened. 'They are my favourite type.'

'My car has gone missing from the parking lot.'

'Oh that is terrible, ma'am, have you called the cops?'

'No, no, I haven't.'

'Do you want me to call them?'

'No, no.'

'But your car has been stolen, right?'

Moran gestured for the young guy to lean in. She whispered in his ear.

'It's embarrassing, I'm not supposed to be here.'

'What? How do you mean?'

'I'm not supposed to be in this motel.'

The young man stared at her with a look that said 'I'm enjoying this, but please make sense, ma'am'. Then it all made sense.

'You mean you are supposed to be somewhere else?'

'Yes, I met a man here.'

'And this man was not your husband or boyfriend?'

'No, he wasn't. And now my car has gone.'

The young guy nodded as though the situation she'd described was an everyday occurrence.

'But if it has been stolen you will need to report it.'

'It might not have been stolen.'

The boy was back to being confused.

'My boyfriend may have taken it. Before I go and call the police I need to know if it's him.'

'And why do you think it could be your boyfriend?'

'He's done it before. You know, to teach me a lesson.'

The young guy raised an eyebrow, pleased that he'd been right all along – this woman was well up for sex.

'How can I help?'

'You have CCTV covering the parking lot?'

'Yes, we do, but not at the side.'

'Could you let me see the recording? That way I will know if it's him or if I need to contact the police.'

'Well, I suppose I could—'

'Please, I would be so grateful,' Moran interrupted.

The young man gave her a theatrical wink.

'Step right this way, ma'am.'

He swung open a hatch and beckoned her in. The TV monitor she'd seen previously was on the desk at the back. She squeezed herself between him and the counter. She felt his body tense.

'Where were you parked, ma'am?'

'I don't know.'

'What car were you driving?'

Moran scanned the screen. 'Er, a blue one?'

'What make and model?'

'I don't know.'

She berated herself for having just substantiated the stereotype of women and cars.

'Can you wind the tape back?' she said.

'What am I looking for?'

'I'll know the car when I see it.'

The guy opened a cupboard on the wall above the desk and Moran saw the tape machine.

He pushed the reverse button.

The figures on the screen moved around like a Harold Lloyd movie, cars and trucks whizzing in, cars and trucks whizzing out.

He kept his finger on the button. Moran kept her eyes on the screen.

After fifteen seconds she said, 'Stop.'

'There.' She pointed to a man getting into a blue car. 'Let me do this.'

Moran shouldered him out of the way and took control of the video recorder.

'Is that your boyfriend?' asked the young man, his hip brushing against hers. Moran kept her cool, when all she wanted to do was deck him and take the tape.

'Yes, it's my boyfriend.'

The car backed out of a space and drove away.

'Are you sure?'

'Yes, that's him.'

The guy looked at the grainy figure on the screen. A sixty-year-old man with thinning hair and a beer gut was not what he was expecting. But Moran wasn't looking at the man or the car, she was focused on the white van.

'Thank you,' she said. 'Can I take this?'

She pushed the eject button and the cassette tape slid out into her hand.

'Er, no ma'am, you can't take that.'

She slipped her arm around his waist and leaned against him.

'I would be ever so grateful.'

He went weak at the knees.

Moran hurried from the reception, leaving the young guy wondering when he would get his reward. She jumped in the driver's seat next to Harper.

'Mechanic bundled Lucas into a white Ford Transit. The time stamp said 9.39.'

'Shit, they've been gone forty minutes. How did he look?'

'Not good, like he was drunk.'

Moran swung the car around and drove to the parking lot at the back.

'There's another thing.'

'What.'

'Mechanic had someone with her, a man.'

She continued to cruise around.

'What did he look like?'

'Tall, broad, wore a hunting jacket. Dark hair.'

'Who the hell is he?'

Moran jammed on the brakes and leapt into the road leaving the door open. Harper followed. She stood in an empty parking space.

'It was here. The Transit was parked here.'

Harper walked around the white line perimeter of the space.

'Look,' he said, kneeling down and touching the floor with his finger. 'Lucas was hurt.'

He pointed his index finger at Moran. The tip was red with blood.

Moran got back in the car.

'We need to get to my place. I got a video player.'

Chapter 43

Moran drove like a woman possessed, cutting up other motorists and running red lights. They burst through the front door. Harper shoved the cassette into the video recorder and switched on the TV.

After much cursing and fiddling with the remotes the black and white image of the Jackpot parking lot came on the screen. Moran snatched the remote from his grasp and handed him a pen and paper.

'There,' she said. 'That's the Transit parking up at nine thirty.' The white van pulled into a vacant slot with its back to the camera.

Mechanic got out and slid the side door open. She disappeared for a second then re-emerged with a black bag over one shoulder. She closed the door, made her way across the lot to the back of the motel, and walked out of shot. Moran hit pause.

'I know, I'm getting it,' Harper said scribbling down the licence plate.

'Look at this.' Moran pointed at the screen. Emblazoned across the back window was a sticker. 'What does it say?'

Harper moved closer to the picture. 'There are blue letters on a red background but I can't make it out, it's too blurred.'

Moran jumped up and rummaged amongst a pile of old newspapers.

'I've seen that somewhere before.' She rifled through the pages and held one up. 'It's from a car rental company.' There in the classified ads section was a quarter page advert for Drive-Right Car Rentals. The ad had the same blue letters on a red background.

'It must be them. It's the same style and colour scheme.'

Moran tapped play and the tape ran forward.

Nothing happened for the next nine minutes. Then Mechanic staggered back into shot and the lights on the van blinked as the doors unlocked. She had her arm around Lucas's waist while his arm was draped across her shoulder. A man was standing on the other side of Lucas doing the same thing. Lucas dragged his feet, unable to support his weight. His head lolled forward.

Mechanic left Lucas and opened up the side door. The man edged Lucas along the van. Lucas struggled and could be seen kicking his legs and flailing his arms around. The man hit him on the side of his face and he flopped inside. Mechanic jumped into the van and hauled Lucas inside. The man opened the driver's door, and then turned to check the sliding door was secure. Moran hit the pause button.

The man's face was partially obscured by the peak of the baseball cap.

'That's Jameson,' said Harper.

'Are you sure?'

'Yep, I'm sure.'

Moran pressed play and the Transit eased out of the lot and disappeared from view.

They were both sitting on the floor, stunned.

'Jameson didn't arrive in the van with Mechanic,' Harper said. 'He must have already been in place when she parked up.'

'When you had your rehearsal last week, did you do it properly? Did you do exactly what we did today?'

'Yes, while you were being given the run around by Mills we stuck to the plan: Lucas in his lookout position and me on the roof.'

'They were there. Either Jameson, or Mechanic, or both of them were there. They watched you work through the plan. They knew Lucas was isolated. Mechanic turns up at the right place at the right time, Lucas sends the signal telling us it's game on. And we're holding our position on the roof, while they lifted Lucas.'

'Shit. That bastard Jameson set us up from the beginning.'

Moran picked up the Drive-Right ad and stood up.

'Let's go talk to these people.'

* * *

Drive-Right was located in an out-of-town mall surrounded by outlet stores selling branded goods at knockdown prices. It was on the end of a row of shops and had a parking lot behind, full of cars ready to rent. Lucas and Moran went inside.

A man in his early sixties sat behind the counter surrounded by pamphlets. He was sorting them into piles and placing them into zip-lock bags. He wore a company bomber jacket and a baseball cap with the logo splashed across the front. He looked up when they entered.

'Can I help you?'

Moran took the lead.

'We are looking for a couple who rented a white Transit van from you. We need to get hold of them.'

'Okay, do you have a name?'

'No, but we have the vehicle's licence plate. I wondered if you could help us.'

'Why do you want to get hold of them?'

Moran flashed a look at Harper that said 'I should have thought this through better'.

'They hit our car and drove away,' she replied all in a rush.

'That's not good. I'm sorry about that.'

'I have the licence plate number here.' Moran dug out the piece of paper from her pocket and gave it to the man. He consulted a thick file of rental agreements.

'No, it wasn't one of ours.'

'It had your company logo on the back.'

'You must have been mistaken, lady. It's not one of our vehicles.' The tone of his voice hardened.

'No, this was the licence plate number and it had your logo on the back.'

'I can only say again, it's not our vehicle.'

'It is. Can you look it up again?'

'No. I've done it once, and now if you don't mind I'm busy.'

The man turned and attended to his pamphlet packing.

Harper had heard enough.

He turned to the door and closed it, pulling down the blind. He unwrapped a fifty-dollar bill from the roll in his pocket and pulled his gun from the back of his belt. The guy looked up.

'Hey! Now what are you doing?'

Harper put both his hands on the counter. Under one was the money and under the other was his gun.

'When you read the licence plate number it registered in your face. You need to practice in front of a mirror more if you're gonna lie. We are not interested in making an insurance claim if that's what you're worried about, but we are interested in the people who rented that Transit. My colleague has already asked nicely. Now I'm asking.'

The man didn't know what to look at. His head flicked around as if he had a nervous tick –from Harper to the gun, from Moran to the gun, from the money to the gun.

'I don't want no trouble,' he said, raising his hands in surrender.

'Which one is it gonna be?' Harper pushed the hand with the money under it towards him first, followed by the gun.

The man was paralysed. His eyes flitted between the two.

'Which one?' said Harper.

The man nervously fingered the note, tugged it from under Harper's hand and stuffed it in his pocket. He returned to the register and unclipped a rental agreement from the file. He held it out, the end of the paper was shaking as Harper took it.

'Thank you. Now talk me through what happened. Who came to collect the van?'

'It was a man and a woman.'

'And what were they like?'

'He was dark, about six foot, she had short hair. They looked like outdoor types, you know, dressed in camouflage gear. I don't remember much.'

'How did they pay?'

'Cash. They paid for three weeks' rental. Asked if they could have a refund if they brought it back early.'

Moran leaned forward. 'Did they say where they were going?'

'Yes, they said something about renting a cabin up in Mount Charleston.'

'Did they say where?'

'No. I asked if they were going hunting.'

'What did they say?'

The man thought for a moment.

'They said, kind of.'

* * *

Mechanic veered off the road onto a dirt track. The wheels rattled in the ruts while the Transit bounced around. The sun disappeared behind the treeline as they drove deeper into the pine forest.

Half a mile further on she swept right and brought the vehicle to a stop. Jameson jumped out and yanked opened the back doors. Mechanic slid from her seat to join him. He reached inside and dragged something heavy and black towards him. It was a body bag.

Mechanic dived into the back and came out with an aluminium frame and some poles. She set about assembling them on the ground. In three minutes she had constructed a low gurney on big rubber wheels. Mechanic stood one side of the body bag and Jameson on the other.

'Two, three.' They lifted it from the van onto the gurney. Mechanic tugged at a telescopic arm that was bolted to the front and slid a four-foot metal tube through the end making a T-shape. Jameson grabbed one end and Mechanic grabbed the other. They pulled the gurney into the woods.

Chapter 44

Harper ran his eyes over the rental paperwork.

'The name says Henderson. They must have had a fake driver's licence. And look at the date.' He passed it to Moran.

'Shit, they rented it a week ago.'

'Yes, while we were running around looking for her in San Diego she was here all the time.'

'Doing what?'

'I don't know.'

'It's good you intervened,' Moran said.

'He wasn't getting the message.'

'Maybe the old ways are sometimes the best.'

'He could see himself being hit with an insurance claim. He was stalling, and I speeded things up, that's all.'

'No, I mean it was good you intervened because I was about to break his fucking arm.'

Harper flashed her a look.

'How do we find out where Mechanic's taken him?'

'I got an idea,' she replied.

Moran jumped out of the car and ran back to the rental place. The guy behind the counter tried to duck out of sight when she burst in. Two minutes later Moran was back.

'Okay, there are a couple of camping stores a few miles away. The man said we should be able to find the names of companies who rent out lodges from there. He was much more cooperative.'

Harper looked at his watch, it was 11.30am. Lucas had been gone almost two hours.

They drove east to the intersection with Charleston Boulevard. A few miles further on was a parade of shops set back from the road. Located in the middle was Camping and Climbing World.

'No guns this time,' Moran said as they walked across the parking lot to the store. The large plate-glass doors hissed open as they approached. It was huge, with what looked like a tented city in the centre surrounded by mountains of equipment. There was every conceivable piece of equipment from sleeping bags to stoves, to fold-up tables and chairs. Around the walls hung the climbing gear.

Moran stopped one of the sales assistants, a woman dressed to survive a week in the forest.

'Excuse me, I wonder if you would be able to help us? We have a couple of friends who have rented a lodge somewhere on Mount Charleston. Unfortunately, they have had a bereavement in the family and we are desperately trying to get hold of them.'

'Sorry to hear that,' said the woman.

'The problem is we have no idea where they are and have no contact details. Do you have a list of companies who rent out lodges? We could contact them to find out where they are.'

'We don't keep a list, but I'm sure we could help. Follow me.'

The woman clomped across the store in her hiking boots and disappeared into a back room. After a few minutes she emerged with a stack of magazines.

'This is the best I can do. These are camping journals which advertise sites and lodges on Mount Charleston, it's a good place to start.' She handed them over.

'Thank you so much. We are really stuck, do you think we could use your phone? We will pay for any calls we make.'

'Oh, well …'

'Please, it is an emergency,' Moran said.

'Sure, you can use our admin office.' The woman showed them into a small room crammed full of ledgers and invoices. There was a phone in the corner and one chair.

'Thank you,' Moran said. The woman left them to it.

'Nice work,' said Harper.

They flicked through the magazines. The pages at the back contained the advertisements, and they started to compile a list.

Moran made the first call. She used the same cover story.

'Hello, I'm trying to trace some friends who may have rented a lodge from you on Mount Charleston. They've had a sudden death in the family and we're trying to trace them. Their name is Henderson.'

A rustling of paper later and the woman on the other end said, 'No, I'm sorry we don't have anyone by that name on our books.'

She rang a second company, with the same result.

Harper glanced at his watch. Lucas had been gone three hours.

'Maybe they booked the lodge under a different name. That is, if they booked a damn lodge at all,' he said.

'Maybe, but it's all we have to go on at the moment. What's the next one?'

Moran dialled another number and went through the same routine.

Harper was striking ads through with a pen. Some companies only did camping holidays, while others offered outdoor experiences and group activities.

He stopped.

The pen hovered above one of the ads. He dropped his chin onto his chest and let out a long sigh. Moran was in full flow describing how they had to contact their friends urgently. He leaned over, took the receiver from her hand and disconnected the call.

'What did you do that for?'

He handed her a magazine with the pages folded over.

'It will be this one,' he said pointing to the ad.

She furrowed her brow and looked at Harper.

'Mechanic wants us to find her. This is all part of the game.'

'How do you mean?'

'I've been so busy rushing around I couldn't see what was right in front of us.'

'What?'

'Let's back up a little. Mechanic could have easily killed Lucas. But she didn't, instead she chose to take him while we were on the roof. She then proceeds to make a series of rooky mistakes. She parks her vehicle in full view of the surveillance camera with the name of the rental company all over the back of the van. She tells the rental guy where she intends to go and leaves the paperwork for us to find with the name Henderson on it.'

'Shit. Why would she do that?'

'Not sure. But Mechanic is the best at what she does, she would never be that careless. If she wanted to take Lucas and disappear into thin air, she would have. If she wanted us dead, we would be. She loves nothing better than to play games. I can't believe I didn't see it before. Tracking her was way too easy. She's already given us the name of the damn company where she rented the lodge.'

Moran looked at the ad.

The first line read, Henderson Camping Lodge and RV Rentals.

'Henderson,' Moran said.

'Mechanic wants us to find her.'

'No, she wants you to find her. She doesn't know I exist.'

Moran picked up the phone and dialled.

Chapter 45

Moran and Harper were flying along US 95 towards Mount Charleston, thirty-five miles northwest of Vegas. They hung a left on to Kyle Canyon Road looking for the highest elevation in Clark County at almost twelve thousand feet. In the distance they could see the snow-capped summit of their destination.

The mountain loomed large as they sped past the intersection with the 158. Two miles further on they turned left to Cathedral Rock. Mount Charleston and the surrounding area had one hundred and sixty campsites and about the same number of vacation lodges. Thanks to her conversation with the man at Henderson Camping Lodge and RV Rentals, they had narrowed the search down to one, and Moran was looking for a dirt track off to the right.

The man had told her that Mr and Mrs Henderson had rented a log cabin for two weeks and were in their second week. He remembered the booking because Mrs Henderson was insistent that the place had to be in a remote location.

'They wanted to get as far away from civilisation as possible,' he recalled them saying more than once. He was surprised when they went ahead with the booking, even after he had explained that the place had no electricity.

Moran found the turning, heaved the car away from the main road and drove onto the gravel track. Within two hundred yards they were engulfed in a forest of white birch, ponderosa pine and juniper. It was a sharp incline and the wheels bounced and spun in the ruts as she nursed the vehicle across the rugged terrain. The man had said the log cabin was located at the base of a cliff half a mile off the main drag.

Moran pulled onto the grass verge and rolled the car under the cover of the trees. She came to a stop behind a clump of bushes and killed the engine. They got out and retrieved their kit from the back. The air was crisp and, apart from the birds and the treetops swaying in the breeze, it was silent. Harper checked his gun and pushed it into his belt. Moran locked the car and placed the key on top of the wheel on the driver's side. She drew her weapon from her bag.

'We go the rest of the way on foot,' she said.

Harper nodded.

They kept off the dirt track and moved under the cover of the treeline. The woodland floor was a combination of grass and shale with patches of soft soil. The place smelled pine fresh. They edged their way forward. About four hundred yards ahead they could see a clearing carved out of the woods and the outline of a building. Harper held his fist in the air and they both stopped. He took out his field gasses.

Through the lens he could see a log cabin with a tall pitched roof and four large windows running down one side. The roof was stained green and the walls had the classic corrugated look of cut logs. Wisps of white smoke drifted from a chimney. They crept along for another hundred yards, stopped, and made out a front porch running around the whole width of the property with an extended decking area over to the right. The Transit was parked up at the side. Wicker chairs were ideally placed to take in the spectacular view of the valley with a cold beer.

They pressed on.

At fifty yards out from the lodge Moran stopped and fished out her binoculars. She was scanning across the building, focusing on the windows for any sign of life. Mechanic strolled out onto the veranda. She was dressed in the same clothes they had seen earlier. She looked around and sat in one of the wicker chairs.

'It's her,' Moran whispered.

'I see her. Is she armed?'

Moran shook her head. 'Not that I can see. No sign of Jameson.'

They edged closer and stopped. This time they both held binoculars. Mechanic was lounging in the chair.

'What the hell's she doing?' Harper asked.

'I'd say she was waiting. Waiting for you.'

'Damn well looks that way to me too.'

'No sign of Lucas or Jameson.'

'Jameson could be in the cabin or the van.'

'Where do you think she's holding Lucas?'

'No idea, he could be anywhere.'

They moved forward but this time skirted to the right, taking them deeper into the undergrowth. They settled behind a thicket.

'We could wait till nightfall,' Harper whispered.

Moran checked her watch. It was four o'clock, another three hours till dusk. Lucas had been gone six and a half hours.

'But we need to strike, we don't know what condition Lucas is in.'

'Let's wait and get eyes-on for longer. If she is expecting us, it will be a trap.'

They crouched beneath the trees and bushes and watched. The time ticked by. Mechanic sat in her chair and did nothing.

After thirty minutes Harper said, 'I say we go. I'll circle around the treeline to the back of the house. From there I got about fifteen yards of open ground to cover before I reach Mechanic. When I break cover you hold your position, and when Mechanic turns to confront me, that's when you make your move. Remember, we need her alive.'

'Got it.'

Harper set off and inched his way around the perimeter, keeping well under cover. Mechanic continued to sit in her chair, taking in the view.

He reached the back of the clearing and took out his field glasses. Mechanic was twenty yards away with her back to him. He placed the binoculars on the ground, gripped his gun and crept forward.

There was one almighty whoosh.

Harper was catapulted into the air, cocooned in a cargo net. He was swinging upside down, crashing against the tree that had just propelled him skywards.

Moran heard the violent rustle of leaves being swept through the air. Her view was obscured but she heard Harper yell out.

Mechanic leapt from her seat and picked up a baseball bat that was propped up against the side of the house. She leapt over the balustrade and strode across the clearing, twirling the bat like a cheerleader. Moran could hear the sound of laughter.

What the hell was happening?

Moran was paralysed.

Harper was flailing about trying to right himself. The net had him jack-knifed with his head on his knees as he bounced amongst the pine trees. He fought against the net but it was no use. His gun was gone.

He saw Mechanic emerge from beneath the branches, bat in hand.

'I wasn't expecting you yet,' she laughed. 'You are so predictable, straight out of the Korean War handbook.'

'I'm gonna fucking kill you,' he yelled.

Mechanic stood next to him. Harper's facial features were forced through the netting, he snarled at her. He was hanging five feet off the ground like a trawled fish. She grabbed the net and spun it around.

'I laid a trail of crumbs and you followed them, like the good detective you are. You made excellent time, though I suppose I did make it so easy a kid could work it out,' she said laughing.

'I'm gonna—'

'No, you're not.'

Mechanic stepped back and swung the bat.

* * *

Lucas was aware of the sound of his own breathing. He felt as if he was floating, gently bobbing around in still water. He was groggy and his head hurt. His mouth was dry. He could taste acid at the back of his throat.

He tried to open his eyes but they would not respond. The fog in his brain made everything woozy. He slipped back into unconsciousness.

He came back to the surface again and flicked open his eyelids. It was black. The world swam back and forth as Lucas began to orientate himself and realised he was lying on his back.

He tried to focus but all he saw was darkness. He raised his hands to his face and felt a thick ridge running down his left cheek. It stung like hell. He raised his leg, and his knee struck a hard surface. A dull thud echoed around him. He reached out in front and his fingers touched something cold. It was flat and metal.

His mind was clearing fast.

He remembered seeing Mechanic get out of the van. He remembered the black backpack slung across her shoulder. He remembered a noise coming from behind. Then nothing.

A knot of fear rose in his chest.

He held his hands out in the darkness and pushed his palms flat against the surface above him, it was cool to the touch. Lucas slid his hands across the metal and felt two corners, one on either side. He tried again to move his legs but they struck against the metal.

His eyes were becoming accustomed to the dark and he realised there was a small cone of light above his head. He dug his heels into the base and shuffled his way towards the light. When he was directly under it, he could see blue. His brain struggled to compute all the sensory information he was gathering. He stared at the circle above his face. How the hell could he see blue?

Lucas dropped his hands to his sides and felt around. His fingers touched a collection of small hard objects along with soft material. He brought his hand to his face.

Panic gripped him.

He could smell soil.

He jerked around, smashing his knees and elbows into the metal with dull echoing thuds.

Lucas screamed until his lungs burned.

He was buried alive.

Chapter 46

The back of Harper's head felt like someone was going at it with a steam hammer. He was sitting on the floor with his hands by his sides and his legs straight out in front of him. When the thudding in his head subsided he could hear birds and felt a cool breeze brush across his face. He was outside. He kept his eyes shut.

Mechanic clomped around the wooden decking in her hiking boots. Harper could feel the boards shift beneath him as she walked by. The footsteps faded away. He opened his eyes to see her disappear into the lodge.

Harper looked around. His hands were cuffed to a thick leather belt fastened around his waist and his ankles were shackled to a metal ring set in the floor. He was leaning against the balustrade at the back of the extended decking area. He could see the wicker chairs to his right and the dark treeline to his left. He searched beneath the trees hoping to find Moran. She wasn't there. How long had he been out?

Harper could hear the footsteps returning. He closed his eyes with his head bowed. The floorboards shifted as Mechanic strode towards him. The footsteps stopped.

'Wakey, wakey,' she said, tapping his cheek with her fingers. Shards of pain rocked through his head. He groaned and winced.

'Come on, sleepy head. Time to wake up. Your friend needs you.' She was singing the words.

Harper lifted his head and opened his eyes. The whole of his vision was filled with Mechanic's face. She was tilting her head, first one side, then the other, as though she was examining a quizzical object.

'You've had a little sleep,' she said, 'but now it's time to wake up because you have important work to do.'

'Fuck you.' Harper cleared his throat.

'That's not very nice.' Mechanic drew back as Harper spat a plume of gob past her face.

'Tut, tut,' Mechanic said. 'Such bad manners.'

'Where is Lucas?'

'All in good time, you've only just got here.' Mechanic walked to the front of the decking and leaned against the rail.

'Where's your boyfriend?'

'You are full of questions today. I sent Jameson away, he had things to do, people to kill. You know what it's like.'

The sun was going down, and Harper estimated the time to be about six thirty, which would mean he'd been unconscious for two hours. He felt slow and groggy. Mechanic dragged one of the wicker chairs and sat in front of him.

'There are three things you need to know,' she said. 'The first is that your friend is alive. The second is that whether or not he remains alive depends on you. And the third is, if anything happens to me, he will die.'

Harper stared daggers at Mechanic. She leaned forward with her elbows on her knees.

'Let me be absolutely clear. Should the cavalry roll in and take me captive, I will not talk, and Lucas will die. If you overpower me, I will not talk, and Lucas will die. If you kill me, Lucas will die. You will never find him in this wilderness. I figure he has four days, maybe five at the most, before he dies anyway. Without me, that's what will happen. Is that understood?'

Harper said nothing.

'Is that understood?'

Harper said nothing.

Mechanic leapt from the chair and drew a hunting knife from her belt. She straddled Harper and dug the point of the knife into his cheek below his right eye. Harper fought against his restraints. Mechanic gripped his throat. He could feel a warm trickle of blood run down his cheek as the knife broke the skin.

'Is that understood?'

'Yes,' he croaked.

'Yes, what?'

'Yes, it's understood.' He gasped for air.

Mechanic released him and returned to her chair, replacing the blade back in its sheath.

'That's better. And just so you know, that's precisely the kind of behaviour that's going to get your friend killed. I figure you'll do anything for Lucas. Am I right?'

Harper was sucking in air. He nodded.

'Can't hear you.'

'Yes, I would do anything for him.'

'I figure you would do anything to keep him alive. That's true, isn't it?'

'Yes, it's true.'

'Good, that's what I thought. Do you recall the penance?'

Harper looked at Mechanic and shook his head.

'Let me refresh your memory. The last time you tried to set me up and have me killed, I told Lucas I would only stop murdering people if he paid a penance. Do you remember now?'

Harper thought back. He recalled the killings in the motels didn't stop when they gave back Jo. The killings continued until Lucas paid a penance.

'I remember,' he said.

'Lucas had to choose between you and Bassano. I wanted to kill one of you as punishment for my sister being dead. Lucas's penance was he had to choose. He had to give me one of you to kill. He chose you.'

Harper racked his brain and churned through the events of the previous year. He remembered he had put himself forward as bait to trap Mechanic. But he was not aware that Lucas had given him up to Mechanic as his penance.

Harper's face flushed with anger.

'Oh, you didn't know? You didn't know Lucas offered you up as a sacrifice? You were to be his penance. Well, it's good for you that I have a sense of humour and blew a hole in his wife's head instead. It was great fun.'

Harper tore himself away from the past. He had to figure out how to survive the present.

Mechanic continued, 'So the penance was never paid. My sister is dead because of you three and no one has atoned for her death.'

'You killed Bassano.'

'I did. But I took his life rather than it being offered to me as a penance. In the same way I took the life of Darlene Lucas. You and Lucas must take responsibility for your sins. You need to pay the penance.'

Harper said nothing, his head was racing. Where the hell was all this going?

'I want to be fair, so I'm giving you the opportunity to choose. That's only fair, isn't it? Lucas had a choice and now you have a choice, that's only fair, isn't it?'

'Yes, that's only fair.' Harper could taste blood in the corner of his mouth. 'You sick bitch.'

'Yes, I suppose compared to most I am a little different. But I am nothing if not fair.' She slid from her seat and straddled Harper's legs, drawing her knife.

'Paying a penance is a voluntary self-punishment to atone for a wrongdoing. You are in a sorry predicament but believe me, compared to Lucas, you are on vacation in the Florida Keys. So if you want to save your friend you have to pay the penance. You must atone for your sin and I will let him live.'

'You won't, you lying bitch!' Harper flung his head forward trying to smash his forehead into Mechanic's face. She rolled back, and he missed.

Mechanic seized his neck and shoved him into the banister. The knife bored into his cheekbone.

'Maybe I will, and maybe I won't. But one thing is certain, if you choose not to pay the penance, Lucas will die. You can refuse at any time but Lucas will die.' Mechanic stepped off him. 'So I ask again, do you understand how this works?'

Harper tasted blood in his mouth.

'Yes, I understand how it works.'

'Good.' Mechanic reached into her pocket and brought out a ring holding four silver keys. She knelt down beside Harper and unlocked the cuff on his left wrist. It snapped open. She moved back with the blade in her hand.

'I need to know you understand the consequences, because I'm not convinced you do.'

'I understand,' Harper said.

Mechanic threw the knife and the blade stuck in the wooden floor, inches from Harper's left hand.

'Pick it up.'

Harper gripped the handle and worked it back and forth until it was free. Every muscle in his body told him to throw it at Mechanic. He fought the instinct.

'Cut the top off the little finger on your other hand.'

Harper's mouth dropped open.

'What?'

'It's not difficult to understand. I want you to cut the top off the little finger on your right hand. Sever it at the knuckle joint.'

'What?'

'This is your penance. You need to do this to atone for your sins, and the sins of your friend. You choose not to do it, Lucas dies.'

Harper stared up at Mechanic, tears welling in his eyes. He twisted the knife in his hand. It was heavy and razor sharp. The blade flashed in the last of the evening sun.

'You have five seconds.'

'I can't.'

'Then he dies. It's your choice. One …'

'This is fucking madness, you murdering bitch.'

'Two …'

'You're gonna kill him anyway.'

'If you fail this small penance, I will get in that van and drive away. You will probably survive out here in the elements, you have a chance of yelling for help. But you will never find your friend. I promise you on my sister's life he will die. Three …'

'Jesus Christ.'

'Four …'

'Aarrgh!'

Harper flattened his right hand on the floor with his fingers outstretched. He twisted his body and levelled the knife. The edge scored his skin above the first knuckle.

'Five.'

Harper shifted his weight and thrust the blade down. The knife cut through the cartilage and tendons. The top of his finger rolled away in a spurt of blood.

He screamed and writhed on the floor clutching his wounded hand. Blood poured through his fingers and he tried to stem the bleeding.

Mechanic reached into her pocket and pulled out a cloth.

'Here, bind it with this.' She tossed it onto his chest.

Harper grabbed it and wound it around the bloody stump.

'Fuck!' he yelled as the pain kicked in, his exposed nerve endings sending excruciating signals to his brain.

'There, that wasn't too hard now, was it?'

Mechanic bent down and picked up the knife. She wiped it on her thigh and strolled into the lodge. Harper was bent double trying to block out the pain.

After a couple of minutes Mechanic was back. She took the keys, removed the shackles from his ankles and snapped his free hand back into the cuffs attached to his waist. She heaved him up. Harper was shaking.

'I need to take a walk now, and it's going to get cold out here so you'd better come inside.' She pushed Harper and he shuffled along the deck to the lodge. Blood leaked from the tightly wound cloth, leaving a spotted trail on the floor.

Mechanic opened the door and Harper went inside.

'I won't be long and I want you to be comfortable.'

Harper's eyes adjusted to the gloom of the cabin. He was standing in a living room decorated with woodland rustic charm. It had a sofa and two easy chairs upholstered in garish blue and green check, and a table and chairs covered with a cloth of the same pattern. Around the walls were trophy heads of animals shot for sport. The vaulted ceiling went right up to the roof and heavy wooden beams spanned the room. The large windows gave a panoramic view of the valley below.

Harper felt a surge of uncontrolled panic.

In the centre of the room, dangling from a beam, was a hangman's noose, with a chair placed below it.

Chapter 47

Lucas had stopped fighting against the metal coffin. His elbows hurt, his knees hurt and his fingers bled. He forced himself to stop when his head began to spin, as the oxygen in the confined space was replaced with nitrogen and carbon dioxide. His heart thumped loud in the confined space. His throat was raw from yelling.

He spent his time staring up at the disc of blue sky visible through the air pipe. He watched it glow pink as the sun sunk below the horizon, and change to a bluish grey as the day disappeared into dusk.

It was now black. The sliver of light which had cascaded down the metal tube was gone. Lucas's world was cloaked in darkness. When he raised his hands in front of his face, he saw nothing. He knew they were there because he could feel his breath on his skin, but all he saw was black. He fought the ball of claustrophobic panic that wound itself tight around his chest. The dark vacuum was crushing him.

Every single noise was blocked by the metal box. Lucas strained his ears, but all he heard was the sound of his own breathing and the blood pumping in his head. The silence roared in his ears.

He closed his eyes and began to drift. He dreamed of the time he was with Darlene in New Orleans. They had partied until their feet hurt in the carnival atmosphere of the French quarter. She had berated him for ogling the hookers, he had berated her for flirting with a crowd of bare-chested college basketball players. They wore heavy, beaded necklaces around their necks and fell into bed when the sun came up. It was a magical time.

He snapped open his eyes. There was a sound.

Above him he could hear the faint crack of breaking twigs. He turned his head and lay on his side, trying to put his ear up to the hole. Yes, yes, there was a sound. It could be an animal, but it could be a person.

'Help!' Lucas yelled. 'Help me.' His voice echoed around the confined space.

He arched his body to scream through the hole.

'Help, somebody help.'

He stopped to listen. More cracking twigs, it was the sound of someone walking. Someone was up there.

'Help. I'm down here. Somebody help!'

He stopped again to listen. The sound was gone. Lucas strained his neck to get his ear as close to the hole as possible. There was nothing.

'Did you think someone had come to rescue you?' It was Mechanic. Lucas's heart sank to the pit of his stomach.

'How are you getting on in there. Still alive?' Mechanic flashed a white light down the tube. The beam hit Lucas in the face.

It burned his eyes. Lucas screamed.

'So you are still there.'

Lucas strained every muscle to keep control. He wanted to throw open the box to murder the psycho bitch, but he knew it was useless. He had to conserve his energy if he was to make it out alive.

'Your friend Harper is doing very well. He's helping me not to kill you by paying a penance. You remember all about the penance, don't you, Lucas? I told Harper you had given him to me as part of your penance. He didn't know about that, but he does now. Of course, I chose to kill your wife instead. I must say it was very satisfying to see the blood erupt from the back of her head as the bullet tore its way through her skull.'

Lucas covered his ears with his hands.

'She was so pretty. Well, she was without that fucking great hole. You listening to me, Lucas?' Mechanic shone the beam down the tube and peered in. She could see him squirming around trying to protect his eyes from the piercing light.

'Harper has a long way to go if he is to atone for his sins. I'm not sure he realises how big a penance he has to pay to win your life. You killed my sister and that is going to take a ton of atonement.'

Tears ran either side of Lucas's face and he bit his hand to stop himself sobbing. The light above went off and he was once again plunged into darkness. He heard the faint noise of footsteps fading away.

* * *

Moran had seen Mechanic slip away from the lodge. She crossed to the van and looked through the window, it was empty. She tried the door but it was locked. She ran across the veranda and peered through the first window. It was an empty bedroom with a double bed and single wardrobe. Through the second window she could see a large room with animal heads displayed around the walls.

At the third window she gasped.

Standing on a chair in the centre of the room was Harper. He had his hands manacled to his sides and a noose around his neck. The rope ran up to the ceiling and was looped over the rafter above his head. It stretched diagonally across the room and was tied onto a set of coat pegs on the far wall. The knot on the noose was against the left side of his neck, tilting his head over to the right. Harper was gulping in air as he tried to remain still and upright.

Moran darted around the front of the house and through the front door. Harper wobbled on the chair when he heard the door.

'Fucking hell,' Moran said as she rushed to the pegs and started untying the rope.

'No, no, stop,' Harper said.

'What? I need to get you down.'

'No, stop. When Mechanic gets back I need to be here otherwise she will kill Lucas.'

'What the hell are you talking about?'

'She has Lucas held somewhere. If I don't do exactly what she says she'll kill him.'

'Your hand.' Moran spotted the bloody bandage and the red patch on the floorboards.

'Look, you need to go. I don't know when she'll be back. If we try and take her out, Lucas is a dead man.'

'Where is she?'

'I think she may have gone to see Lucas. I think he's being held nearby. The best thing you can do is find where she's holding him.'

'What about Jameson?'

'She says he's not here, but—'

The sound of heavy boots on wooden decking stopped them dead.

'Shit.' Moran made it into the bedroom just as the front door opened.

'Getting cold out there,' Mechanic said removing her jacket. 'We'll get a fire going.' She busied herself taking logs from a basket and pushing them into the wood-burning stove.

Moran eased her way to the window and slid back the catch, the handle creaked as the frame swung open. She looped her leg over the sill and lifted herself onto the ledge. She pivoted and sank down onto the walkway outside. She pushed the window shut, inched her way to the back of the house and bolted for the treeline. The window was now unlocked but there was nothing she could do about that.

Mechanic collapsed onto the sofa. Harper was still tottering on the chair trying to keep his balance.

'I told Lucas you were paying penance for your sins. I told him you were doing it to keep him alive. He seemed grateful enough.'

Harper snorted as he tried to calm his breathing. He shifted his weight to relieve his cramping legs. His back ached.

'I told him that you had a whole bunch of atoning to do to make up for killing my sister. He was confident you wouldn't let him down. You're not going to let him down, are you, Harper?'

Harper glared down at Mechanic, holding his composure.

'No.' He choked the words out.

Mechanic got up to check the fire. She rubbed her hands together in the hot air rising from the grille at the front.

'That's the problem with wilderness living. What do you do to kill the boredom? Don't you think?'

Harper nodded.

'If only we had some entertainment to while away the time. What do you say?'

Harper nodded again.

Mechanic flopped down on the sofa again, leaned forward and kicked away the chair.

Harper dropped. The rope stretched under his weight and the noose tightened. His legs flailed around and he choked as the ligature cut deep into his neck, crushing his windpipe.

Mechanic sat back and watched while Harper twisted and jerked, trying to free his hands. His face turned purple as the cord closed off the arteries and veins feeding his brain, sending the blood pressure in his head rocketing. His mouth was open and his tongue stuck out. Harper was being strangled to death.

Mechanic got up from the sofa and started dancing around Harper's twisting body.

'You dance, Harper!' she called out. 'You shake that ass.' Mechanic put her hands in the air and gyrated her hips.

'Woo, you go, boy.'

His eyes bulged out of his skull and his wrists bled where the cuffs cut into his flesh. Popping candy was going off in his head, and he could see flashing lights. The oxygen to his brain ran out and he blacked out. His legs continued to spasm.

Mechanic stopped dancing and tugged the loose end of the knot tied around the coat peg. The rope unfurled from the rafter and Harper crashed to the floor, his body twitching and convulsing. She leaned over, loosened the noose and removed it from his head.

She shook him and a rasping torrent of air rushed into his lungs. He gagged and coughed. Mechanic rolled Harper into the recovery position and went to make coffee on the stove.

Chapter 48

Lucas was concentrating on staying alive. His only hope of getting out of there was to be rescued and it was no good if when that happened he was a dead man. He had drifted in and out of sleep during the night and had shifted positions as often as he could to prevent cramp setting in. At one point his mind ran amok and he couldn't tell if he was awake or asleep. The blackness engulfed him.

He kept looking up at the hole above his head and watched it turn from black to grey, as the night slipped into dawn. He figured it had to be about 5.30am.

Lucas had another more immediate problem – he needed to pee.

He undid his pants, shuffled them down and removed his penis. He allowed a short burst of urine to escape and caught it in his cupped hand. He brought it to his mouth and drank.

Lucas had once watched a TV programme where a fighter pilot had crashed his plane in the desert and had kept himself alive by drinking his own pee. He recalled that so long as you were well hydrated to start with, the first flow of urine was fine to drink and could buy you extra time before the crippling effects of dehydration took hold. Lucas slurped at the liquid, he needed all the extra time he could get.

It tasted disgusting. Warm and salty with a bitter back taste. Lucas repeated the exercise over and over, each time releasing a small amount of pee and drinking it from his hand. After fifteen minutes he was done. The hole in his coffin had turned bright blue and the cone of light had returned.

* * *

Moran was dozing in her car, hidden beneath the treeline. She had spent hours in the night searching for Lucas amongst the woods and rocky outcrops. It was hopeless. The forest was pitch black and it was impossible to see anything. She had persevered, using landmarks to map out a grid in her head. She paced out each one in turn but by 2am she gave up.

She woke, pulled a bottle of water from the bag and ate some cookies. She wanted to be at the lodge early to catch Mechanic when she went out. She reached the cabin at 6.15. Harper was tied up on the decking area, sitting upright. Moran took a chance.

She crossed the open ground at the back of the lodge and approached Harper from behind. He was asleep with his head and shoulders propped against the wooden balustrade. His hands were secured to the belt around his waist and his ankles manacled to the eyebolt in the floor. She shook his shoulder, he jumped a mile.

'Shhh,' Moran whispered. 'It's me.'

Harper turned to look at her.

'Fuck, what did she do to you?' Moran said. The twist of the rope had imprinted deep furrows around his neck. The whites of his eyes were speckled with burst blood vessels and his face bore patches of red and purple spots where capillaries had ruptured under the skin.

Harper shook his head. 'Never mind, did you find him?'

'No, I tried but it was too dark.'

Harper slumped down. Moran rummaged in her bag and brought out the water and some chocolate. She held the bottle to his lips, and Harper drank thirstily. She snapped off squares from the bar and pushed them into his mouth. Harper chewed and swallowed fast.

'You gotta find him,' he said, his voice unrecognisable.

'I know, I'll follow her today. You sure about this? I could shoot her and then we could beat it out of her.'

'No, that won't work. She won't talk. You have to follow her and find him. It's the only way to get Lucas out alive.'

Moran fed him more chocolate. A noise came from inside the cabin. Moran ducked away and dashed back to cover. Mechanic came out onto the veranda with a cup of coffee in her hand.

'Beautiful morning for a penance, don't you think?'

Harper said nothing.

'Did you sleep okay? You should have, you were half asleep when I dragged you out here last night. Or was that you being unconscious? I can never tell the difference.'

She strolled across to Harper and pulled up a wicker chair.

'We had some fun, didn't we? When you get in the groove you can really dance.'

Harper looked at the floor, avoiding eye contact.

'I'm a great believer in starting the day off right. You know, a little gentle exercise, a healthy breakfast, followed by a hot shower. And I was thinking, the breakfast is shit, I can't exercise because you're here, and I don't have a shower. So what should we do to get the day off to a great start?'

She reached behind her back and drew the hunting knife. She threw it and it stuck in the wooden floor a foot from Harper's injured hand. She pulled the keys from her pocket.

'I think removing the top of your ring finger is exactly what we need to get the day off on the right note.'

Moran watched from the safety of the treeline. She saw Mechanic kneel beside Harper. Next thing he was struggling with her. There were raised voices. Mechanic stepped away.

She heard the muffled sound of Mechanic's voice, and then she heard Harper scream. He rolled on the floor, sobbing, clutching his right arm. Moran's immediate instinct was to run at Mechanic and put a bullet in her head. But Harper's words kept her rooted to the spot.

Mechanic went into the house and returned a few seconds later carrying something. Moran couldn't see what it was. Mechanic let it drop to the deck while she knelt down and released Harper's ankles. She stood up and Moran saw the noose dangling from her grasp. She forced it over Harper's head, pulled it tight and hauled him to his feet.

She yanked on the rope and Harper shuffled after her into the lodge.

* * *

Ten minutes later Mechanic re-emerged. She stepped off the veranda and walked into the woods. Moran followed keeping well back.

She kept about thirty yards between herself and Mechanic and crept though the trees and bushes. After fifteen minutes Mechanic stopped. Moran took cover in a copse of trees and pulled out her binoculars.

What the hell is she doing? Moran thought.

Mechanic was walking around in a clearing, talking to herself.

'Did you really believe this was going to work?' Mechanic said. 'I had Jameson compile intel reports on you, Harper and Bassano a long time ago. That's how I was able to relieve Bassano of his cock and balls. He squealed like a stuck pig.' Mechanic laughed. 'It was a beautiful sound.'

Lucas lay in his coffin listening to Mechanic rant above him. The metal tube distorted her voice but he could make out every word. She continued.

'So when you showed up at Jameson's door he recognised you. I mean, all that shit about insisting on the same shooter or the deal was off, and that nonsense about your client needing to know the details of the hit. Jameson would never have allowed that to happen on a normal contract. We played you along and you sucked it all up. Me and him go back a long way, he is loyal to the core, and with your level of stupidity, you didn't stand a chance.'

Moran skirted away to the right to find a better vantage point and crouched down, peering through the glasses. Mechanic was walking around in a circle, talking and gesticulating. Moran was too far away to make out any of the words.

'The choice of Bonelli was a good one. Who thought of that? Was it you or Harper? I enjoyed that, but it was such an obvious trap. You listening to me?' Mechanic called down the pipe. Her voice reverberated against the metal, bursting against his ears.

'Anyway, what else do I have to tell you? Oh yes, you could be out soon. Your man Harper is doing a great job of atoning for his sins. He didn't look so good this morning and he won't play the piano again, but he's hanging in there.'

Lucas's heart lifted at the prospect of getting out but then sank when he thought of Harper and the terrible things he must be enduring to save him. He had to stay strong. He had to stay alive.

Moran's eyes were glued to Mechanic watching her every move. For the next fifteen minutes she looked like an evangelical preacher with no congregation. Round and round she circled, talking to herself and throwing her arms in the air.

'Well, that's it for now. I'll be back later. Got to go, I have some meat to hang,' Mechanic said and trooped back towards the lodge.

Moran watched her disappear. When Mechanic was gone she crabbed forward to where she had been standing. There was nothing there. She scouted around, the place was covered in bushes and tufts of long, dry grass. There were young trees dotted around and the rest of the ground was soil and shale. This had to be the place. But what the hell was she doing?

Moran paced out every inch, combing the area like a crime scene.

Then she saw it.

Chapter 49

Hidden in a thicket, sticking out of the ground, was a two-foot length of metal tubing. It was painted green and shrouded by twigs and branches while a clump of grass surrounded the base. Moran cleared them away. It was two and half inches in diameter and made of steel. She put her face close to the end and peered inside.

'Lucas?' she whispered. The sound of frantic scuffling travelled up the pipe.

'Moran? Is that you?'

'Yes, Mechanic has gone.'

'Get me out of here,' he cried. 'Please, please get me out of here.' She could hear the panic surging in his voice.

'Okay, keep quiet.'

Moran cleared the vegetation. It came away easily to reveal an oblong patch of freshly dug earth.

She leapt to her feet, scoured the woodland floor and found what she was looking for, a length of wood about three inches thick. She gripped it with both hands, sank to her knees and thrust the end into the dirt. The wooden stake dug into the newly turned soil and she dragged it to the side. She wielded the pick like a canoeist wields a paddle and drove it into the dirt over and over again, digging a trench. Moran shovelled the earth with her hands and piled it up at the sides.

The bark on the wood cut into her hands but she pressed on ignoring the pain. She could hear the sound of Lucas sobbing below. The soil piled up around her and she dug deeper. Then suddenly she hit something hard.

'That's me,' Lucas called out.

Moran removed her shirt and wrapped it around her hands. They were bleeding. She dug into the earth like a crazy woman, pulling at the mounds of earth with her forearms to clear the way. The metal box was about two foot down, and she hit the lid again with a metallic clunk. This galvanised her into more frenzied digging.

She eventually found the edge of the metal coffin and scraped the pole along its length. She brushed the earth away with her hands to find four clasps locking down the lid. She unfastened them and heaved against the weight of the top and the remaining soil. Lucas saw a crack of light opening up down one side. He shoved with all his might with his hands and his knees. The lid hinged upwards.

He could see Moran, red in the face with exertion, straining to lift the lid. Lucas brought his knees up, thrust his feet under it and pushed. Soil and rocks fell into the coffin covering his face and body. The lid flew open, sending Moran toppling backwards.

Lucas shielded his eyes from the brightness, hauled himself out and rolled across the ground.

'I got to go,' said Moran putting on her shirt. 'I'll come back for you.' She reached in her bag and pulled out the bottle of water and what remained of the chocolate. She sprinted off in the direction of the lodge.

* * *

Mechanic threw open the door to the cabin. Harper almost fell from the chair in shock, the noose tightened around his neck as he shifted position.

'What a fantastic day for a penance,' she crowed at the top of her voice.

Harper steadied himself. Blood was dripping from his hand and pooling on the wooden floor. The grubby bandage was now wrapped around two fingers. He was struggling to stand up straight, his back kept going into spasm and the muscles in his legs screamed with cramps. His breathing was shallow as he tried to remain focused.

'You know, your friend wasn't very talkative today. I'm not sure he's doing so good.' Mechanic walked to the stove and lifted off the coffee pot. She busied herself at the kitchenette filling it with water and ground coffee.

'But he's pleased that you have his best interests at heart. You do, don't you?'

Harper nodded his head.

'I can't hear you,' she barked with her back to him.

'Yes, I do,' Harper croaked.

Mechanic walked back placing the pot on the stove and threw herself onto the couch.

'What shall we do today? I fancy doing some more of that dancing we did last night. You were really good. What do you say?'

'Go to hell.' The words hissed from his throat.

'Don't you be bad mouthing me, it will only get your friend killed.'

'Sorry.'

'That's better.' She jumped from the sofa and flitted around tidying the place up. It was a bizarre scene. Mechanic hung her coat up and collected dirty cups, while a man dripped blood on the floor, standing on a chair with a noose around his neck. She washed the cups in the sink. The coffee pot glugged and bubbled on the heat.

Mechanic dried the cups and started singing. It was a tuneless, wordless song which she belted out. She swayed her hips and shoulders and pirouetted around the room.

'You sing too,' she said, drifting past him and knocking his leg.

Harper wobbled and the noose gripped tighter.

'Come on, you sing too, it will raise your spirits.'

Harper began to emit a low groan.

'That's better. See, you feel much better now, don't you?'

Harper nodded and continued to croak out a sound.

'Now how about we dance a little?'

Mechanic sashayed up to him and gyrated like a stripper. She rolled her hips and dipped her knees with her hands on her head.

'You want to dance with me, Harper? I bet I turn you on.' She ground her hips some more and spun around in front of him. 'You're not dancing.'

Harper steeled every sinew in his body.

'I said, you're not dancing.' She raised her voice, pulling out the knife.

His body shook with the expectation of what was to come.

'I said, dance!' she yelled and kicked away the chair.

Harper dropped like a stone and the rope yanked tight around his neck. His legs jerked and his body twisted in the air.

The bullet shattered the window, slammed into Mechanic's right shoulder and exited through her upper chest. The force spun her around. The second shell demolished her right knee sending blood and bone gushing into the air.

Mechanic collapsed onto the wooden floor and rolled into the base of the sofa holding her knee.

Moran ran down the side of the lodge and crashed through the front door. Harper was convulsing wildly and his head looked like it was about to burst wide open. Moran reached the coat hooks but couldn't untie the knot. Harper was choking and gagging as he jerked at the end of the rope.

Moran saw the knife on the floor. She reached down to grab it. Mechanic seized her wrist. Moran toppled over and fell in a heap. Mechanic was snarling and hissing as she held on to Moran.

Moran struggled to break free and swung the Beretta. The butt of the gun cracked hard into Mechanic's temple. She went limp and released her grip. Moran grasped the knife, leapt up and took an almighty swipe at the rope. The blade severed it in one and Harper slammed onto the floor. Moran scrambled over and yanked the noose from around his neck. His face was completely purple.

She laid Harper on his back and shook him, striking at his chest with her fists and blowing in his mouth. Harper convulsed and took an enormous gulp of air. He coughed and gagged blood onto his chin.

She left Harper where he was and rolled Mechanic onto her front. She ripped the keys from her pocket, crawled back to Harper and snapped open the cuffs. Harper groaned as the metal bracelets came away from his wrists. He lay on the floor wheezing and gasping while Moran unbuckled the belt and removed it from around his waist.

Moran stood up and walked over to Mechanic. She was out cold and there was a widening pool of blood around her shattered knee and another emerging from under her right shoulder. Moran secured the thick leather belt around her middle and snapped the cuffs on her wrists.

Harper was rolling around trying to sit up. Moran put her arms under his and dragged him towards the front door propping him against the wall. He was rubbing his neck with his hands and coughing.

Moran took the rope, went back to Mechanic and tied it around the top of her thigh as a makeshift tourniquet to stem the bleeding. She stripped the cloth from the table, balled it up and stuffed it against the chest wound under Mechanic's shirt.

Harper was looking around, dazed.

'What the fuck happened? Did you find Lucas?'

'I found him.'

'Where was he?'

'He was buried underground in a metal coffin. No wonder I couldn't find him last night. You stay here, I need to go get him.' She handed Harper her gun. 'If she moves put another hole in her.'

* * *

Moran ran back to Lucas. She found him staggering around, stretching his limbs and arching his back.

'Hey, you need to be careful,' she said.

'Where's Harper? How is he? Where's Mechanic?' He fell to his knees.

'Wow, take it easy. Harper is safe. He looks like he's been run over by a truck and he needs a doctor but he'll survive. Mechanic is out of commission and she's bleeding out. We need to get back there. You up for a walk?'

'Yes.' He held out his arm and she pulled him to his feet.

'Take it slow.'

'I thought I was going to die in there.'

'I think that was Mechanic's plan. And Harper nearly died as well, several times.'

They walked back at a slow pace. Lucas had to stop every so often to steady himself. Along the way, Moran filled Lucas in with the details of what Mechanic had done to Harper and how he had kept her occupied while she searched for him. Lucas described how Mechanic would visit him and taunt him. The outflow of emotions was too much for Lucas and he couldn't stop crying.

They reached the cabin and went inside. Harper was still sitting, leaning against the wall with the gun by his side. Mechanic was coming round, groaning on the floor.

'Fucking hell,' Lucas said when he saw the state of Harper. Moran went to the sink, drew water into a bowl and tended to the deep wounds around Harper's neck and wrists. She unwound the bandage from his fingers, Harper gritted his teeth as the material separated from his exposed flesh. Moran found some salt in one of the cupboards, made a solution in a bowl and handed it to Harper.

'It will hurt like a bastard.'

Harper dunked his fingers into the fluid and almost hit the roof.

Lucas found the coffee and something to eat. He sat on the floor next to Mechanic and watched her writhe around. Moran fixed food for Harper and a mug of water.

'Thanks,' he said. Everything hurt.

'Why did you patch her up?' asked Lucas.

'Because the holes in her are from my gun and I didn't really think it was my place to kill her.'

'What do we do with her now?'

Lucas and Harper flashed each other a look.

* * *

Moran and Lucas dragged Mechanic outside. She lay on her front, blood oozing from her chest. Harper hobbled out and sank into the wicker chair. Moran had found the keys to the van in the bedroom and opened it up. Lucas helped her heave the gurney onto the floor.

Mechanic came round and started to struggle against the cuffs.

'What the fuck?' she said twisting herself to lie on her side staring at Harper. She let out a yell as the shattered bones crunched in her knee.

'Careful now,' Harper said.

'You stupid fuck. Now your precious friend Lucas is a dead man.'

Moran stepped up onto the decking.

'You!' spluttered Mechanic. 'I saw you once with Lucas in an ice-cream parlour on the Vegas Strip. You must be a cop too.'

Moran nodded. 'Yeah, we were there but I don't recall him introducing me to you.'

'Have you told her, Harper? Have you told her that this means Lucas is a dead man?'

'No, I thought I'd leave that up to you.'

Mechanic laughed. 'You fuckwit, you killed him. You'll never find him now.'

Lucas walked up and stood behind Moran. Mechanic for once was lost for words, her mouth opening and closing like a landed fish.

'Ready,' Lucas said.

'Yup,' said Moran.

They marched forward and hauled Mechanic across the floor to the edge of the walkway. They rolled her over the edge and onto the gurney. She landed hard and yelped in pain. Moran stepped down, pulled out the extendable handle and inserted the crossbar. They towed Mechanic away from the lodge.

'I'm going to kill you all,' she snarled as she bounced around. Once or twice Mechanic tried to get off the gurney but her injuries were too great and she slumped back down. They walked in silence through the undergrowth and came to a clearing. Thirty yards ahead stood the mounds of earth.

'We thought you'd like to try it out,' Lucas said.

Mechanic twisted around and saw where she was. She laughed.

'You think you're going to scare me with that? Be my guest. None of you have the balls to kill me. You're all cops and law-abiding citizens.'

'That's right, we are. But before we call the cops to have you taken in, I want you to feel what it's like. Besides, we are all a lot safer if you are locked up in there.'

Mechanic laughed again. 'I knew it. You're gutless pieces of shit. Put me in the box, I don't care.'

Moran pulled open the lid and Lucas tilted the gurney up onto two wheels. Mechanic rolled off and hit the side of the hole before landing in the metal box with a thud.

'You should be ripping me apart right now, not putting me away for some limp dick cop to arrest me.' Moran slammed the lid and fixed the clasps.

The sound of Mechanic laughing drifted up through the air pipe.

'You haven't got the balls.' They could hear her voice screaming from the box. Moran kicked the soil on top, filling in the trench. Lucas and Harper followed suit, pushing the earth into the hole. A few minutes later it was covered over. The dirt had a sound-deadening quality, but they could still hear Mechanic's cackling voice rising from the tube.

All three stood around. Nobody spoke. Each one in their own personal quiet zone, taking in what had just happened. Each one thinking 'It's over'.

Lucas picked up the branch Moran had used to dig him out and took out Mechanic's hunting knife. He sat on the floor and drew the blade across the wood. Slivers of bark peeled away. He rotated the wood and repeated the process.

'We used to do this when I was a kid. Me and my dad would go camping and we'd sit around whittling away at old branches. I had one of those Swiss Army knives with the twenty-seven blades, I thought I was the kingpin with that. We would make spears and bows and arrows and go hunting. My mum would never have approved of such things so we never told her.'

He turned the wood over and over in his hands, slicing at the end, whittling it down into a point.

The sound of Mechanic's voice drifted up from the air pipe.

'You do realise I will spend my days in a high security mental hospital having three square meals a day and watching daytime TV while your wife will be decomposing in the ground, Lucas. Lucas, do you hear me?' She screamed with laughter.

Lucas put the wood on the floor and sawed the end off.

'Yeah, I used to do the same thing except neither of my parents would have approved,' said Moran, 'so I didn't tell them either.'

They allowed the moment to pass between them.

Moran looked at Harper.

'Are you ready? We got some serious cleaning up to do in that log cabin.'

'Yes, come on, let's go.'

They turned and left Lucas sitting on the ground.

Lucas thought about the families Mechanic had murdered, he thought about the women left alive with nothing to live for. He thought about the kids who would never see their next birthday. He thought about the couples she had killed in the motels and how in the end she did it for fun. He thought about Chris Bassano and his grieving family, and of course he thought about his wife, Darlene. It would have been their wedding anniversary next month. A tear ran down his cheek.

He rooted around in his jacket pocket and brought out the Polaroid camera which Harper had presented him as a gift. He had found it on the floor of the van when taking out the gurney. He slid the lever on the side and it popped open.

He put the viewfinder to his eye.

Lucas pushed the button.

Chapter 50

Exactly one year on
June 1985

Lucas heard the familiar sound of alloy wheels striking concrete. Harper had come to visit and he was late. They were watching the afternoon baseball game and Lucas had prepared a feast. A feast of chili dogs and beer that is. There was a rapid knock at the door.

Lucas opened it and Harper pushed past him into the hallway.

'It's hammering down out there,' he said shaking water from his coat and onto the walls as he tossed it in the corner. He left dirty footprints on the carpet on his way to the living room, carrying with him a suitcase of forty-eight cans of beer.

'Come in, why don't you,' Lucas said as he breezed by.

Lucas hung up Harper's coat and went into the living room to find him with a beer already in hand, pulling back the tab on another. He handed it to Lucas.

'Cheers. Here's to drinking in the afternoon.' They hit the cans together and drank.

'You hungry?'

'Always hungry, man. You of all people should know that. Always hungry and always thirsty.' He took a massive slurp and burped.

Lucas clanked around with pots and plates in the kitchen.

Harper went to the sideboard and picked up a framed photograph.

'This always makes me smile,' he said holding it up.

'Yeah, me too. You know it was a year ago today.'

'Yup, I got up this morning and smiled so wide my head almost broke in half. It is truly a day to celebrate.' He emptied the can down his throat and cracked open another.

Harper took another swig and continued, 'I keep mine stuck to the dashboard of my car. Every time a light turns red or I can't find a parking space or someone cuts me up, I take a look at it and smile. It works every time.'

'What could be better – the New York Yankees versus the Tampa Bay Rays on a day of celebration.' Lucas laughed and handed Harper a plate overflowing with a foot-long hot dog, chilli, onions, grated cheese and a fist-sized helping of jalapenos on the side.

'You got sauces?' Harper asked.

'What?'

'You know, like condiments.'

Lucas skulked back into the kitchen shaking his head.

Harper balanced the photograph on the top of the TV.

Lucas returned with ketchup and sat down ready for the game.

'That way we can look at both,' Harper said pointing to the picture and holding his can out towards Lucas.

'Yes, that way we can look at both.'

'Cheers.'

* * *

Two thousand miles and three time zones away Moran was waking up. It was late, but that was fine because she had nothing planned and all day to do it in. She got up and padded into the kitchen. The plates from last night's dinner were still on the table along with the wine glasses. She clicked on the kettle and turned the TV to a twenty-four-hour news channel.

Moran pottered around loading the dishwasher and fixing coffee. She fetched her bag from the hall, unzipped a pocket and pulled out a photograph. She laid it on the table and ran her finger across it.

The kettle boiled and she poured water into the coffee pot to let it brew. She pulled two cups from the cupboard.

'Come back to bed,' a voice came from the bedroom.

'In a minute, just making coffee.'

She returned to the photograph, it made her smile.

'Hurry up!' The voice was playfully insistent.

Moran had finally worked out why her track record with dating men was so crap. Judy was an elementary school teacher and was everything Moran was not. She was soft, girlie, colourful and a touch on the crazy side. They met at a job fair and hit it off straightaway. Three months later she moved in. Judy was now waiting for her late morning coffee.

Moran had left the force. The charges that were levelled at her melted away. Mills couldn't prove she'd been at the public records office, and she managed to convince the disciplinary hearing that she was unfit for duty at the time she investigated the Nassra Shamon accounts. Having fifteen people testify that she threw up her breakfast during the morning briefing certainly helped. And quietly pointing out to Mills that he was on Bonelli's payroll had helped a great deal.

Despite escaping with nothing more than a severe dressing down from the chief and a disciplinary note on her file, her heart was no longer in the job. Two weeks later she handed her badge in for good.

Now she worked at the University of Las Vegas lecturing in criminology. It was challenging at times but at least people didn't tend to fire guns at her. For the first time in years she was happy and relaxed. She still wore black, but Judy had it as her life's ambition to see her girlfriend dressed in pink one day.

Moran replaced the picture in her bag and zipped the pocket shut. She poured the coffee and headed back to bed.

* * *

Fabiano Bassano was watching baseball in his man-cave. The room was full of excited chatter as the additives from the fizzy drinks and chocolate snacks began to kick in and the kids went a little crazy. He liked nothing better than watching the game with his five grandchildren. They were mad about baseball and mad about Grandpa.

Whenever they got together it was always the same. The kids talked over the commentary, walked in front of the TV, and bombarded him with questions about the rules, but that was fine. For Fabiano Bassano, enjoying the ball game with his grandchildren had nothing to do with the ball game.

'Hey, what's going on,' he cried, holding up an empty beer bottle. 'Who's on bar duty?'

One of the children reached up, snatched it from his grasp and dashed into the kitchen, returning a minute later with a frosted replacement, courtesy of Grandma.

Zak, the youngest, snuggled onto the chair alongside him.

'Grandpa, why do you have this silly picture?' His shock of black tousled hair hid his face as he gazed at a silver framed photograph in his tiny hand. He looked up, his moon face and bright eyes waiting for his favourite playmate to respond.

'Yes, that is a silly picture, isn't it?'

They both laughed.

'What is it?'

'I don't know. Someone gave it to me. I like it, don't you?'

'Yes, I like it too.'

'It makes me smile.'

'It makes me smile too, Grandpa. Who gave it to you?'

'A friend of Uncle Chris.'

'Is he the one who died?'

'Yes. He died when you were small.'

'I like it.' Zak turned the picture over in his hands and the frame caught the light.

'I'll let you into a secret.' Fabiano bent his head and whispered into the child's ear. 'Do you know what today is?'

'No, what?'

'Today is its birthday.'

'Its birthday?' Zak was fixated, not taking his eyes off the image. 'How can a picture have a birthday?'

'Well, it's one year ago today that the photograph was taken.'

'Wow, then it does have a birthday.' Zak and his grandpa sang Happy Birthday. But Grandpa struggled on occasion to get his words out. When they finished he dabbed his eyes with his sleeve.

'Now put it back and we can watch the game.'

Zak shuffled off the chair and placed it on the shelf.

It was an odd photograph.

It showed a length of green metal tubing poking out of the ground with a carved wooden plug jammed in the top.

The End

Acknowledgements

I want to thank all those who have made this third book possible – My family Karen, Gemma, Holly and Maureen for their blunt, painful feedback and endless patience. To my band of loyal proofreaders Yvonne, Lesley, Christine, Penny, Christine, Nicki, Jackie and Simon who didn't hold back either and finally my superb editor, Helen Fazal, who once again did an amazing job and made me a better writer in the process.

I would also like to mention my wider circle of family and friends for their fantastic support and endless supply of helpful comments. Who made marketing suggestions such as, 'You should have a battle bus Rob like they do in elections', provided excellent advice on plot development, 'You need more teachers in your books' and gave constructive critique on my attempts at media promotion, 'Just been listening to some knob on the radio rambling on about coffee and writer's block'. With such an abundance of quality guidance, how could I possibly go wrong.

Finally, I would like to say a special thank you to the brilliant bloggers Caroline Vincent, Sharon Bairden and Susan Hampson. They saw something in my writing when I was initially setting out that made them want to shout about it, and fortunately for me they still do. They are very special people and I am a lucky man to have them in my corner.